PETI
I'LL S

REGINALD Evelyn Peter Southouse Cheyney (1896-1951) was born in Whitechapel in the East End of London. After serving as a lieutenant during the First World War, he worked as a police reporter and freelance investigator until he found success with his first Lemmy Caution novel. In his lifetime Cheyney was a prolific and wildly successful author, selling, in 1946 alone, over 1.5 million copies of his books. His work was also enormously popular in France, and inspired Jean-Luc Godard's character of the same name in his dystopian sci-fi film *Alphaville*. The master of British noir, in Lemmy Caution Peter Cheyney created the blueprint for the tough-talking, hard-drinking pulp fiction detective.

PETER CHEYNEY

I'LL SAY SHE DOES!

DEAN STREET PRESS

Published by Dean Street Press 2022

All Rights Reserved

First published in 1946

Cover by DSP

ISBN 978 1 915014 03 0

www.deanstreetpress.co.uk

AUTHOR'S NOTE

The time has come when I must say a few words about Mr. Lemuel H. Caution and this book.

I'll Say She Does is the result of a promise I made to two brave officers in the Australian Forces. Lieut.-Commander Al Palmer, D.S.C., and Major Brooke Moore. I told them I would do a Lemmy Caution novel especially for them and prisoners of war. This is it.

In 1944 my wife was one of the St. John Welfare Officers who went to Sweden to repatriate British Prisoners of War on the *Drottningholm*—called by the Repatriates the "Trotting Home." On the voyage home it was discovered that she was Mrs. Peter Cheyney and Palmer and Brooke asked her to bring back to me a letter, written by them on behalf of the people on board. Many of these men had been in prison camps for years.

I have always been rather pleased with inventing Lemmy Caution who has, during the last ten years, found his way into a large slice of the world and acquired a popularity with many people; but I can say without undue sentimentality that the proudest moment in my life as a writer was when I read this letter.

They said that during their years of captivity the Caution books had brought them entertainment and laughter—at times and under circumstances when laughter was not particularly easy. They told me stories of Lemmy Caution in the *Stalags*—one, of the *padre* who, walking about the camp with his nose in a large book of Devotions, was discovered, eventually, to have *Dames Don't Care* inside the covers.

The letter ended ". . . and thanks for what you've done for us."

Afterwards, when I met Skipper and Brookie and we had the historic "four-fingers" together, I heard the rest of it and said that, as soon as possible, I would do a Lemmy

Caution book for all Prisoners of War and especially the *Drottningholm* people in whom I had a particular personal interest.

Brookie is back in Australia but this book will find him there. I don't know where one-armed Skipper is at the moment but he'll get it sometime.

I am very proud of being thanked by prisoners of war for what I have "done for them." May I, on behalf of Lemmy Caution and all his readers, thank them for what they have done—and suffered—for *us*.

CHAPTER ONE
AND HOW!

LIFE can be goddam wonderful. And how! It can be so beautiful that every time somethin' swell happens you don't believe it. Some guys call this cynicism an' other bozos describe it as wishful thinkin' like the guy who made himself up like Santa Claus so's he could put a ladder in some babe's stockin' at Christmas.

Me—I am feelin' so depressed that I would cut my throat, only then I would not have anythin' to worry about—except my throat. An' the reason for all this depression which is now settlin' over this piece of Paris in the month of March 1945 can be summed up in one word . . . dames! Even if I was Aladdin an' rubbed the lamp like hell, I reckon the genii would not produce anythin' I wanted unless I handed in the coupons first.

So now you know.

The guy who called this alleyway the Place des Roses has got a sense of humour, because believe it or not it smells plenty. It looks as if everybody round this place had been throwing away everything they didn't want an' leavin' it there. Or maybe it's because the Germans ain't been outa Paris for very long. I wouldn't know.

Me—I am feelin' a little high because the guy who told me that Dubonnet mixed with rye was a good drink certainly knew his vegetables. But my head is not so good an' I am also mixed up a little bit about the babe I had dinner with. I reckon I am gonna call this babe V. 2 because she is so goddam unexpected.

The place is dark, but at the end I can see a crack of light comin' outa the first floor window. I reckon this is the house all right. Fours told me in the old days when the Gestapo boys was runnin' the job around here that he an' the English Secret Service guys usta meet up there. So the place has sorta got atmosphere if you get me. An' if you don't what do I care?

When I get to this dump I see an iron bell-pull hangin' down one side of the door. I give it a jerk an' stand there waitin', a cigarette hangin' outa the corner of my mouth, wonderin' about that dame—the one I had dinner with. Maybe I've told you guys before that three-quarters of the trouble in life is through dames an' the other quarter is just financial an' don't mat

ter. Anythin' that don't happen through a dame you can stick in your eye. It wouldn't worry anybody.

A minute or two goes by an' the door opens. There is a little light in the hallway, an' standin' lookin' at me is a tall thin bronzed guy. He has got a humorous sorta face an' nice grey eyes. I like this boyo.

He says: "Would you be Lemmy Caution?"

I say: "Yeah, that's what my mother said."

"I'm Jimmy Cleeve," he says. "I'm a private dick from New York. Maybe they told you about me?"

I say: "Yeah, I heard about you. How'ya, Jimmy?"

He says: "Not so bad. I find life in Paris these days after the German occupation a little bit enervatin'. I don't know whether it's the liquor or the babies. As I don't go for dames in a big way it must be the liquor. Come on up."

I go into the hallway. In front of me is a windin' flight of stairs an' on the right of the hallway is a door lookin' inta a side room. Everything about this place is goddam dusty except the brass door handle on the inside door. I follow on up the stairs after Cleeve. Halfway up he says to me over his shoulder:

"There's a pal of yours here. He's lookin' forward to seein' you."

I say: "Yeah? Who is that?"

He says: "A boyo named Dombie. I reckon he's worked with you before."

I say: "Yeah, I like him. He's a nice fella. He talks too much, that's all. An' he's got a leery eye for dames. But he's a nice guy. Has anybody got anythin' to eat up there?"

He opens the door at the top of the stairs. He says: "Yeah. Dombie's got a bottle."

We go in.

The room is not bad. There are a coupla chairs an' a truckle bed, an' at one end is something that looks as if it used to be a bar sometime. There is a bottle that looks like whisky called Veritable

Cognac written on the label, which makes me a bit suspicious, a few glasses an' some water.

I say: "Hello, Dombie. How's it goin'? I ain't seen you for two years. You remember that job we did in London?"

He says: "Yeah—I remember, you dirty so-an'-so, you hooked a lovely dame off me. How could I forget?"

I say: "Listen, I never hooked a dame off anybody. She gave up of her own free will—that one. But I can understand you bein' annoyed about it."

He says: "Feller, I should worry about dames. The trouble is keepin' away from 'em. I got something; every dame in Paris sorta knows it. At least that's the idea I get."

I say: "*You* got somethin'! Say, Jimmy, do you hear that one? Listen to this big lug. *He's* got something. *He's* got allure."

Cleeve says: "Yeah—that an' a gumboil!"

Dombie says: "O.K. O.K. You guys are just gettin' jealous. Jimmy here, is needled to me because of the baby I got. You wait till you see her. She's terrific. She goes for me like hell. She even thinks I'm *good*."

I say: "Yeah. She must be marvellous."

"Sure she's marvellous," says Dombie. "I tell you that baby's intellectual. She's got a sixth sense."

I say: "You're tellin' me. She's gotta have because she ain't got the other five if she's stuck on you."

Cleeve says: "Wait a minute, you two. Ain't there a little business goin' around here?"

I say: "Yeah? What's the business?" I have got a good idea why the hell this guy Cleeve, who as I have told you is a nice lookin' guy, an' a good private dick, is kickin' around with the "G" office in Paris. It looks like something's broke.

Dombie takes a swig at the bottle; then he corks it, throws it across to me, an' a glass after it. I give myself a shot.

Dombie says: "Listen, Lemmy, you're a guy who has gotta reputation for keepin' his nose clean, but it looks as if you're in bad with the big boy."

I say: "No? Don't tell me you're gonna spoil my night's sleep. What have I done now?"

Dombie goes on: "I reckon it's a matter of janes again. That last job you did—there was a sorta leakage or something. Somebody wised up the boss that you were gettin' around a bit with a hot dame—Marceline—you know, the one they knocked off. He's got the idea in his head that maybe you shot your mouth a little bit."

I say: "Well, he's a goddam liar. I can get around with any dame without shootin' my mouth."

Dombie says: "Yeah. Well, I hope you're gonna persuade him about that, because he's got an idea that somebody did a little talkin' outa turn an' that somebody was you."

I say: "You don't say?" I give myself another drink.

The guy Cleeve says: "Take is easy, Lemmy. Look, I'm just sorta musclin' in on this business, see? But I've been dragged over here from New York because the chief reckoned I knew something. So he took me away from the agency an' got me over here. He asked me plenty an' I had to tell him what I knew."

I say: "That's all right by me, but I'd like to know who gave him the big idea that I'd been shooting my mouth to a dame."

Dombie shrugs his shoulders. Nobody says anythin' for a minute; then Cleeve says: "But I can tell you that one. She did. The Marceline baby told him that."

I don't say anythin', but it's like I've been kicked in the face by a mule. I say: "Listen, do you mean that?"

He says: "Yeah, Lemmy. I mean it all right. It don't rate a lot because when they pulled her in for questioning they reckon she's liable to say anythin' that she thinks is gonna help her. Maybe she thought if she stuck a medal like that on you she'd make it easier for herself." He yawns. "I reckon this Marceline had one helluva imagination," he says, "but the thing is to get the chief to think that. There is also another thing. You remember that guy who was working with you on that?"

I say: "You mean the guy Ribban—a Federal guy—the man from Connecticut. Well, he is a good guy an' he knows all about it."

Cleeve says: "That's what I thought. I thought you might like to have a talk to him before you saw the chief. I sorta fixed it."

I say: "I think that is pretty swell of you, Jimmy. When do I see the big boy?"

Dombie comes up for air. He says: "I reckon he wants to see you around ten o'clock to-night. He's burned up about this thing, Lemmy, because there's some more strings on it. You know there's a lot of stuff getting round. He says there are leakages everywhere—Paris, London, and everywhere else. Goddam it, they even say that somebody gave the Arnhem show away; that the Jerries knew when the British paratroops were gonna drop an' where."

I say: "Yeah! Maybe the chief thinks I told 'em that too."

"Aw shucks!" says Dombie, "with *your* record. Take it easy, Lemmy. I reckon he thinks you did a little too much talkin' to this dame. Well, why not? You thought she was on the up and up. How the hell were you to know she was workin' for the other side?"

I say: "That makes no difference so far as I'm concerned. I never talk to blondes anyway."

Dombie says: "I wish I could say the same thing. I don't talk to 'em about anythin' serious, but what I do talk to 'em about seems to get me inta plenty trouble."

I take another swig outa the bottle. I say to Cleeve: "O.K. So I see the boss at ten. Maybe it's a good idea if I have a talk with Ribban first. You said you fixed something up?"

He says: "Yeah. There's a little dump he goes to—a little bar place just off the Place Pigalle—Leon's place. He said he'd be around there at nine o'clock. It's a quarter short of that now. Maybe you just got time to get around there an' have one with him an' hear what he's gotta say before you see the old man."

I say: "O.K. I'll get movin'. Well, I'll be seein' you."

Dombie says: "Yeah. Soon I hope, Lemmy."

Cleeve says: "I'll be seein' you to-night, Lemmy. I think the old boy has got something on the ice for us."

I get up an' go down the stairs and out into the Place des Roses. I start walkin' towards the Place Pigalle.

I think: What the hell!

I stall around for a bit. An' why not? Me . . . I am not in any great hurry to contact up with this Ribban guy an' I am certainly not dyin' on my feet to get around to this interview with the big boy. I reckon that little meetin' is goin' to be so goddam interestin' when it comes off that you'd be surprised. So the longer I stall seein' Ribban the longer I stall the showdown. Anyhow, Ribban has gotta wait till I show up.

I walk around lookin' at the sights and comparin' Paris in this year of grace—or disgrace—whichever way you like to play it—with Paris in 1926 an' Paris in 1939. I was there on cases both years an' it was "good goin'" then. Maybe I liked it better in 1939.

I get around to thinkin' about this babe Marceline. A clever babe that one. A little cute jane who knows how to mix the poison good an' plenty. I would give a coupla months' pay to know what that cutey told the chief about me an' just how much of it was straight stuff. Maybe I did do a spot of talkin' when I oughta have kept my trap shut. But whether what I said meant a goddam or not is somethin' I do not wish to talk about right at this moment. No, sir. . . .

You gotta realise that it is not all roseleaves an' bourbon working for the "G" service with the Army in Paris. I'm tellin' you. In the good old days in New York when I was a top guy in the Federal Bureau an' in line for bein' made a Field Agent, things was pretty good. Maybe I didn't know when I was well off. Now when a bunch of us mugs is workin' with the Army Intelligence an' Secret Services over here, everybody is rushin' around in circles, playin' it off the cuff an' gettin' so goddam busy that they're fairly trippin' over each other.

But I wish to heck I knew just how much that babe Marceline had shot her mouth. . . .

My old mother who was great for knowin' about dames— an' why not she was one herself—usta tell me that nobody was gonna get anywhere in the "G" business if he was playin' around with frails all the time. Well, maybe she was right an' maybe she wasn't but right now I'm wonderin' if I didn't maybe overreach myself a bit over this Marceline. It looks like the kid was cuter than I thought.

Down the end of the little street I am passin' I can see a light. I go down there. It is a dump called Wilkie's. It is one of them places. A bar, some dames, an' a certain amount of bottles stuck around the place. The liquor is so goddam expensive that it takes a guy about four million francs to get a bit high, an' if you drink the cheap stuff you sorta pause when you put the glass down an' wonder if you are merely gettin' a kick or whether you have been hit in the navel with one of Mister Hitler's V 2's.

I lean up against the bar an' make a sign to Wilkie that I need brandy—an' outa the right bottle too. I drink two slugs, a chaser an' then take a look around the bar. I take a look an' I realise that the guy who wrote that number *My Heart Stood Still* musta been thinkin' of yours very sincerely Mr. Lemuel H. Caution—Special Agent of the Federal Bureau of Investigation now attached General Headquarters Intelligence an' Secret Service U.S. Army, Paris, an' if there is anythin' to come back on the empty bottles we shall be pleased to hear from you.

The reason for this shock to my system is that sittin' at the end of the bar an' lookin' just as if she had jumped out of a fashion plate book is my old friend Juanella Rillwater, who is the wife of a guy called Larvey Rillwater who rates as bein' about the best safe-blower in the United States, an' who has been chased all his life by every type of copper that there is in the world, most of whom have just been wastin' their time because there are no flies on Mr. Rillwater. Except once when there were plenty.

Right now I'm tellin' you guys that the sight of this babe takes my breath away for two reasons. The first one bein' the way she looks an' the second one bein' somethin' that I will wise you up to in a coupla minutes.

She is a sweet parcel is Juanella. On the tall side with curves just where they oughta be, an' everythin' pointin' in the right direction. She has got auburn hair that looks as if it had just been done by the world's champion hair fixer an' green eyes. Her figure is what they would call willowy—if anybody ever taught 'em the word—an' she has plenty of that stuff that is worth more than pearls an' platinum to an ambitious dame—the stuff called allure. When they was issuin' out sex appeal I reckon Juanella took a shoppin' bag, winked an' drew double.

She is wearin' a leaf green velvet coat an' skirt that looks as if it had been pasted on to her, a primrose crepe-de-chine shirt-blouse, one of them smart tailor-made hats an' bronze coloured kid court shoes with four-inch heels. This babe is guaranteed to hit anythin' in pants for a home run an' what she don't know to go with it could be stuck under a postage stamp an' not missed.

The second reason why I am sorta intrigued with seein' her around here in Paris is that Jimmy Cleeve, the private dick that I just been talkin' to around at Dombie's dump, is the guy who eventually put the finger on Larvey Rillwater for a bank safe job in Illinois about eighteen months before the war. An' at the present moment I get a big idea that I know exactly what is the trouble with Mrs. Caution's little boy Lemmy.

Figure it out for yourself that I am one of these poetic guys who is always lookin' around for beauty. I have got that sort of eye. Maybe you mugs also know that this palooka Confucius who is the smart boyo who is always ready with a wise spiel, and who has himself a good time tellin' the rest of the world where it gets off the ridin' rods, has summed all this business up when he said: "The beauty of women is like the alligator waitin' in the bulrushes." Just when the sapient bozo thinks he is all set for a big time with some allurin' *femme* he is only on the threshold of havin' the pants kicked offa him an' bein' hit for a home run. "Better," continues this Confucius . . . "better to tickle the sleepin' tarantula than to a make a false pass at the geography of some seductive blonde who woulda been given a good conduct medal by Henry The Eighth for knowin' all the right answers, an' who when bein' discovered in the act of four flushin' the monarch in the pantry with the Court Jester, arranges to be A.W.O.L. just at that moment when the royal executioner gets busy sharpenin' up the old battle-axe."

Because it will hit you people like a well-aimed piece of coke that right now the wrong thing for me to be doin' is to get myself contacted in any way whatsoever with any more dames. But life is like that. What you never had you don't miss . . . like hell you don't!

Because the safe baby is never beautiful. Which is maybe O.K. for a guy who goes in for safety. But the safe baby is also plain an' usually dumb. She has one of them mouths that writin' guys call generous because they are too nice to say that it looks like a yawnin' chasm. The safe baby is safe but she also has ankles that look like stove-pipes all the way up an' a figure that makes you wanta rush home, get some drawin' paper an' start designin' false bust developers. The safe baby has dough in the bank an' also intends that it shall remain there until her teeth get as yellow as last year's daffodils. The safe baby thinks she is smart but she is so goddam deficient in the old grey matter that she believes that a blunderbuss is a vehicle used for conveyin' spinsters to a maternity home.

And that is the safe baby!

Because when a dame is beautiful she also has to develop a certain amount of horse sense even if it is only through self-protection. All the time guys are tryin' to make this dame in a very big way. She has also to have herself a very snappy line in comebacks just so's she can tell the smart boyos where the 'bus stops.

Me . . . I remember a very swell dame is Oshkosh where the women are all easy on the eyes, an' the men don't wear braces, who was so marvellous to look at that it hurt. She was also a very hot number an' she had a lotta brains.

One day she is walkin' down the main stem an' one of these good guys that you read about rushes up to her an' he says: "Esmeralda," he says, "I do not like the sort of life you are leadin'. Every man around this hick town is nuts about you. Last night I was thinkin' about you, an' prayin' for you."

To which she replies with dignity an' a slight droopin' of the upper eyelid: "Home come, palsie? Why the heck do you have to start prayin' for me when my number's in the telephone book. Why didn't you call through?"

After which the good guy had himself four double ryes, joined the Marines an' was last seen manicurin' a Japanese machine gunner with a pickaxe.

An' if you cannot see the moral to this story then all I gotta say is that you oughta go see some quack about it.

However, all that is sorta on the side an' revertin' to Mrs. Juanella Rillwater I would like to say that right now her husband, the said Larvey, is stuck safely away in a Federal prison in U.S.A. an' I reckon that Juanella has thought she might as well make hay while the sun shines an' has by some means known only to herself an' the guy who pulled it off, got herself over here in Paris just to see if there is anythin' worth pickin' up.

Just for one little minute I think I will lay off talkin' to this babe an' get around an' see what this Ribban guy has got to talk about. Then I think what the hell an' I ease over an' stand behind her an' say: "Well . . . well . . . well . . . if it is not that gift to mankind Juanella an' how's it goin'?"

She spins around on the high stool as if she had been poleaxed. She takes one look at me with those green eyes of hers. She goes red an' white an' blue an' she says:

"Well, for cryin' out loud in Chinese! If it is not the only guy I ever really wanted to make—Lemmy Caution."

She sits there smilin' up at me an' makin' a little grimace at me with her mouth—which is some mouth—an' showin' her little white teeth.

"Lemmy," she goes on, "may I be sugared an' iced an' sold for a wedding cake if I am not very glad to see you. You are a sight for sore eyes an' I love you like death."

I wink at her. Because this sorta stuff is a line with Juanella. Except that she has always told everybody she was a trifle stuck on me in the old days an' maybe she was tellin' the truth for once.

I say: "This is marvellous. I have not had such fun since I was shot out of a cannon in a circus. Talk to me, sweet, an' tell me what you are doin' in this city of gladness an' sorrow, dressed like a film star, an' lookin' like a million dollars. Also how is your spouse—that is if he is still your spouse—Larvey?"

She takes a long an' very knowin' look at me an' she says sorta soft: "The same old Mister Caution, hey? If I didn't like you so much I would call you a heel because you always do something to me. At the same time I hate your guts because you know goddam well that my spouse, as you call him, otherwise Larvey T. Rillwater the safe-blowin' expert, terms on application, is, at this minute, permanently at home to everybody entitled to take a look through the cell bars in Alcatraz. An' what about buyin' me a drink, Mr. Caution? Or may I call you Lemmy?"

I go inta a huddle with Wilkie an' after a lotta negotiation he runs up a couple of cocktails which we take over to a table in the corner an' sit down an' look at each other. I grin at her because to me this is like a coupla light-heavyweights sparrin' for an openin'.

After a bit she takes a sip at the cocktail an' runs her little pink tongue over her lips. She says: "That tastes swell. But you always did buy the best drinks, didn't you, Lemmy? Sorta selective, aren't you? The only trouble is that you never got around to selectin' me."

"Never mind, Juanella," I told her. "While there is life there is hope an' maybe when you are an old dame with iron grey hair an' a puss like a map of the South Atlantic Coastline I will come around an' hold your hand an' tell you some of the secrets of life."

"Yeah?" she says. "Like hell. Anytime I get like that I'm gonna take a powder on myself an' disappear into thin blue smoke. Me, I am never goin' to grow old. I am just goin' to fade away while I have still got *somethin'* left."

I light myself a cigarette an' one for her. "I am just stuck around here, Juanella," I say. "An' I am not doin' so well. They sent a bunch of us 'G' people over here to work with the Army people an' it ain't so easy. Besides which I been makin' a little piece of a fool outa myself. I been a top grade mug."

She raises her eyebrows. She says: "You don't say, Lemmy! Not *you*. Anybody else but you. But you ain't goin' to tell me that Mr. Lemuel H. Caution, the pride of the F.B.I., the big boy who could do no wrong, has blotted his copybook, smudged his slate an' otherwise balled up the works. I don't believe it. No, sir!"

"Well, I wish you was right, Juanella," I say. "But that's the way it is. I been a mug. I was on a job an' I shot my mouth a bit wide to some dame. I didn't tell her a thing that mattered but enough for her to guess a little bit here an' there, an' they are goin' to tear me wide open for it an' I don't mean perhaps."

She says: "That's bad, Lemmy." She looks at me an' there is somethin' like a tear in her eye. She goes on: "If there was ever a guy that I would have bet was permanently gonna keep his nose clean that guy would be you. But I would like to get my hooks on the dame. I would certainly do somethin' to that so-an'-so. An' what are they goin' to do to you, Lemmy?"

I shrug my shoulders. "I'm not worryin', Juanella," I say. "What's the good anyhow? It won't get me any place. But never mind about that. What're you doin' over here? An' how did you fix it? Or who fixed it? It's goddam difficult to get outa U.S. these days an' get a permit for Paris. Especially for a dame with her husband stuck in the cooler. How come?"

She looks at the end of her cigarette. Then she says: "Well . . . I'll tell you, Lemmy. Maybe you know the name of the guy who knocked Larvey off. It was a guy called Cleeve . . . Jimmy Cleeve. A private dick who was workin' in the Illinois State police office. Sorta loaned there for the War. Well, he put the finger on Larvey but he was goddam decent about it."

"He would be," I tell her. "Because this Cleeve guy is a right guy. I know him." But I do not tell her that Cleeve is over here in Paris right now, because it is not always a good thing to tell a dame *too* much.

"O.K.," she goes on. "Well, when they slung Larvey inside I was all sorta broke up. I've always been sorta fond of Larvey an' even if I ain't been crazy about him like I am about some people"—she throws me one of them hot looks—"still Larvey was O.K. I was just sorta moonin' around an' goin' all to pieces an' just when I felt the time had come for me to chuck myself inta East River an' try an' catch a fish in my mouth I run inta this Cleeve boyo an' he says if I like to come over here an' do a job in one of the U.S. Despatch Departments he will fix it an' get me over in spite of my record not bein' so hot."

She sighs. "I was tickled pink to get the chance," she says. "So I pulled myself together an' then another thing broke. Old Mrs. Fayle—Larvey's aunt—the one in Saratoga—who was always tryin' to get Larvey to give up safe blowin' an' go into somethin' straight an' decent like fake-Company promotin'—died an' left me a few thousand iron boys—not a lot, but enough jack to get a girl a haircut an' a few bits of things to match right through—if you get me. So here I am an' all the better for seein' you."

I look at my strap-watch. It is half-past nine. I think that maybe I will get around an' meet up with the guy Ribban an' get wise to anythin' that is goin'.

"Look, Juanella," I tell her. "I got to go. But I'd like to see you again some time. Maybe we could have a dinner together."

She says: "Sure, Lemmy, I'd like nothin' better. I'm stayin' at an hotel—the Hotel St. Denis. Here's the telephone number. Call through some time an' you needn't worry about givin' me any notice because whatever I got on that evenin' I'll ditch it. That's how I feel about you . . . honey."

I give her a big grin. "You got a swell line, Juanella," I tell her. "You oughta been on the stage. But I'll call you just as soon as I got things sort of squared off."

She says: "O.K., Lemmy . . . an' watch your step. You're too good to get yourself into trouble. I'll stick around here for a bit an' maybe have another little drink."

I say so long an' scram. Out in the street I think that the guy who said that the world was a small place musta been takin' brain tablets.

I walk up the Hill pretty slow thinkin' about this an' that. It has got cold suddenly—so goddam cold that even a baby with hot pants would think she was sittin' on an iceberg. Or maybe that's the way I'm feelin'! I've got the idea in my head that there is a lotta trouble waitin' for me one way or another.

I should worry! I reckon I been duckin' trouble for so many years that a little bit more is not likely to do very much to Mrs. Caution's eldest unmarried son. No, sir . . . because I have had every sort of trouble happen to me, an' when things get a bit tough I always remember the French guy who said that most of the things that he's spent his time worryin' about had not happened. The boy definitely knew his artichokes.

I have already told you mugs about this Chinese guy Confucius. Confucius is a boyo that I go for in a very big way, because he has spent most of his life reducin' things to terms of some sayin' or the other. One of the things he said was that there is only three sorts of trouble—dames, dough, an' not bein' well. Well, this is where he slipped up.

Because first of all a guy who has got dame trouble has got all the others anyway. I never knew a mug who was worryin' about some bundle of babe who was not also havin' a lot of trouble about jack an' who was not also feelin' not so well.

But the trouble that Confucius missed was the fourth one. An' that is the one that you have if you have not got any of the others. Work it out for yourself. If a guy has not got a dame to worry about; if he has got dough an' nobody to spend it on; an' if he is also healthy an' has nobody to feel sick about, then all I can say is that the guy must be nuts because any palooka who is goin' through life that way must be headin' for the local bug house. An' you can quote me.

Fifteen minutes' walkin' an' I get to this Club Leon. It is an old narrow turnin' not far from Rue Clichy. It is not really a Club. The ground floor is a sorta *bistro* with a little tiny place at the back for dancin'.

There are a coupla reputed Russians sittin' on a platform at one end of the room an' playin' on *balalaikas* on Mondays, Wednesdays an' Saturdays evenin's. On Tuesdays, Thursdays an' Fridays they play on zithers—but you should worry because the noise is just the same all the week an' anyway if Joe Stalin ever catches up with these mugs he will listen for about two bars an' then order the Kremlin Guard to get busy with a coupla medium machine guns. I have heard music in practically every place where they got feet an' some dames, but the stuff these guys turn out is lousy. Even if it was good I would not like it.

Beyond this, Leon's is just one of them places.

I go in. Comin' outa the cold night air the place is hot. It is fulla smoke an' the Russians are makin' their usual tinklin' noise. There is a hum of conversation from all over the place. There are guys makin' black market bargains, dames makin' guys an' other dames tryin' not to make mistakes.

I go over to the bar at the end of the room. Leon is standin' behind it, leanin' on his elbows, with a thin Spanish cigar stickin' outa one end of his mouth.

I say: "Well, fella, how's it goin'?"

He says; "It's all right. Everythin's perfect—I don't think." He grins. He says: "What do you theenk, my fren'—everything is what you call goddam awful."

I say: "Maybe you're right. Something musta happened to everybody. Maybe it's a guy called Hitler. Look, is there a Mr. Ribban around here?"

He nods. He picks up a duster an' starts trying to polish the top of the bar. He says: "Yes, he's got a room on the top floor. He's up there now. You can go through the bar. Take the door at the end of the passage and go right up."

I say: "O.K." I walk through the bar, through the little dance room on the other side an' through the passage. The passage is dark, an' right in the middle of it some G.I. is neckin' a French girl like it was his last night on earth. I squeeze past, find the door at the end an' go up the stairs. It looks to me like there are millions of stairs. I reckon Ribban musta liked to be near the stars. Maybe he was a bit poetic—the sorta way I get sometimes when I get stuck on some frail.

Because I do not know whether I have ever told you guys that I am very a poetic an' artistic sorta cuss. Most of the time I have spent chasin' around the world after thugs, come-on boys and skulduggers in general; but any moment I got time to breathe I always start gettin' poetic an' thinkin' in a very big way about beauty. An' I am the sorta guy who when he starts thinkin' about somethin' tries to turn these high-class thoughts into action. An' why not an' what would *you* do?

Only I have found that bein' poetic an' thinkin' about certain beautiful things—like a pair of swell ankles an' everything else to match has caused me more goddam trouble than all the crooks I ever been chasin' after.

Maybe there is a moral here. If there is you can have it because I am a very generous sorta guy an' like to go through the world givin' moral thoughts to one an' all an' no charge either.

I walk up two flights an' I take a breather on a little landin'. The last flight of stairs narrows down an' curves around to the left. The stairs are wooden an' there are no carpets on them an' my footsteps make a funny sorta noise. It is goddam dark because there is no light anywhere an' I am feelin' my way along up the wall. Halfway up the stairs I tread on something soft. I reckon somebody musta dropped a handkerchief.

After a bit I get to the top. I switch on my cigarette lighter an' take a look. In front of me is a door. I push it open an' go in. It is a bedroom an' it's empty. On the end of the mantelpiece opposite the door is a candle. I go over an' light it. I wonder what the hell Ribban wanted to keep a dump like this for, but you never know. Maybe he used it for dates or something.

I look around. There is a bed in one corner, a coupla chairs, a chest of drawers with a mirror an' a desk. There is a blottin' pad on the desk—a sheet from one of the U.S. stationery depots—an' on it are a couple sheets of writin' paper an' an envelope. A piece of blottin' paper is folded an' laid across the sheet of notepaper just as if somebody was gonna write a letter or something. The idea strikes me that maybe Ribban was gonna write to somebody an' got interrupted an' went out. Then I get an idea.

I take the candle an' I go down the stairs. You remember I said that when I was halfway up the last flight I trod on something soft like a handkerchief. Well, it wasn't a handkerchief. It wasn't anythin' like that. It was the sleeve of Ribban's coat. The guy is lyin' with his head pointin' towards the bottom of the stairs, bunched up against the banister rail.

I take a close look at him. He's had it all right. I reckon he's as dead as last week's cold cuts. I put the candle down on the stairs an' I slip my hand just inside his shirt. I feel he is still nice an' warm.

I take out a cigarette, pick up the candle, an' light it. I stand there leanin' against the wall just above the boyo lookin' down at him. Then I bend over an' hold the candle close to his head. Just inside his right ear, which is the uppermost one, I can see a little yellow fluid.

I stand there lookin' at him, thinking: This is not quite so good.

A telephone bell starts ringin'. It is ringin' in the room at the top—the one I just come out of—Ribban's room.

I ease up the stairs. There is a telephone on a little table in one corner of the room. I go over and grab it. I say hello.

Some guy says: "Is that you, Ribban?"

I say: "Yeah. What can I do for you, an' who is it?"

He says: "This is Jimmy Cleeve speakin'. Is Caution with you? If he is, you might put him on to me."

I say: "Listen, Jimmy, this is Caution."

He says: "Yeah? I thought you said you was Ribban."

"So I did," I say, "only because I wanted to know who it was ringin' through. I thought I might find something out. Things are not so good around here."

He says: "What do you mean? Another thing," he goes on, "things are not so good around *here* either. The chief is raisin' hell an' devils because you have not showed up. He asked me to get through to you. It's after ten now. What goes on around there?"

I say: "Look, you tell the big boy that something that looks as if it might be important has broke—something big, see? You get yourself a jeep an' come around here as quick as you can, but don't bring the jeep up to the Club, send it away at the end of the street an' come here on your own. You don't wanta make any sorta fuss, see?"

He says: "O.K., Lemmy. What you say. I'll be with you in no time at all."

I say: "Thanks a lot, Jimmy," an' hang up. I pick up the candle an' I go down the stairway an' take another look at Ribban. He is lyin' like I told you—sorta bunched up against the wall with his head pointin' towards the lower floor landin'. I kneel down on the stairs an' take a close look at him. His left arm is sorta caught up underneath him, but the hand is stickin' out. It is clenched an' there is something stickin' out between the fingers. I look at it. It is the end of a fountain pen that has still got the cap screwed on.

I take out my handkerchief, get hold of the end of the pen an' ease it out of Ribban's fingers. I look at it. It is a French pen—the sorta thing you can buy on the black market if you feel that way. I put it in my pocket; then I feel in the left hand lower pocket of Ribban's vest an' I find a little two-inch stub of pencil. I put the pencil back an' button up the middle button of his coat. I think: Well, that is that. Then I sit down on the stairs an' wait for Cleeve.

I light myself another cigarette an' wonder what the hell is poppin' around here. None of this business seems to make any sorta sense to me, but life is like that. If ever a thing made sense it would be easy, which is what the dame said when her boy friend went off with a blonde. I give up thinkin' an' relax.

Ten minutes go by an' Cleeve comes easin' up the stairs. He is comin' up two at a time nice an' quiet. I watch him over the banisters come out on the stairs below where there is a little light. He is a slick an' easy mover. I think that this Cleeve is an attractive guy. I like the cut of his jaw, the way he talks an' most other things about him. Maybe he will have some ideas about this.

He comes round the turn of the stairs an' stops dead when he sees me sittin' there with a candle beside me an' Ribban givin' an imitation of the sleepin' babe in the wood.

He says: "Jeez! For cryin' out loud! What d'you know about that?"

"I don't know a thing, Jimmy," I tell him. "*You* tell me."

He says: "Look, Lemmy. What's happened?" He stands there with one hand on the wall lookin' down at Ribban.

"You know as much as I do," I say. "I got here about fifteen minutes ago. A coupla minutes before you telephoned I saw Leon downstairs an' he told me Ribban was up here in his room. I came up the stairs an' I hadn't got a light, so I didn't notice him. I just trod on his coat as I went past. I thought maybe somebody had dropped something. Then I went to his room an' found it empty. Then I came down here an' took a look. Then you telephoned."

He nods. He says: "This is not so good. I don't like this one little bit. Have you taken a look around his room?"

I say: "Yeah. There's some notepaper an' an envelope an' a piece of blotting paper all set out on the desk just as if he was gonna write a letter."

He says: "Yeah. He was always writing letters to somebody— Ribban. He was like that." He looks at the stairs. He says: "Of course it would be goddam easy for anybody to fall down these stairs, you know."

I say: "Is that your theory, Jimmy?"

He says: "Why not? Look, was there a pen an' ink or anythin' up on the desk or just the paper?"

I say: "There was no pen an' ink. There was only just the paper an' the envelope an' the blotting paper."

He nods. He says: "I get it. The guy is waitin' for you an' he sits down to write a letter, or maybe he is gonna make some notes or something, an' he suddenly realises that he hasn't got a pen or ink, see? He goes trippin' down the stairs to get one off Leon. He falls down an' he breaks his neck. That's how it is."

I say: "Yeah? Come again, Jimmy."

He looks at me. He says: "What do you mean?"

I say: "Take a look in his right ear." I hold the candle up. He bends down an' looks.

He says: "So what? There is some yellow wax or something in his ear."

I say: "That is not wax. That means the guy's got a fractured base of the skull. Take another look an' you will see where the fracture is. He never broke his neck. Somebody let him have it. Somebody decided to sandbag the boy."

He says: "What—on the stairs! You mean someone's gonna wait here for him to pass an' sock him as he goes by? That don't make sense to me, Lemmy."

I say: "It don't make sense to me either. Nobody was waitin' for him on the stairs. Look, I reckon he was sittin' at that desk upstairs just startin' to write that letter without noticin' that there wasn't any pen or ink. O.K. Well, somebody comes gumshoein' up the stairs in the darkness. The door is open because Ribban is expectin' me. They go in an' they hand it to him. His head's just in the right position to get it like that. Then they lug him down here an' push him up against the wall, so some mug"—I grin at him—"like you will think he fell down the stairs an' broke his neck."

He says: "Well, you might be right at that. Have you got a weed?"

I give him a cigarette. He lights it, stands leanin' up against the wall. He is thinkin' hard.

After a bit he says: "Look, I reckon he was gonna write a letter an' then he hadn't got a pen an' ink. I reckon he got up an' started comin' down the stairs to borrow one off Leon, tripped up an' broke his neck. That's my story an' I'm gonna stick to it. About this yellow fluid in his ear an' this fractured base of the skull stuff, that's O.K. They ain't gonna worry too much if we send him round to the mortuary an' *we* tell the authorities what happened, are they? That's gonna be O.K."

I say: "It's gonna be fine. But what's the big idea? Somebody creased Ribban."

He says: "Jeez, Lemmy, won't you get some sense in your head? Look, you got a date with the old man to-night. You're gonna see him about puttin' out a little explanation about shootin' your mouth to this dame Marceline. He's not so pleased with you."

I say: "I know that. So what?"

He says: "So this: Who was it Marceline talked to? Who was it examined her when they brought her in? Who was it put her through it an' got the story about you? Wasn't that Ribban?"

I say: "Yeah, I suppose it was."

"All right," he says. "So Ribban is the guy who talked to her. He is the guy who knows all about what you told her and what you didn't tell her. O.K. Well, you come around here an' see him an' the pair of you are gonna see the big boy to-night, an' I ring up because I wonder what the hell is happenin' because you two don't show up. An' you're here an' he's dead, an' he's been creased. Well, it don't look so good for you, does it?"

I say: "Meaning that I creased Ribban because he'd got something on me?"

He says: "That might be an idea. Maybe there are one or two people not so well disposed towards you, Lemmy. Maybe they'd go for a story like that. After all, supposin' you *did* tell this Marceline baby something that mattered, supposing to save her own skin when she was pulled in she shot the works to Ribban an' told him, it wouldn't be so good for you, would it? If he'd shot his mouth?"

I say: "No. But you're forgetting one thing. We've still got Marceline. If I'm supposed to have told this baby so goddam much, maybe she can tell *us* what I told her as well as Ribban. Maybe if she talked to him she'll talk to somebody else. Because I think it's a lot of hooey. So let's get outa here an' let's see the big boy an' give him the works, an' let me talk to this Marceline dame. I wanta get my hooks on that frail."

He says: "That would be swell, Lemmy. If you could work it that way, but you can't."

I say: "Why not?"

He says: "Because Marceline is no longer with us. They had her stuck in the local cooler, you know, the No. 14 French police base. O.K. Well, about an hour or so ago, somebody walks in there with a forged order from the big boy an' got her out. You got that?"

I say I've got it.

"O.K.," says Jimmy. "Well, about twenty minutes ago they found her on a doorstep, in the Rue Zacherie. She'd been shot twice an' dumped there. You got that?"

I say: "I get it, fella."

He says: "So now you go leapin' around to the big boy an' tell him that somebody killed Ribban. It doesn't matter what he says, he's gotta think something, hasn't he? And it's not gonna look so good for you."

I do a little quick concentrated thinkin'. I say: "Jimmy, I reckon you're right." I point my finger to Ribban. "If this is murder," I say, "it don't look so good for Mr. Caution."

He nods. He bends down an' puts his hand on Ribban. "He hasn't been dead long," he says. "The fact that you just arrived wouldn't have meant a thing. It wouldn't have taken you half a minute to have done this." He smiles at me. He says: "He was going down to borrow a pen an' some ink. He tripped up an' broke his neck."

I say: "Jimmy, I think you're a good guy. One day maybe I'll be able to do something for you."

He says: "Forget it, pal. I know about you, an' I know your record. I know you wouldn't do a thing like this. But there are one or two guys who have maybe got it in for you. So we play it this way."

I get up. I say: "O.K. I'll get an ambulance."

He says: "You can phone from downstairs. I'll go up to Ribban's room and call through to the big boy. I'll tell him what happened. I'll tell him we'll be a little late gettin' round there."

He goes up the stairs. I go down an' use the telephone in the *bistro*. I think that maybe there is a helluva lot in what Jimmy has said. I reckon that this mighta been not so good for me. I reckon I don't like it a lot anyhow. Because it looks as if somebody is layin' for Mr. Caution in a very big way.

Me . . . I think that if I was a guy who worried I would be worried.

So now you know.

CHAPTER TWO
STRIP TEASE

I HAVE seen the big boy lookin' tough one or two times before, but I have never seen him looking as tough as he is right now.

The office at Headquarters is in darkness except for the one desk lamp on the corner of his desk. When we go in he is reading some papers in front of him, an' Jimmy Cleeve an' I stand sorta twiddlin' our thumbs lookin' at him. He don't even look up. The big boy is a pretty good guy. He has got a nice round face an' iron grey hair, but in spite of the flesh around the jaw you can still see it juttin' out like a rock. A tough egg that one. The light from the desk lamp is reflectin' on the General's star on his shoulder. I reckon he is amused at the idea of bein' a General officer—this guy, who was probably the top line Federal dick in the Bureau of Justice, but war is a funny thing an' all sorts of guys are doin' all sorts of jobs in all sorts of uniforms.

He looks up. He pulls a switch down an' the light right above our heads goes on.

He says: "Well, good-evening. I'm glad to see you here."

Jimmy says: "Good-evening, sir."

I don't say anythin'. I think maybe it's a good idea if I keep my trap shut for once. Flash takes a long look at Cleeve, and then one at me.

Then he says: "Well, I reckon I know you well enough, Caution, to talk straight to you. I know your record and I've known your work for a long time. You've always been regarded as one of the best agents in the F.B.I. If anybody had told me that you'd do too much talking; that you'd shoot your mouth, whether you'd taken too much liquor or not, I wouldn't have believed it. Well?"

I don't say anythin'.

He goes on: "Well, you know the story. What have you got to say about it?"

I say: "Look, General, what the hell does it matter what I've got to say about it? I know what I've been *told* about it."

He says: "Yes . . . maybe you're right." He opens a drawer, takes out a cigar an' lights it. He goes on: "The position is even more unsatisfactory because there's no means of checking on the report. You know what's in it, don't you?"

I say: "I got a rough idea what's in it."

He says: "All right. I'll just go over the salient details so that we understand each other. Marceline du Clos—a French citizeness—and an American named Varley—at least he was a reputed American; there seems to be a little mix-up about his passport—have been operating an interior decorating business in New York practically since the war started. They came under the notice of the F.B.I. They were suspect. The idea was that they were in the pay of the Germans or the Japanese or both. Two agents of the F.B.I. were detailed independently to take care of the job. One of them was George Ribban and the other was you, Caution. You both had your own instructions and you both worked separately.

"The next thing is du Clos and Varley, by some interesting means which nobody has yet discovered, got themselves permits and passports to get out of New York and come to Paris. Well, we didn't mind that. We thought maybe we could get on to something over here. They got over here two or three weeks after the American and British Armies got into Paris and the Germans got out. Ribban came over here after them and so did you, Caution. The next idea was that you should try and get next to this woman Marceline du Clos."

He sits back in his chair, draws a lungful of cigar smoke, blows it outa one corner of his mouth. He says: "Your record shows that you've always been pretty successful in handling women. Well, you contacted du Clos. You got around with her. One night you took her out and it looks like you hit the liquor. They find you cockeyed the next morning in a dump off the Rue Clichy. Nobody knew where du Clos was.

"By this time certain information had got out about troop movements. Intelligence over here believed that du Clos and Varley were responsible for the leakage. Ribban was put on to pick up du Clos. We couldn't find Varley. We still don't know where he is. Ribban got du Clos. He found her. He threw a scare into her. Maybe she thought she was going to get shot or something. Possibly Ribban encouraged her to think that way. He thought it might help her to talk. Well, she talked.

"She told him a certain amount, but the main thing she said was that you, Caution, had shot your mouth good and plenty. You told her what you were doing and it looks as if you did a little bit of beefing about what our Secret Service and Intelligence organisations are doing over here and how they're working. Ribban didn't like that. He didn't like it because as a good Federal agent he couldn't understand it. Neither can I.

"All right, you haven't got anythin' to say. I think you're right. If you talked to this woman when you were drunk you wouldn't know what you said anyway. If Ribban was here so that he could tell us what she'd actually told him we'd know a lot more about it. But he's not here. Perhaps that's a little convenient for you. I'm told that he fell down some stairs to-night and broke his neck. That was a bad break for him and a good one for you—maybe."

I say: "Maybe it was. General, an' maybe it wasn't. Me —I woulda liked to have heard what George Ribban had to say. I woulda liked to hear what I am supposed to have told this dame."

He says: "Yes, I expect you would." He looks at me hard. "And so would I."

I say: "There's another tough angle to this thing too. General. I reckon I would have liked to have talked to this Marceline du Clos myself, an' at a time when I wasn't supposed to be cockeyed, an' in front of you. I woulda liked to have heard this goddam jane tell *me* what I was supposed to have told her when I had all this liquor aboard."

He says: "Well, you won't hear that. You know what's happened to her. Somebody presented a forged pass to-night at the 14th Police Post here and got her out. Who it was we don't know. The pass is a good imitation. It bears a very nice imitation of my signature. Anyway, it was good enough for them. They let her go and they seem to be vague about the person—man or woman—who took her away.

"All right. Later they found her shot in the Rue Zacherie. That's very inconvenient too." He looks at me again.

I say: "Yeah. Look, General, what is the big idea? Is the idea that I got this Marceline du Clos out an' shot her? Because I wanted to stop her talking about what I'd told her. It looks as if I'm qualifyin' for murder on a big scale."

He puts his cigar back in his mouth. He says: "Don't talk like a damned fool, Caution. Personally, I don't think the matter is as serious as one or two people have tried to make out. Du Clos was apparently a temperamental sort of woman. When Ribban pulled her in and she got scared, she may have said anythin' that she thought might help her a little. Espionage suspects are often like that, but it's the first time that anythin''s happened to this organisation in this war like this, and I don't like it."

I say: "Neither do I. It looks to me like I am the bad boy around here, an' nobody knows why. Everybody's shootin' off their mouth about Lemmy Caution an' nobody knows what he's done or what he's said. O.K. Where do we go from here?"

He blows out some more cigar smoke. He says: "I'll tell you. I've been looking through your record, Caution. It's pretty good and I find it very difficult to believe that an operative like you could slip up with a woman like Marceline du Clos. I am taking the point of view that she was talking nonsense; that she just told Ribban one or two things that came into her head, because she wanted to say *something* because she was scared. If Ribban had been alive he might have put that job right. But he's not alive. Well, his death is just one of those things. Cleeve here gave me all the details on the telephone. Obviously, he fell down the stairs and broke his neck."

He stops talkin'. There is a pause. Nobody says anythin'. Then he brings a box outa his desk drawer an' puts it on the desk.

He says: "You two men give yourselves cigarettes and sit down and listen to me." He looks at me first of all. He says: "I'd like you to know I'm going to keep you on this job, Caution. Maybe one or two people think I'm going to take you off. Maybe they thought I might even send you back to the States. I'm not doing that. I don't see why an agent with a good record should suffer for accusations which have been made against him but which can't be substantiated."

I say: "Thanks a lot. General. But I'm still not dyin' with gratitude over bein' given a break for something I didn't do."

He says: "Forget it. Now we'll be constructive. This Varley has got away. We believe he's got over to England. He's going to start making some trouble over there. Possibly he has contacts over there. Maybe what he and du Clos started in New York, continued with over here in Paris when they got here, is something that is going to finish in England. And it is not going to be particularly easy to put a finger on him over there. There are a lot of American troops in England. If he's got friends there; if he's got forged papers, maybe he could give our people and the English authorities a run-around over there for a long time."

He looks at Cleeve. He says: "Cleeve, you know this Varley?"

Cleeve nods.

The chief says: "What do you know about him?"

Cleeve takes a drag on his cigarette. He says: "Two years ago I was loaned to the Illinois State Police because I'd been in a case—a private case—that was brought to the agency I was working for in New York—where Varley was concerned. The Illinois police were lookin' for Varley. There was a Federal drag net out for him an' he was believed to be out there. I know what he looks like an' I think I know what his game is or was. Varley is one of the guys who was workin' in with the Hitler Bund in U.S. before America declared war. He's got some tie-up over here an' he's probably got a tie-up in England."

The chief says: "I reckon you're right. Did du Clos tell you anythin' about Varley, Caution?"

I say: "She told me plenty an' most of it was hooey. But here an' there a little bit of sense was stickin' out. The night I contacted Marceline du Clos an' took her out for a little drink hopin' she would talk, I threw a scare into her. Ribban didn't throw a scare into her. He may have tried it afterwards, but I did it first. I think she sorta got the idea in her head that her number was up. I think she got the idea in her head that she'd slipped a little, and that if our people didn't get her here in Paris, the Germans would. For some reason which I don't know that baby thought she was unpopular with them, an' Varley, the man she'd been workin' with. Mind you," I go on, "she didn't say anythin' sorta specific. She was vague. But that's the impression I got. O.K. Then I did do a little talkin' deliberately. I told her one or two stories about what had happened to other dames who had stuck their necks out in the espionage game. You can understand that, can't you, Chief?"

He says: "Yes. That's understandable. That's an old technique."

I say: "Well, it seemed to work. She told me that Varley hadn't been trustin' her much for six or seven months; that he'd been stoogin' her around, using her as a front. The idea was that Varley, who was a tough egg, believed she was gettin' scared an' might do some talkin'. She got the idea in her head that that's why he brought her over here."

The chief says: "I see. She didn't give you any ideas about any of Varley's associates?"

I wait for a minute. I knock the ash off my cigarette inta the ashtray. I take a long look at the Chief, an' I say: "Yeah, she told me one thing. This Varley has got a sister. I sorta got the idea that this dame is in England. According to what the Marceline piece said about her she must look like Venus de Milo. She said she was lovely. She said she was so goddam bad that she'd make Satan look like the President of a Bible Corporation. I got the idea in my head that she didn't like this baby."

The Chief thinks for a long time; then he looks at Cleeve. He says: "Did you ever hear anythin' about his sister?"

Cleeve says: "No. But why should I? I wasn't interested in Varley's family. I was interested in him an' we weren't so lucky. We didn't find out much about him."

There is another pause. Then the big boy says: "Did she give you a description of this sister, Caution?"

I say: "And how! You know, General, when a dame really hates another dame she notices every goddam thing about her. Maybe as suggested I was pie-eyed when all this talk was goin' on, but I wasn't so pie-eyed that I couldn't remember the exact description that Marceline gave me of this sister of Varley's.

"She said first of all that she was a brunette with a lovely skin an' big amethyst eyes. Besides that, she had everything—figure, style, knew how to dress, spoke a coupla languages—maybe more. A fascinating dame, this sister of Varley's."

The Chief says: "That's a pretty general identification, isn't it? I reckon every good-looking woman thinks she looks like that. Maybe she thinks like that, but she doesn't say it about another woman."

"There's one other point," I say. "This baby has got one peculiar identification mark. The little finger of her left hand is twisted. Du Clos told me that she'd got lovely hands with long fingers, beautifully manicured nails, an' that the contrast of this little finger bein' twisted was terrific. It was so fascinatin' that people used to watch her hands while she was speakin', because she always used that hand to make gestures with rather as if she had a complex about the little finger being badly shaped, see?"

He says: "I see. We'll write that description down." He takes a pad an' he writes it down. He reads it out to me. He says: "Is that O.K.?"

I say: "Yes, that's all right."

He puts the pad away. He puts the cigar back in his mouth. He says: "Now look, I'm sending you and Cleeve here to England. You find this Varley and you fix it. If you can, get him back here to me alive. I'd like to talk to him. He's bad medicine. It's going to be difficult, but Cleeve here knows him and if he's gone over there to make contact with that sister of his—supposing she's over there—a couple like that ought to be found some time or other. You'll get all the help you want from the English authorities. It's all laid on. All right. When do you start?"

I say: "Well, I'll start when you like. General, but I'd like to have another day or so around Paris. There are one or two little things I'd like to do."

He says: "All right. Leave the day after to-morrow. I'll have a plane laid on for you in the early morning." He looks at me and his blue eyes are not quite so hard. He says: "I'd like you to pull this off, Caution."

I say: "You mean it would be a come-back for me?"

He says: "We've got a lot of good F.B.I. men working for us and they are all looking for promotion. This Marceline du Clos business hasn't been exactly a recommendation for you, you know. Anyhow, do your best. Find Varley. Find out what he was doing, bring him in, and"—he says with a sorta grin"—while you're doin' it, I'd like to have a look at this lovely sister of his." He draws some more cigar smoke inta his lungs. "I've got on idea we've either got a firing squad or a nice cell at Alcatraz for twenty years for those two guys. All right."

I get up. I say: "Good-night, General."

Cleeve says good-night and we go out.

Outside in the corridor Jimmy looks at me an' grins. He says: "Well, it's O.K., big boy. You're in, Caution."

I say: "Like hell I'm in. I'm in if we find Varley. If we don't I reckon I'm out. Let's go get ourselves a drink."

We start walkin' down the street. I don't say anythin' much because I am busy doin' a little thinkin'. After a bit, Jimmy says: "What's eating you, Lemmy? Maybe you're letting this thing get into your system too much. Maybe you've got the wrong idea about it."

I say: "Wrong idea nothin'. Work it out for yourself. It's stickin' outa foot that Flash thinks I said *somethin'* that mattered to the du Clos dame. But he can't find out anythin' an' he can't prove anythin'. She is dead an' Ribban has also got his. But the General is pretty busy right now believin' that there is not any smoke without some fire. So he tells me to get on with the job. He reckons that if I really did shoot my mouth to the Marceline babe I'm gonna give myself away somehow. An' if I do he's gonna tear me inta little pieces. That's what I think."

He don't say anythin' for a minute. Then: "What the hell!" he says. "You should worry. All we gotta do is to get our hooks on this Varley mug an' this sister of his. Then you'll be in the clear and maybe I'll be in line for a job with the F.B.I. that I've always wanted. Let's go an' have a little drink on that."

I say: "O.K. I could do with a snifter."

An' between you an' me an' the gatepost I reckon this is a good idea. Because if ever a guy is plenty worried there are always three things he can do. He can go an' hit the liquor an' forget everything; he can rush off an' lay his head on some baby's chassis an' spill the works an' get a lot of sweet womanly sympathy; or he can go to bed an' sleep.

An' you guys can take it from me that the sleepin' business is the best because it's the safest. I have known mugs rush off to some sweet momma an' tell her all their troubles, an' then about a week afterwards they find they got more trouble than they ever had before.

Sleepin' makes you more tired than you was before an' liquor makes you even more goddam sleepy. But dames don't even make you sleepy. They make you dizzy an' that is why they are very dangerous things.

But guys are very funny people. If a guy got himself wrecked on some desert island with everything laid on; with a cask of liquor, some food an' a coupla good books, do you think this palooka would sorta settle down in the sunshine an' be happy?

No, sir. . . . I'll bet you a coupla stale eggs to all the tea in China that before the sun goes down this mug is easin' all over the place, crawlin' through the thick grass an' generally rushin' around to see if he can find something with a nice shape in a grass skirt.

Because guys are like that, which is why that old serpent in the Garden of Eden just usta stooge around in the tree laughin' his head off at Adam who was the biggest mug that ever went bust in the fruit business.

It is just after midnight when I ease outa headquarters an' start walkin' around. It is not a bad sorta night—a bit cold but I don't mind that. I'm thinkin' about Ribban. I am also thinkin' that it was very nice of Jimmy Cleeve to fake that nice little story about Ribban goin' downstairs for a pen. I reckon this guy has gotta very quick brain because he was on to the pen business directly I told him that there was a piece of writin' paper an' an envelope on Ribban's desk just as if he was gonna write a letter.

An' Cleeve knew that Flash would not stand for Ribban bein' murdered—with me around the place—that woulda been a bit too much. First of all there is this Marceline du Clos gettin' herself creased out an' then Ribban. Cleeve reckons that it is stickin' out, like a dead mackerel on the seashore by moonlight, that the guy who has to gain most by these two people bein' no longer with us is Ma Caution's little boy Lemmy. An' I don't mean maybe. An' he is a good enough guy to wanta get me sort of straightened out on this business.

I reckon Cleeve is a pretty smart investigator even if he was only a private dick who has been lent to the "G" service for the war. I reckon it would be fun if we had some more guys like him.

I get around to thinkin' about Juanella Rillwater. I believe I told you guys before that the world is a small place but I did not think it was so small that I'd meet that honeybelle around here in Paris at a time like this, all of which shows that a mug never knows what's waitin' round the corner.

Because this bozo Confucius that I have already introduced to you fellas once shot an earful when he said: "The unexpected woman is like the dew rose seen in the hedge. She springeth suddenly. She cometh from no man knows where and disappeareth after she hath smacked some poor fish a sweet one across the beezer like nobody's business." All of which will show you guys that this Confucius certainly knew his packaged goods an' you can quote me.

I light myself a cigarette an' start walkin' to the Hotel St. Denis. This is a place not far from the Boulevard St. Michel, an' as far as I can remember it is just one of them places. When I get there I see I'm right. It's a coupla old-fashioned houses which have been knocked inta one with an entrance in a side street. I ring the bell an' after a bit a guy in a baize apron opens the door. This guy has got about fourteen days' growth of beard on his chin an' looks like Methuselah after comin' out of a deep hangover.

I say good-evenin'. He don't say anythin'. He just stands there lookin' at me. He looks like the sorta guy who is always waitin' for a funny crack an' is not very surprised when he hears one.

I say: "Look, there is a lady by the name of Mrs. Rillwater livin' here. Is she in?"

He says he wouldn't know, but anyway her number is twenty-three on the second floor. He says why don't I go up an' take a look.

I say thanks a lot. I start walkin' up the stairs. The place stinks an' when I say stinks I mean it smells plenty. All sorts of strange and mysterious odours hit me. The carpets have not been swept for weeks an' here an' there bits of the ceilin' look as if they might drop on your head at any moment.

When I get to No. 23 on the second floor I tap quietly on the door an' wait. Nothing happens. I try it again but still nobody answers. I turn the handle an' give the door a little push an' I go in. The room is dark but on the other side is a door leadin' to some inner room, an' I can see a crack of light comin' round the corner. I feel beside the doorpost for the electric light switch, put it on an' shut the door behind me. As I do this the door on the other side opens an' a dame comes out.

Me—I am not a guy who is ever very surprised at anythin'. I have seen some funny things happen in my time an' this dame is one of the funniest ones. She is wearin' Turkish slippers, a pair of harem trousers that anybody but a blind man could see through, a *brassière* made out of a coupla rhinestone G strings, an' an amused expression. She has got one of the finest sets of legs I ever saw in my life, a swell shape, a face that looks like a piece outa your geography book, an' a squint. In addition to these she is also a strawberry blonde an' the dye is beginnin' to fade a bit. Also—an' maybe I forgot about this in my hurry—she has got a silver paper star stuck over her navel.

I say: "Well . . . well . . . well . . .! If you are not the swellest little picture I am an Indian Princess with a cork leg."

She says: "Listen, mug, what d'you think you are—the Gestapo? Maybe they didn't tell you that this part of France is unoccupied now an' the free list is entirely suspended."

"Don't you believe it, babe," I tell her. "Me—I am practically an Army of Occupation. But maybe you might satisfy my curiosity just for once. What are you wearin' all that stuff for—or are you rehearsin' for a strip-tease act?"

She looks down at her trousers. She says: "Maybe I was thinkin' of the old days."

"Even if you was, honeybelle," I tell her, "you oughta wear a pair of step-ins, because my old mother, Mrs. Caution, who is a very wise one, once told me that a lady's step-ins are like the Rhine because they are practically her last line of defence. An' the way it looks to me you would not even have half a chance if somebody put out a flankin' movement."

She says: "So you're the smart guy, hey? Maybe it might surprise you to know I was a stripper one time. Maybe you'd be surprised to know I had a feature spot in the programme too."

"Some feature," I tell her. "I take you six to four that if any of the customers took one look at that squint of yours you wouldn't see 'em for dust."

She says: "Never mind the squint, boyo. The customers never paid to look at my face. Now maybe you'll tell me what it is you want around here. This is private."

I say: "Look, I am merely tryin' to satisfy a little curiosity. I'm lookin' for a dame called Juanella Rillwater —Mrs. Rillwater. This is her room. Maybe you know where she is?"

She says: "It is *not* her room an' I don't know where she is. Anyhow," she goes on, "I do not wish to know anythin' about a dame called Rillwater. I do not like the name."

I stand lookin' at this baby. There is something about her that sorta touches a sorta memory chord in my brain. Then I get it.

I say: "Well . . . well . . . well . . . life can be very strange. If you are not Marta Frisler who used to do a striptease act in Metzler's Burlesque in Chicago I'm Adolf Hitler."

She says: "You're right, fella. That's me—an' was I a hit or was I? I remember one night . . ."

I say: "I'll take it for granted. I reckon one night at Metzler's was like any other night. So you don't know Mrs. Rillwater?"

She says: "No. I never heard of her. Now maybe if you've finished talkin' you'll get outa here an' let me get on with my rehearsal."

I say: "Look, there are just one or two little points I'd like to take up with you before I scram."

She says: "Yes, an' who are you to take up anythin'?"

I take my badge outa my pocket an' I show it to her.

"My name's Caution," I say. "I'm a Federal man attached to the Army Intelligence here. What are you doin' here an' how didya get here?"

She turns her wrist over an' looks at her wristwatch.

She says: "Well, it's a long story but maybe it's a very interestin' one. Maybe a guy like you would like to hear it from the beginnin'?"

I say: "Why not? I'll try anythin' once."

She says: "All right. Take your weight off your feet."

She points to a chair. I sit down. She goes over to a sideboard, pours a coupla glasses of rye, brings one over to me. I drink it. It is good stuff.

She says: "Well, this thing starts a long way back. I'll tell you all about it."

Then she looks over my shoulder an' a little grin comes over her face. I am sittin' with my back to the door I came in through. I screw around on my chair an' take a look. A guy has come inta the room. He is standin' with his back to the wall. He is a thin guy with a thin face an' pinched nostrils. He is wearin' a blue shirt an' collar with horizontal stripes an' a white silk tie. He looks like a Cuban—one of those acts you sometimes see in the cheap vaudeville shows. He is smilin', showin' a very nice set of white teeth an' he has got an automatic in his right hand. The automatic is pointin' at the back of my stomach, a process which I do not like at all.

I finish my drink an' put the glass down on the floor. The guy at the door looks over at my girl friend an' he says in a funny sorta accent:

"Well . . . what is thees?"

She says: "Oh this . . . this is really *something*! This is Mr. Caution. He's a 'G' man. He's got a little badge. He's lookin' for some dame called Rillwater."

He says: "Oh, yes . . .!" He comes into the room. He goes on: "You know, we don't like people who stick their noses into our beezness, Mr. Caution. Especially, we do not like policemen—even if they are working with the U.S. Army."

I say: "Maybe that makes you dislike 'em a bit more. Why don't you put that gun away? You might hurt yourself."

He grins. It is not a nice sorta grin. I reckon I do not like this bozo.

He says: "Me—I nevaire get hurt—ver' seldom. It ees always the other one who gets hurt."

He undoes the button of his tight waisted coat with his free hand, puts his hand in his trouser pocket. When the coat opens I can see that he has got a fancy pencil stuck in his top vest pocket— that an' a thin gold-coloured chain. But it is the pencil that takes my eye. He goes over to the sideboard, puts the neck of the bottle in his mouth an' takes a pull. But all the time he is watchin' me an' the gun is still nice an' easy in his hand.

I come to the conclusion that I am dead right in not bein' fond of this guy. To me he looks like a first-class heel. I have also the definite idea in my head that he would think nothin' of squeezin' the trigger of that automatic, thereby removin' a large lump of my lower anatomy, which as any dead guy will tell you is not a nice business.

I take a look at the gun and from where I am I can see that the safety catch is off. Maybe this guy means business. The girl in the fancy pants is leanin' up against a wardrobe on the other side of the room lookin' at him outa the corner of her eye—at least I think she is because this baby has got such a squint that any time she got high she couldn't even stagger.

I say: "You must be a very lucky guy. But this is one of the times when you are liable to get hurt good an' plenty, because it is a very unhealthy thing for a mug like you to threaten a guy like me with a hand gun up in Room 23 at the Hotel St. Denis. Maybe they didn't tell you we got an Army here?"

He says: "Yes, I know all about that, but accidents, *senor*, will sometimes 'appen."

I say: "You're tellin' me! I reckon your father thought that when your mother told him you was on the way. But maybe," I go on, "you wasn't even born or perhaps you never had a father." I grin at him. "That's what it is," I tell him, "just another love child!"

He says: "Yes? You're ver' clever, aren't you? Supposing I knock some of your teeth down your throat. Maybe you are going to like that."

"I wouldn't like it at all," I tell him, "but where's that gonna get you? Look, you interest me."

He puts the bottle in his mouth an' takes another pull. Then he puts it back on the sideboard.

He says: "Oh yes! All right, Mr. Caution, you tell me why."

I say: "There is nothing like the truth. It's that pencil you got. It sorta fascinates me. When I was a kid," I tell him, "I always went for fancy pencils in a big way. I reckon I'd have been stuck on that one."

He looks at me for a moment as if he thinks I'm nuts. The woman is still leanin' against the wardrobe nice an' easy an' relaxed. She looks as if she is enjoyin' the situation.

He puts his hand in his pocket an' he takes out the pencil. He says: "What's so funny about that?" He looks at it.

"Nothin' very funny about it," I tell him, "except I saw the pen that goes with that set to-night. That pencil is the sorta thing that's sold with a fountain pen, but you haven't got the fountain pen, have you, fella? You got an odd one."

He looks at the dame an' shrugs his shoulders. He says: "I theenk he mus' be mad."

She says: "All right. Well, if you think he's mad you gotta do something about him."

I say: "Listen, baby, what is all this? Why does anybody have to do anythin' about anybody. I come up here to make a nice little social call an' there is this guy gettin' around totin' artillery along as if he's proposin' to start a new world war. Why can't you guys be sociable an' relax?"

He says: "All right, senor. I am relaxed. Now you tell me what it ees you want?"

I say: "O.K. Let's do a little straight talkin', shall we? You wouldn't know a place called the Club Leon, would you?"

He shrugs his shoulders. "Maybe," he says. "Maybe not. But"—then he remembers—"I theenk I know the place."

"I think you know it too," I tell him. "O.K. There was a guy called Ribban—an American—a 'G' man. Somebody sandbagged him to-night in a top floor room there. At the present moment he's extremely dead. I suppose you wouldn't know anythin' about that?"

He shrugs his shoulders again. He grins. When he grins he looks like the devil.

He says: "*Senor*, I think you're mad. Why should I know anythin' about it?"

I say: "It might be very convenient for me to *think* you did, because I can take you in on that. I can hand you over to the American authorities an' it wouldn't do you any good either."

He says: "I don't know what you're talking about. I was never near the Club Leon to-night."

I say: "That means you've got an alibi—a real cast iron alibi—one that I could maybe check without goin' outa this room."

He says: "You know, *senor*, you are a leetle bit of an optimist. You're not quite certain you're going out of zis room."

"I'll take a chance on that," I tell him. "All right. Well, supposin' you got an alibi, I wonder what that would be."

I get up sorta casual. I put my hand in my pants pockets an' start walkin' up an' down the room sorta slow. I say: "Maybe the alibi would be this. There was a babe called Marceline du Clos. She was stuck in a cell at the 14th French Police Post to-night. She was waiting around there for somebody to come an' take her to headquarters. They wanted to ask her some questions. They were sorta curious about her.

"Well, somebody went round there with a forged police pass to get her out. It was a phoney but they fell for it at the 14th Post an' they got her out. After that somebody takes her along over the river to the Rue Zacherie an' puts a bullet in her where she's gonna feel it most. They found her on a doorstep. That wouldn't be your alibi by any chance, would it?"

He don't say anythin'. He just looks straight in front of him at the sideboard. I take a quick look over my shoulder at the dame. She is lookin' at me an' she has even forgotten to squint. I get an idea that there is a scared look in her eyes.

I say: "Look, maybe I am doin' a little bluffin'. Maybe I am only tryin' to throw a scare into you pair of near humans. But the point I am goin' to ask you to realise is this . . ."

I put my hand out an' wag a finger at him if I am comin' to some big point. Then, suddenly, I take a jump at him, shoot out my left leg an' give him a king kick in the guts.

This guy does not appear to like this one little bit. He looks at me for a second with a sorta surprised look on his face. Then he lets out one helluva holler, drops the gun, doubles up on the carpet an' starts moanin' an' rollin' around.

I take a step towards the gun. But as I reach out for it the girl friend in the zephyr pants is there first. This baby shoots across the room as if she was shot out of a cannon. She grabs the gun an' starts loosin' off.

She yells: "You louse . . . I'm gonna fog you for this, you crawlin' Federal so-an'-so!" Then she has another quick shot at me but what with bein' all steamed up an' cross-eyed she misses.

She now has another go an' this time she gets too near to be pleasant, an' I can hear the bullet smack inta the wall behind me. I make a grab at the rye bottle on the sideboard, an' as she is about to start shootin' some more I throw it at the electric light globe. I get a direct hit an' the light goes out.

She now tells me some more about myself an' what she hopes is gonna happen to me. I reckon that either the gun is empty or else she is waitin' for me to go outa the door when she has gotta see me against the light in the corridor.

I ease quietly over to the guy who is still lyin' on the floor writhin' about. I grab the pencil outa his pocket, crawl across to the door on my hands and knees, get a hold of the door handle, throw the door open an' wriggle round the corner.

I was right. She starts some more shootin', but the bullets go high—where I woulda been maybe if I had been standin' up straight.

I scram down the corridor an' down the stairs. When I get to the hallway the palooka in the baize apron is still there leanin' up against the wall.

He says: "M'sieu . . . I 'ope you found Mrs. Rillwater."

I turn around in the doorway. I say: "Bozo, you are a lyin' guy. I do not like you at all. Anyhow I reckon you directed me to the wrong room. The dame up there must be called Mrs. Ditchwater. Also one of these fine days I shall come back here an' practically tear this place apart."

I then make a dignified exit through the front door. Me . . . I do not like these shootin' gallery scenes. I have seen plenty of 'em. An' one of these days somebody is liable to get hurt.

When I get back to my hotel I take off my coat an' my shoes. I give myself four fingers outa the rye bottle, lie on the bed an' do a little quiet thinkin'. Me—I have always found the trouble with life is that things go past a guy very quickly. Sometimes they go so goddam quick that he has not time to grab 'em off or even make any mental notes about 'em. Maybe that is what is happenin' in this business. At the same time I reckon that I can still put two an' two together without making seventeen out of it. Maybe I am beginnin' to get some ideas.

Takin' it by an' large, I reckon the interview to-night with the General was O.K. I start thinkin' about Cleeve. One thing is stickin' out like Connecticut pier an' that is this guy is gonna get all he can outa this case an' he is not gonna worry very much about Mr. Caution in the process. Why should he? He is just a private dick an' he reckons that if he can make a good showin' in this job he is gonna do a lotta good for himself. Maybe he thinks that. It might easily be that he put on that big act about Ribban fallin' down the stairs because he wants me stringin' along doin' all the work while he takes all the credit. Private dicks can be like that. An' why not?

The next picture that goes across my mind is Mrs. Juanella Rillwater. I told you mugs before that the world is a small place, but at the same time I think it is a little bit queer that I should run into Juanella right now here in Paris. I think it is even more funny that I should run inta the packet of trouble I have just got out of with the Cuban an' the striptease baby Marta Frisler through gettin' that address from Juanella. I wonder whether Juanella *is* livin' at the Hotel St. Denis. Maybe she is not. Maybe she wanted to dodge me an' gave me the first address that came into her head. Either that or she mighta had some other idea.

I reach out for the telephone an' call Dombie's number. I hang on for a minute; then I hear him say hello. Before I can say anythin' I hear some French dame with a high pitched voice bawlin' at the other end. I reckon that that Canadian mug is doin' a big Casanova act with some baby. An' I am right.

She starts screamin': "Dombee . . . You give me ze large pain in ze neck. Eef you make one more pass at me I will clock you wiz ze flat-iron. . . ." She then relapses inta French an' tells the boy just where he gets off.

I say: "Hello, Dombie. This is Lemmy Caution."

He says: "Yeah! You have to ring up at this time of night just when I got a beautiful dame here who is nuts about me."

I say: "You're tellin' me! I just heard all about that. Why don't you lay offa some of these French women? Why don't you give 'em a chance? One of these fine days someone's gonna stick a knife in you; not because they love you but because they don't."

He says: "Yeah, wise guy! Well, what is it you want?"

I say: "Look, Dombie, you get yourself outa that dump an' come round here. I wanta talk to you."

He says: "All right. Life can be very tough. Me—I never get any time for relaxation. I'll be seein' you."

He hangs up. I get off the bed, give myself another drink an' start walkin' up an' down the room. In spite of myself I am gettin' sorta interested in this set-up.

Twenty minutes go by an' Dombie gets around. He brings a bottle of rye with him an' we get down an' do a little quiet drinkin'.

Then he says: "Well, fella, what's it all about?"

I tell him. First of all I would like you palookas to know that I got quite a respect for this guy Dombie. He is a very deep feller. What they call a would-be dumb sorta guy. On top he is always pretendin' to be worryin' about some dame but underneath he's a wise guy all right. Also he is very tough.

This guy started the war off in the Canadian Commandos, went from there to British Intelligence, an' is now workin' with us as a sorta *liaison*. Ever since he's been with us there's been less liquor flyin' around than there ever was before.

I say: "Look, Dombie, you heard about Ribban?"

He says: "Yeah, I heard about him. Cleeve told me. He fell down some stairs an' broke his neck."

I say: "He broke nothin'. Somebody creased him."

He says: "No! How come?"

I say: "I wouldn't know. But there's something very funny goin' on around here. To-night somebody hands in a forged pass on the No. 14 Police Post with a very good imitation of General Flash's signature on it, an' they get that baby Marceline du Clos out. All right. So then they knock her off. You know about that. The next thing is that somebody gives it to Ribban. Well?"

Dombie says: "That's not so hot, is it? It's sorta odd. These are two guys who know all about you. Marceline is the baby you are supposed to have shot your mouth to, an' Ribban is the guy she told all about it." He yawns. "You oughta be the guy to be suspected," he says. He grins at me. "You wouldn't have knocked these two guys off, would you?"

I say: "No. But I think it's very funny. It looks as if somebody is tryin' to do me a good turn, hey?"

He says: "Yeah, it might be that, an' it might not be." He goes on: "Listen, Lemmy, all this stuff about you shoot-in' your mouth off to this Marceline, I reckon that was hooey, wasn't it?"

I nod my head.

He says: "That's what I thought. Well, Ribban is the guy who started this story. He is the guy who goes to Flash an' says that Marceline has told him that you shot your mouth off about this an' that, an' Ribban was a good pal of yours, wasn't he?"

I say: "Yeah, he was."

Dombie says: "Well, it looks a little strange to me that he didn't come to you an' talk to you about it first of all."

I shrug my shoulders. "Maybe," I say.

Dombie goes on: "Listen, there's only one reason why he wouldn't have done that. Can't you think of it?"

I say: "Yeah, I can think of one. The reason would be that the stuff that I was supposed to have told Marceline was pretty big stuff; an' even although Ribban was a pal of mine he took a tough view of it. He thought it was his duty to kick in with it to the General."

"That's what I think," said Dombie. "An' for some reason or other which nobody knows about some guy wants to stop 'em talkin'. Some guy wants to stop 'em tellin' this story that Marceline told Ribban, an' they take goddam good care that nobody's gonna tell the story. They crease Marceline an' they crease Ribban. An' where do you go from there?"

I say: "I wouldn't know." I take another pull at the rye bottle.

Dombie says: "What happened to Ribban?"

I say: "Somebody hit him with a black-jack."

He looks surprised. He says: "A new technique, hey? I wonder what they did that for? How come!"

I say: "It looks to me as if Ribban was sittin' at a desk an' was just gonna write a letter, see? There was a sheet of notepaper with some blottin' paper folded across it just like it would be if he was gonna write. I think somebody eased up behind him an' let him have it as he was bendin' over the desk. Ribban goes out cold, an' they drag him down the stairs an' leave him there, so some mug's gonna think he fell down the stairs an' did it that way."

He nods. He says: "You got any ideas?"

I say: "No, not many. But something funny happened earlier this evenin'. I ran into a baby I usta know in New York—a swell piece. Her husband's got a record as long as your arm. He's a guy called Larvey T. Rillwater, a top-grade safe blower in the United States. I had a drink with her an' she gave me an address where I could call through. O.K. Well, after I left the jane to-night I go around there. It's a dirty little dump near the Boulevarde St. Michel. Juanella is not there, but when I go upstairs to her room I find a comedy duo performin' around the place. Some baby rehearsin' for a strip-tease act an' a guy who arrives a little later who looks like a Cuban or an Argentine. He is not so pleased with me because I am askin' questions. In fact I get so unpopular with this mug that eventually he unlimbers some artillery an' he starts loosin' off at me. He don't like me, see?"

Dombie says: "No? It just shows you the sorta things that can happen in time of war, don't it?" He gives himself another drink.

I say: "There is just one other thing. When I found Ribban he had something in his hand. He had a fountain pen." Dombie says: "Yeah! Well, that's O.K., ain't it? He was just gonna write a letter."

I say: "The cap was screwed on the fountain pen an' Ribban never used to use one. He always used a stub of pencil. The stub of pencil was in his vest pocket. He had it all right."

Dombie says: "So what?"

I say: "The pen was a French pen—fairly new—one of those coloured things—the sort you buy in a set with a pencil in the Black Market." I go on: "It might be a coincidence but the boyo who was doin' the shootin' to-night at the Hotel St. Denis had a propellin' pencil stickin' outa his vest pocket that matches up with the pen Ribban had. I took it off him. Here it is." I throw the pencil across to him.

He says: "Lemmy, you got something in your mind?"

I say: "Yeah, I got this in my mind. You get out early to-morrow mornin'. You try an' find where that pen an' pencil set came from. You can do it easy enough. Find out the mug who's sellin' the things. Usually there are only two or three of each sort in a set. If this pencil belonged to the set that Ribban's pen belonged to, maybe we got something."

He says: "O.K. I always get the leg work, don't I?" He lights a cigarette an' throws one across to me. Then he says: "What's the idea, Lemmy? You got something at the back of your mind. Maybe I got a theory."

I say: "Yeah? What's the theory?"

He says: "This Cuban or Argentine mug has bought this pen an' pencil set for himself. It's the sorta gaudy thing a mug like that would carry. All right. Well, he has a date with Ribban. He goes round to see him. Maybe he's got some information or something, an' what he says is so important that George Ribban wantsta write it down, an' it's so important that this time he don't wanta write it in pencil, but he hasn't gotta pen. So the Cuban guy hands Ribban his pen an' the boy is just about to unscrew the top when the other mug lets him have it with a black-jack. How's that?"

I say: "It might be. But I can't see that mug leavin' the pen behind. He'd know Ribban had it. He'd have taken it."

Dombie says: "O.K. I'm only guessin'."

I say: "Well, look, Dombie, you can go back to that French dame of yours, if she's still waitin' for you, which I very much doubt. You get crackin' on this pen an' pencil job to-morrow. There's another thing you might do. You get in touch with one of the 'I' Sections an' find out just where Mrs. Juanella Rillwater is really livin'. Come through on the phone an' let me know. An' I'll bet a lotta money it's not the Hotel St. Denis either."

He gets up. He says: "O.K. But maybe I got an idea where that baby is livin' right now."

I say: "So you knew she was over here, Dombie. How did you get that?"

He says: "Well, the other night was Cleeve's birthday. We have a little party an' he gets high. He's gotta scheme about this Rillwater baby." He looks at me sideways. "You know this Cleeve is a brain guy all right. He's gotta lotta brains. That's why Flash sent for him. I reckon he's pulled some sorta story about why he got Juanella Rillwater over here, but I reckon it ain't the true one."

I say: "No. Well, maybe you can give me the genuine article?"

He says: "Maybe I can. I got in idea in my head that the Juanella baby knows plenty about the guy Varley that Marceline du Clos was gettin' about with. I got an idea that when he was runnin' that interior decoratin' business in New York he used to get around with Larvey Rillwater. I think they pulled off one or two little jobs on the side together; bond robberies—jobs like that. Maybe," he goes on, "this Varley, who seems a clever sorta mug, was using Rillwater. Maybe the stuff that Rillwater was knockin' off was much more important than he ever knew. Maybe it wasn't always bonds."

"I get it," I say. "You think this Varley used Rillwater to steal documents an' things he wanted; that Rillwater didn't know what he was doin'."

"That's my idea," says Dombie. "Work it out for yourself. Rillwater gets slung in Alcatraz where he is now, Cleeve brings Juanella over here to work for him. She knows Varley. She knows Varley's habits. If she runs across Varley, Varley is gonna tie up with her, ain't he? He knows her old man is in the cooler, an' he knows Juanella ain't no better than she oughta be. So Varley is gonna be inclined to talk, more especially as Larvey Rillwater got knocked off through him."

"I get it," I say. "You're dead right about this Cleeve. The boy certainly has got brains."

Dombie says: "He knows what he's doin' all right. I reckon he's out to make a killin' here. I reckon he's out to get Varley, after which he gets the credit an' you maybe get a kick in the pants."

I say: "Well, that's the way it goes. But my old mother thought I was a guy who could always look after himself. Thanks for the tip-off."

He gets up. He says: "If I get anythin' on this fountain pen thing I'll ring you, an' I reckon I'll have the Rillwater dame's address by ten o'clock. So long, Lemmy."

He has one for the road an' scrams.

A nice guy, Dombie.

CHAPTER THREE
JUANELLA

I WAKE up at nine o'clock. It is a nice mornin' an' there is some sweet sunshine. I reckon I like sunshine. I have told you before that I am a very poetic sorta cuss. I am a mug who goes for beauty in all sorts of ways, which is maybe the reason I am always gettin' tied up with some baby or other. Because work it out for yourselves. If a guy likes sunshine an' the moonlight an' the leaves comin' on the trees in the spring an' the birds singin'; then it will be stickin' out a foot to you guys that he also goes for the dame that has a swell shape, a well-cut ankle an' all the rest that goes with it.

I get out of bed an' I start walkin' around thinkin' about this an' that. Mainly I am thinkin' about Juanella Rillwater, because as you may have realised I am not a guy who believes too much in coincidences, because they are things which only happen sometimes an' usually when you are not lookin'.

An' there are coincidences an' coincidences if you get me; but I reckon that a few minutes' concentration is gonna show you guys that Juanella is not the sorta babe who is a coincidence at any time. No, sir . . . that honeybelle is more of an accident at sea while the life-boat's bein' repainted an' is not available.

After a bit I ring down for some coffee an' sit on the edge of my bed drinkin' it.

I am immersed in such very great an' deep thoughts that the telephone bell is janglin' for about five seconds before I do anythin' about it. It is Dombie.

He says: "Hello, fella. Look, I been doin' a lotta leg work for you. I started good an' early this mornin'. First of all the fountain pen thing; this thing was not at all difficult, because there are not a lotta fountain pens in Paris at the present moment. There were about six dozen of those sets—a fountain pen an' a pencil in a box. There were only four of each colour. The one that your boy friend has is sold by a black-marketeer called Le Fevre—first name Paul. You'll find him kickin' around any mornin' you want to about twelve o'clock in Fritz's bar near the Grand Hotel, Montmartre. You got that?"

I say: "I got it. Go on from there, wise guy."

He says: "The second thing is Mrs. Rillwater. Look, she's a sweet dame, this dame, ain't she? I wanta tell you something. I been listening about this dame. She's beautiful an' when I say beautiful I mean but beautiful. Why don't you put me in next to her? Maybe I could find something out."

I say: "Yeah!" I laugh—one of those laughs they call cynical. "I put you in next to her an' what you could find out would be nobody's business. Also it would probably land you in the cooler. Be your age, Dombie. Where is she?"

He says: "Well, I don't know where she is, but there's some dump out near Auteuil. There's a big house out there—usta belong to some Count or other. It's called the Villa des Fleurs."

I say: "Yeah! An' what goes on there?"

He says: "Well, it's a gamblin' *spieler*. All the guys in the *Marche Paralel* get around there, an' get rid of some of their ill-gotten gains or else win some more off somebody. There's big play there every night. I reckon you'll find Juanella around there any night about twelve."

"You don't say," I tell him. "Look, what goes on around here? Is she a come-on girl for this dump or what?"

He says: "Don't ask me, Lemmy, because I wouldn't know. She's around there most nights from about twelve to two. She takes a powder about two a.m. They tell me she wears some very nice clothes an' the customers like her."

I ask: "What d'you mean the customers like her?"

He says: "Well, just that. They go for her in a big way."

I say: "Do they get any place, Dombie?"

He says: "I think not. My information tells me that she's still very badly stuck on that husband of hers—Larvey Rillwater—the boy in Alcatraz."

I say: "Yeah, that's what I think."

He says: "All right. Is that O.K. by you? An' where do I go from there?"

I say: "I wouldn't know."

There is a pause; then Dombie says: "Look, Lemmy, what's goin' on around here? You've got something stuck in the back of your head an' you're not talkin' to me about it."

"No!" I tell him. "Don't tell me that I'm not a guy who talks. I been hearin' that I am the biggest talker in the F.B.I. I talk to spies like Marceline du Clos. Me—I talk to everybody. Why don't I talk to you?"

He says: "I wouldn't know. The only thing I can think of, you're just a big fat-headed basket who does not know who his pals are."

I say: "Well, that's how it is. I'll be seein' you, Dombie."

He says: "How d'you know?"

I say: "I'm not askin' you, I'm tellin' you. Have you got that?"

I hear him laugh. He says: "Maybe I have. I'll be seein' you."

I hear the receiver click down.

I light a cigarette an' start walkin' around the bedroom in my pyjamas. I am feelin' a lot happier. Maybe you guys think that I am stuck on Juanella. Well, if you do you might be right. This dame has got something. She has got allure but she has also got brains an' Mrs. Caution's little boy was always a sucker for brains.

I open the door, go out on the landin' an' bawl down for some more coffee. When it comes up I drink it an' try an' work out a sorta campaign about what I'm goin' to do about all this. I have a little meetin' with myself an' wonder if I shall ring up Jimmy Cleeve; then I think no. I think I will play this off the cuff on my own, which is exactly what this boy Jimmy is doin'.

I sit there drinkin' my coffee, smokin', an' I think about Jimmy. I reckon I got his picture all right.

A small time guy in a private detective agency in New York. Well, you know the sorta work that is stickin' around tailin' guys, handlin' blackmail cases, lookin' after rich guys who've got themselves in a bad way with some dame. All the sort of lousy, cheap an' uninterestin' work that comes the way of a private dick.

But somehow in the way that sort of thing happens he comes across Varley, just by accident. Well, that accident makes him valuable. The F.B.I. get on to Varley. This boy's got his nose dirty over some espionage job. He's checked up on an' they find there's some sort of contact between him an' the Hitler Bund—the German organisation that was workin' in America for years before the war started—an' they wanta know plenty about Varley. Jimmy Cleeve knows just a little bit an' that makes him valuable. So they take him away from the agency an' he gets himself attached to the Illinois State Police. He starts gettin' ideas an' I don't blame him, for a man who's got any brains has also got ambition. Jimmy sees himself as a big F.B.I. shot. He wants to get it an' here's the short way to do it.

O.K. Then this Varley an' Marceline du Clos take a powder an' get outa New York. They come over here to Paris, an' then this thing happens with me. Marceline says I've been talkin' an' the General does not like it. Maybe they brought Jimmy over then. I wouldn't know. Maybe they brought him over afterwards. Maybe for all I know he's havin' a quiet check-up on me. I reckon it wouldn't be the first time they put an outside man in to do a job like that. But all the time he's workin' for himself, tryin' to get himself into the big time. I don't like him for that. But I reckon on this job I'm the guy who's in the spot. So anythin' I know I'm playin' my own way.

I take a shower, dress myself in a quiet dark grey suit. I put on a white collar an' a grey tie. I reckon the idea is I am gonna be one of these U.S. business men who is over here startin' something, gettin' ready for when this war closes down. After which I give myself one little shot outa the rye bottle, stick my hat over one eye, light a cigarette an' walk around to Headquarters.

I go inta the outer office an' tell Sweetie-pie there that I would like to see the General. She goes into his room an' comes out a minute later an' asks whether I wanta see him alone an' if it's important, because he's very busy. I say it's not important—I just want two minutes. She says to go in.

Flash is sittin' behind his desk smokin' a cigar. He looks at me an' says: "Well, Caution? You been getting some ideas about something? Maybe you want to talk?"

Sittin' on the corner of the desk is a guy who is a lieutenant in Intelligence, who is lookin' a little bit uncomfortable. I reckon he has heard about me. I reckon he has heard that I am the big bad boy who goes shootin' his mouth off to little French dames.

I say: "Look, General, I'm sorta bored with this idea about my suddenly thinkin' of something I have done some time an' wantin' to tell somebody about it. My story is I have not told anyone a goddam thing, an' I'm stickin' to it."

Flash shrugs his shoulders. He takes a big draw on the cigar an' knocks the ash off in the ashtray. He looks at the end of the cigar.

He says: "Personally, I think you're very wise. If you've got a good story stick to it. Well, what can I do for you?"

I say: "Just a little thing. There is some dump at Auteuil I wanta get out to. There's a spieler out there; black-marketeers use it." I tell him the name of the place. I say: "The set-up is this. I am an American business man over here on some Government contract work for after the war, an' I want some papers showin' that, an' an introduction to get me inside."

He says: "What's in your mind?"

I say: "Nothing very much."

He takes a long look at me. He says: "Well, you know what you're doing. O.K. I'll have the papers sent round to you in an hour's time. You can be one of the big business men who've come over here on the U.S. steel contract."

I say: "Thanks a lot. I'll be seein' you, General."

He says: "I hope."

I go out. When I get to the doorway I turn around an' the General an' the Intelligence Lieutenant are sorta lookin' at each other. Maybe they think I'm tryin' to pull something else. There's an odd sort of expression on Flash's face. As I walk down the passage I wonder if he really thinks I'm workin' for Mr. Hitler. I give myself a big grin.

Outside the sun is shinin'. The streets look good. It is one of those days when all the men look brave an' all the women look—well, you know how women look on a good day.

I take myself into a little bar en route an' buy myself a Vermouth Cassis, not because I like the goddam drink but because I am feelin' slightly fresh if you get me. Then I look around for a taxicab an' remember suddenly that there are no taxicabs in Paris; that you might as well try to catch yourself a butterfly as get yourself a taxicab in Paris.

I do some leg work an' get around to Fritz's bar. This is just one of those places. The place is full of come-on girls, racketeers, one or two *maquisards* who are tryin' to forget some of the things they've seen during the last few years, an' all the odd palookas you meet around a place like that. I been in here once or twice before.

I go up to the bar an' Fritz comes along. He says: "Good-morning and what can I do for you?"

I tell him whisky.

He says: "Don' be silly." He speaks very good English this guy. I put a thousand franc note down on the counter. He says: "Well, that ees different." He gives me a double shot of some reputed whisky which tastes like petrol mixed with the stuff you put in the radiator when it's cold.

I say: "Look, Fritz, d'you know a guy called Le Fevre—Paul Le Fevre?"

He says: "Yes, he's a very expensive guy."

I ask: "Is he here?"

He looks over in the corner. Sittin' behind a table, drinkin' a Bock is a little fat guy with a bald head an' a very small black moustache. His face reminds me of a bladder of lard. He's got pigs' eyes an' a sneerin' expression. He is not a handsome guy.

I pick up my drink, walk over, pull a chair out an' sit down; I say: "Good-mornin', fella."

He says: "Good-morning, m'sieu. And what can I do for you?"

He sounds fresh. I reckon that this Le Fevre is one of these wise guys who knows all the answers.

I take my F.B.I. card an' my French police pass outa my pocket an' I stick 'em on the table where he can see 'em. I say: "Take a look at that. You try bein' funny with me an' I take you right away an' smack you inside. I know all about you."

He don't look so good. He says: "And what do you know?"

I say: "I'm not tellin' you. All you have to do is to just tell me one or two things I wanta know, an' make it good. Then you're O.K. If you don't, it won't be so hot for you."

He goes inta a long spiel about bein' a great friend of the American people; about wantin' to die for France; the usual hooey you hear from a guy like that.

I listen. I let him talk. When he's finished I put my hand in my pocket an' I bring out the fountain pen—the one I took from Ribban.

I say: "D'you remember that?"

He says: "*Mais oui* . . . but of course. M'sieu, listen. . . . I buy several sets of those pens and pencils. There are four colours of each set. I have only one set in that colour."

I say: "You wouldn't know who you sold it to, would you?"

He says: "But perfectly. Because I could not forget. Three or four days ago I saw an American gentleman. I think he is in your Service. I don't know. He comes round to see me and is very pleased with himself—a little, what you say . . .?"

I say: "Do you mean the guy was cockeyed?"

He says: "Well, a little like that. He's just left a marvellous party and in the evening is going to another one—somebody's birthday party. He comes round to my place and he talks about how good life is and this and that. And he buys the set. Of course I am not very willing to sell it to him, because you know you can get a lot of money for a thing like this in Paris to-day."

I say: "You're tellin' me! What did you charge him for it?"

He shrugs his shoulders. He says: "I let him have it ver' cheap; because he's one of the liberators of my country I charge him only two thousand five hundred francs, and I only do that because I know who he is and what he is doing."

I say: "Fine. Who was he and what was he doin'?"

He says: "M'sieu, he was in your Service and his name was Ribban—M'sieu George Ribban."

I say: "Thanks a lot, Le Fevre. That's all I want to know."

So Ribban bought that pen an' pencil set.

I drink my drink. I say so long to this Le Fevre an' tell him to keep his trap shut. I tell him exactly what I'll do to him if he doesn't. Then I go back to the bar an' buy myself a little snifter.

Me—I've got an idea an' I'm a guy who when he gets an idea sometimes gets happy. So the sun's shinin' an' I'm happy.

So now you know.

I get out to Auteuil around eleven o'clock. It's a dark windy night. After a bit I find this dump. It's the usual sorta big French house that the aristocracy used to own in the old days. It's a big wanderin' sorta place, set back from the main road, with high iron gates an' a lotta cypresses hangin' around. There's a sorta mournful air about this dump, an' I reckon it only wants a few tombstones an' it would look like a graveyard, only better.

I give the iron gates a push an' they open. I go inside, shut the gates behind me an' start walkin' up the long curvin' carriage drive. After a bit I come to a big courtyard in front of the house. There are two three cars parked there, but I don't take any notice of that because if a place is run as a *spieler* they usually keep the cars around the back. There is a wide flight of steps an' a big portico entrance. I go up, find a bell-pull an' pull it.

I light myself a cigarette an' wait. After a bit the big door is opened, an' I find myself lookin' inta a dim sorta hall. There are some suits of armour an' two-handed swords stuck all around the place an' I think to myself that if this is a spieler it's the funniest one I've ever seen. Because it smells damp an' dusty an' unused.

The guy who has opened the door stands there lookin' at me. He is an old grey-haired type an' he is wearin' a striped waistcoat an' a short baize apron—the usual dress of the old-time French manservant who is not on formal duty. He looks at me with a pair of very old an' faded eyes an' he says: "M'sieu?"

I say: "Look, I am Mr. Cyrus C. Hicks, over in Paris on business. I been introduced here by Mr. Paul Laroche. You ever heard of him? I got a card he gave me. Maybe you'd like to have a look at it?"

He says: "I'm not very certain about the name, m'sieu, but I would like to see the card."

I show him the card that the General sent around. It is a visitin' card of some guy called Paul Laroche an' there is something written on the back of it.

He takes a look at the card an' he says: "Very good, m'sieu. Will you come this way?"

We cross the hall an' start walkin' down a long dark passage. The corridor we are in seems to be miles long. There is a thick carpet on the floor an' I cannot even hear myself walkin'. I get around to thinkin' that the guy who is runnin' this place as a *spieler* certainly knows his oatcakes, because anyone takin' a look at this place would think it was uninhabited.

We go on walkin'. After a bit I can hear some music comin' from somewhere—very nice music—sorta quiet if you get me. Then we come to the end of the corridor. The old boy opens the door an' stands on one side.

He says: "Go in, m'sieu."

I go inta another sorta hallway—pretty big an' very well lit. There is a guy in a black coat standin' in the middle of the floor. He is a *maître d'hôtel* type of guy. He comes forward an' he says: "M'sieu?"

I give him the same line of talk as I gave the other bozo.

He takes a look at the card. He says: "Excellent, m'sieu. You want to play immediately or would you like to eat? Or would you like to see a little floor show?"

I say: "Well, I guess I came out here for a game, but I'm a piece tired. Maybe I'll take a little drink an' have a look at the floor show." I put my hand in my pocket for my wallet. I say: "Maybe you'd like some dough?"

He smiles an' he waves his hand. "No, thank you very much, m'sieu," he says. "Here we take ten per cent.—the *cagnotte* only. No charge is made for anythin' else."

I say thanks a lot. He points to a big staircase on the left at the far end of the hall. I go along there. It is a short stairway an' at the top is another passage with a cloak-room. I check in my hat an' overcoat, go along through two swing doors, push 'em open an' go in.

Well . . . well . . . well . . .! It is the old night-club scene an' it could be anywhere—in Bermuda, in Paris, New York, Madrid—any place you like. There is the usual not very big dance floor with a curtained stage on the far side of it. On the left of the curtained stage is a band platform. Sittin' on this platform are about twelve guys dressed in black evenin' pants an' frilled shirts—the usual Argentino stuff. They are playin' an' they are playin' very good. I like the music. Also these orchestra mugs are about the toughest lookin' lot I have ever seen in my life. Stuck all around the dance floor are tables with gold chairs. The table linen an' glass is good an' the cutlery is good. I think that they may be short of a lotta stuff in France but they are certainly not short of anythin' here. There are some people sittin' at the tables—not many—an' there seem to be a lot more women than men. Champagne corks are poppin' here an' there an' nobody seems to be goin' easy on the liquor.

I look at my watch. It is seven minutes to twelve. Then I ease over an' sit down at a table in the corner where I got the wall behind me, which is an old-fashioned habit of mine. After a bit a tired looking waiter comes over. He asks me what I want. I tell him I'll have some whisky to start with. He goes off an' comes back in a few minutes with a bottle of Canadian rye, some ice an' a syphon. He pours me out a glass of the stuff an' it is good. I tell him to leave the bottle.

He says sure an' goes away. I call after him: "Look, what time does this floor show start?"

"Any minute now, m'sieu," he says. "Usually at twelve o'clock."

I sit back in my chair, light myself a cigarette an' drink my whisky. I think maybe things could be a great deal worse than they are. Anyway, right now I have nothing to grumble about.

I keep my eye on the main entrance. Some more people are tricklin' in. Most of them look like Frenchmen or foreigners—well-dressed—an' there are some very fine lookin' frails with 'em. They might be anythin'—Argentinos, Frenchmen, Spaniards or anythin' you like. And they are all wearin' very swell clothes an' the women are showin' some very valuable ice. One woman has a diamond collar that must have set somebody back a whole lotta dough.

The band stops for a coupla minutes. Then it starts off on a hot number an' the curtain goes up. Half a dozen girls wearin' very pretty dresses—an' very modest sorta dresses—come on, sing a number an' go inta a dance. This strikes me as bein' funny because this sorta turn is usually more undressed in this country. But in a minute I get it. All of a sudden all the lights go out except one spot light at the back of the stage where there is an openin'. The girls sorta form up three on each side of it an' through the openin' comes my little pal Marta Frisler!

I give a big sigh, finish off my rye an' pour myself another four fingers. I think this is gonna be very good.

Marta is lookin' swell. She is wearin' a long blue velvet cloak that reaches almost to the ground. She is a graceful mover an' the way they got the lights fixed you can't see she's boss-eyed. An' also I reckon when she said the customers don't look at her face she was right. Then she takes the cloak off. Underneath she is wearin' the normal sorta frock. She starts singin' some goddam silly little song in French an' goes into the old strip tease act that I have seen her do in Metzler's Burlesque years ago in New York.

I finish my drink an' I get up. The lights are still out an' anyway nobody is takin' any notice of me. There is just enough light comin' from the lime for me to edge around, behind the tables towards the right hand side of the stage—the side opposite the band. There is a door here. I open it an' go through.

My guess was right. I am in a little curvin' passage that leads around behind the stage an' on the other side of it are dressin' rooms. I look into the first one. It is empty an' the light is on. It is a big room an' full of clothes. There is stuff hangin' all over the place. I reckon this is the chorus girls' room. The next room looks to me like a sorta store-room, but the third time I go lucky. This is a little room. It is well lit, an' well furnished. There is a make-up table an' mirror with, lights all around it, an' hangin' on a peg is the pair of zephyr pants that I saw Marta wearin' at the hotel.

An' that is not all. Sittin' in the corner lookin' not quite so good is the Cuban guy. He is still wearin' his white tie an' he has got one hand held up over his stomach as if it was still hurtin' him. When

he sees me his dark skin goes pale. He gets up. I walk across an'
put my hand on his face an' push him back into the chair.

I say: "Look, pal, I'm a little bit tired of you. You wouldn't try
an' pull a gun an' start somethin', would you, because I don't like
it. Also I am not in such a good temper as I was the last time I
saw you. An' how d'you like that?"

He looks at me for a long time. His eyes are narrow, like
snakes' eyes. He says in a low sorta voice: "What the hell do you
theenk you are doing here, *senor*? And where do you theenk it
ees going to get you to?"

I say: "Listen, handsome, don't you trouble yourself with
that problem. The thing you've got to ask yourself is where it's
gonna get *you* to. Look, you tell me one or two things. What did
you come to Paris for? How'd you meet up with the Frisler dame
an' what's the big idea? I suppose you're tellin' me that you work
here. Is that it?"

He says: "And why not? Look, I am seeck. I am seeck. because
you kick me, otherwise I'd be workeeng in the bar at this minute."

I say: "Yeah? You try another one." I pull the chair away from
the make-up table an' I stick it down opposite him. I say: "Look,
fella, I got some ideas about you an' I got some ideas about Marta.
The best thing you can do is to make it easy for yourself. You've
already tried to fog me last night an' that's a helluva offence. The
best thing you can do it talk."

He says: "You can go right to hell." He spits right in my eye,
which will prove to you guys as I have told you before that this
guy is not a guy with nice manners.

Outside I can hear the music workin' up to a climax. I reckon
in a minute Marta will be through with her act an' comin' back
to start dressin' again. I take another look at the boy friend. He
is sittin' there starin' at me lookin' very tough, but at the same
time there is a sorta curious look in his eyes as if he does not quite
know what is gonna happen next.

I get up. This guy is scared all right, but he's not gonna talk,
because he's scared of something else more than he is of me. I
say: "All right. Here we go." I put my left hand out an' put it in

the top of his collar. Then I hit him once with my right—a short arm jab that connects with his jaw an' makes a noise like choppin' wood. The guy does not even know what's hit him. He goes out like a light, I pick him up, take him outside in the corridor, open the store room door which is the next door, sling him inside, shut and lock the door. I put the key in my pocket. Then I go back to Marta's dressin'-room, put the chair back in front of the make-up table an' sit down in the chair that the Cuban was sittin' on. I light myself a cigarette.

A minute goes by an' the door opens. Marta comes in. She stands there just covered with a fan an' a lotta maidenly modesty, with the cloak over her arm.

I say: "Well ... well ... well ...! You were right, Marta, when you said they never notice your squint, but if you wanta put that cloak on don't let me stop you. I've seen strip acts before."

I get up, move over an' kick the door to behind her. I say: "Take your weight off your feet an' sit down. I wanta talk to you."

She pulls the cloak around her an' flops down in the seat by the dressin' table. She looks at me like a sour-faced cat. She does not like me a bit.

She says: "What is this? And where is Enrique?"

I say: "D'you mean that guy with the white tie—the fella who tried to crease me last night—the guy who was waitin' here in this dressin' room?"

She says: "Yeah, that's who I mean. Where is he?"

I say: "If you must know, babe, he's knocked off. I got an American military police waggon outside at the present moment. He's inside it with a pair of steel bracelets on. Somebody came to the conclusion that they didn't like him. Maybe that somebody was me."

She says: "Yeah!" She looks at me for a long time. I look at her hands. Her fingers are tremblin' an' the pupils of her eyes are pin-points. I reckon this baby has been doin' a little dopin' in her spare time—which might be a help.

She says: "What have they got on Enrique? He ain't done anythin'."

I say: "No? Let me tell you a little story, baby. I told you last night that a very good guy in the Federal Service named Ribban was killed up at the Club Leon. He was sandbagged. O.K. A couple days before, he bought a fancy fountain pen set—a pen an' pencil—off a guy I know. There was only one set like that in Paris. Here's the pencil that belongs to it. It's the pencil I took off Enrique last night. O.K. That's good enough."

She says: "What d'you mean—that's good enough?"

I say: "Look, are you tryin' to tell me that he didn't bump Ribban?"

She says: "Goddam it, there is always a helluva lot of *trouble* around this dump. A girl can't even do her work without something bustin'." She changes her tone. She says: "Listen, can I have a drink?"

I say: "You can have twenty if it's gonna help you, but you gotta make your mind up on one thing an' you gotta make it up good an' quick." I draw my chair a little closer to her, an' I put on a quiet an' sympathetic tone of voice. I say: "Listen, Marta, if you don't talk you're goin' out to that waggon too. If the U.S. Military police get their hooks on you it's a stone certainty you're gonna find yourself in bad over this Ribban business. Maybe you can say you don't know anythin' about it but you're Enrique's girl friend."

I laugh. "For all I know you might have done it. Yeah, that's an idea. I reckon Enrique woulda used a gun or maybe a knife. Yeah, he'd have used a knife. But it'd be easy for a dame to sandbag a guy like Ribban when he was gonna write something down. An' he'd trust a dame. He'd turn his back to her. Listen," I say, "*you* didn't kill Ribban, didya?"

She goes as white as death. She says: "I'm tellin' you I didn't do it. I wasn't even there."

I say: "But you know Enrique was?"

"Yes, he was," she says. "What else do you want to know?"

I say: "Look, sweetheart, you talk an' say your piece. Let me know all about it. I wanta know everything that's been happenin' to you an' Enrique since you've been in Paris. How long have you been here?"

She says: "Not very long—two or three weeks."

I say: "How'd you get over here?"

She thinks for a minute. Then: "There was some guy called Varley. I don't know him. Enrique knew him. He fixed it."

I say: "Yeah, that's very interestin'. That bein' so, what did Enrique wanta crease Ribban for?"

She says: "I think Ribban had an idea about Varley. I think he was on to something—I don't know what. Varley was aimin' to get outa here, an' he could do it. He'd got it all fixed."

I say: "Where was he aimin' to go to? Do you know that?"

She says: "Yeah, he'd got a seat fixed in a transport plane for England."

"Yeah," I tell her. "Well, come back to Ribban. Why did Enrique have to fix him?"

She says: "Varley wanted it. Varley wanted Ribban fixed because he knew too much."

I say: "Yeah! You know what, Marta, I think you're tellin' the truth. The story sorta matches up. O.K. I'll leave you out of it."

She says: "Willya? Honest to God I never had anythin' to do with it. I knew about it, but I couldn't stop it."

I say: "Well, you know what they'll do with Enrique, don't you?"

She says: "Yeah, I know."

I say: "An' you won't even miss him, hey?"

She shakes her head. "I won't miss him one little bit."

I say: "All right. When is your next show?"

"Not for another twenty minutes," she says.

I tell her: "Fine. You stick around here an' don't go outa this room for another ten or fifteen minutes at least. You stay here. I wanta get that police waggon away before you're seen around the place. Otherwise somebody might wanta take you in, which is a thing I don't want because I may wanta talk to you some more. But if you keep your trap buttoned up maybe you'll be all right."

She says: "Thanks a lot, Mr. Caution. I'll do what you say."

I get up, go outside an' shut the door. Outside the passage is quiet. I open the store room door with the key, go in.

Enrique is still lying where I left him. I look around the place. There are two or three theatrical baskets corded in the corner. I take the cords off an' I truss this guy up so that he can just breathe. He's got a big silk handkerchief in his pocket an' I gag him with that. An' I toss him in the corner, shut the door an' lock it again.

I reckon it's gonna be some time before they find that guy. I ease back along the passageway, through the pass door, into the dance room. I go back to my table. I sit down an' give myself another shot of whisky.

The band is playin' a dreamy waltz number. After I have had a coupla drinks more I begin to feel good an' poetic. Maybe it's the music or maybe it's just my temperamental nature. I get to thinkin' that if I was not forced to spend all my time bustin' people like Enrique on the beezer an' generally raisin' hell an' devils around the place I would like to be sittin' in the moonlight talkin' to some honeybelle an' handin' her a line of poetic talk that would grow hair on a horse-radish. Me—I am like that.

Then I get around to ponderin' on my little pal Marta Frisler. I reckon this baby is the biggest goddam liar that I ever listened to. Everything that she has told me—except perhaps one thing—is just punk. But because she thinks that her boy friend Enrique is knocked off an' all set for the cooler she is willin' to say anythin' just to save her own carcass. An' maybe she is right.

Maybe it's gonna be easier for her if Enrique is outa the way. Maybe that is what she wants. Maybe she is playin' to get into the big time with this mysterious Varley.

Figure it out for yourself. She says that Enrique was the guy who killed Ribban. She says that because I have suggested that very thing to her. She knows I got corroborative evidence because I got the pencil that Ribban bought with the fountain pen set. She reckons that everybody is gonna think that Enrique took it off Ribban after he'd busted him with that sandbag. An' so she is gettin' herself in right.

Anyway, she thinks, nobody is gonna believe what Enrique says. She also thinks that if she plays ball with me an' supports

anythin' I say that I am gonna forget that she took a coupla shots
at me in the Hotel St. Denis.

All of which will prove to you mugs that this guy Confucius is
one hundred per cent, right when he says: "The lyin' woman is
like a gin ricky without any gin. She is also like a martini without
any ice. All the time she is tryin' to remember what she said the
time before last, an' is therefore all the more interestin'. Because,"
says Confucius, "the dame who has got nothin' to lie about is as
shapeless as a piece of cold veal an' as uninterestin' as last week's
hamburger. But she that is beautiful an' passionate has got a line
of fancy talk that woulda made Casanova sound like a dumb guy
with a stutter. An'," he concludes, "you can quote me any time
you like without payin' a copyright fee."

It is half-past twelve when I get up from my table, ease quietly
through the curtains by the main entrance, walk along the corridor
an' push open the big doors at the end. Inside is a helluva scene.

This dump is one of those places that you read about an' don't
believe in. It also makes you wonder whether it is you or the
other guys who are screw-eyed about the way the world is goin'.
The room is a very big one—nearly as big as the local dance hall.
There are hangings an' suits of armour all around the walls, an'
a smell of some heavy sort of perfume hanging about the place.
There are settees an' couches an' what-will-you all around the
place, an' in the middle of the floor are four big tables—faro,
roulette, an' *chemie* games. In one corner of the room some
boyo, who looks so pretty that he might be his sister wearin' her
brother's pants an' a sickly grin, is runnin' a caged dice game. In
the opposite corner there is what looks like a poker school with
five guys playin'. One of these palookas looks like the picture on
the wall of the original owner an' the others like they just been
let out on parole from sixty-five year sentences.

There are men in tuxedos an' women wearin' frocks that cost
a bundle. There are babies stickin' around with whatever is the
French for Sugar Daddies an' other frails playin' a lone hand
with a watchful eye for any boyo who gets himself in the money.

I reckon if one of these honeybelles gets her hooks on him he will wonder what hit him an' where the dough went so quick.

All of which will show you guys that whatever may be goin' on in this great big world—it don't matter whether it may be war, murder, mayhem or skulduggery—there will always be guys who like playin' the dough an' dames who like to stand around an' watch—just in case a roll falls inta their laps.

I start lookin' round for Juanella because I reckon I gotta get my business finished with this baby, otherwise some curious guy may go inta the store-room an' discover the Cuban. If they do an' if Marta finds I've been stringin' her along about havin' knocked this guy off things may not be so hot for me.

I start walkin' around, lookin' at the play. The people playin' are all sorts an' conditions of guys, but most of 'em are well-dressed an' look as if they've got jack. The stakes are pretty high. When I get around to the other side of the room I see Juanella. An' what a sight she is!

She is wearin' a very tight watered silk frock, cut high in the neck, with gold Spanish epaulettes on the shoulders. One side of the skirt is slit up to the knee an' I can see a very nice sheer gold stockin'. She is wearin' black shoes with four-inch heels with little gold studs in 'em. I'm tellin' you that Juanella looks a picture.

I wonder what the hell she is doin' around here. Juanella is a funny sorta cuss. She has got looks an' brains ail' everythin' else that you want but she is one of these dames who are always chasin' moonbeams if you get me. Whatever she wants, well when she gets it I reckon she wants something else. Knowin' this brings me to thinkin' about Larvey. I reckon that just because Larvey is well an' truly stuck behind the bars in Alcatraz the only thing she wants is to get him sprung. An' I reckon that once she got him sprung she would not be interested very much more an' would not mind very much if they slung him inside again just so she could get him out some more. All of which will show you that this baby is like the rest of us because she is always after some thin' she *thinks* she wants.

She is standin' there talkin' to some fat bozo with a bald head. I lean up against the wall an' watch. After a few minutes the fat guy goes off an' Juanella turns an' sees me. Her mouth curves inta a smile an' she comes over to me like I was her long lost boy friend just back from the war.

She says: "Lemmy, am I glad to see you? An' what are you doin' around here?"

I say: "Hush, Sweetiepie. My name is Mr. Hicks. I am a U.S. steel magnate over here on business."

She says: "Like Hell! I reckon what you are doin' here is nobody's business. Why don't you come an' talk to me an' have a little drink?"

I say: "That sounds a very good idea to me, Juanella. Where do we go?"

She says: "You come with me." She takes me by the hand an' she leads me through some velvet portieres at the other end of the room. We go along a little passage, through a doorway. She shuts the door behind her an' switches on the light.

It is a very nice little sittin'-room. The furniture is good an' there is a bottle of rye an' a syphon on the table.

She says: "Sit down, Lemmy, an' have a drink."

I say: "Look, Juanella, tell me something—what are you doin around this dump?"

She says: "Well, a girl's gotta live. I gotta job here. I'm a hostess."

I say: "What does that mean? You talk the boys outa gettin' steamed up when they're taken for a big roll?"

She smiles at me. She says: "Something like that." She pours out a drink, squirts some soda in it, hands it to me. Then she gives herself one. She holds up the glass an' she says: "Well, here's to you, Lemmy."

I say: "An' here's to you, Juanella. You're a wonderful sight. I haven't seen anythin' like you since I worked in the circus. You look younger every minute."

She says: "Yeah, that's as maybe, but I'm sorta sad."

A faraway look comes inta her lovely eyes. This dame looks as if she's gonna burst into tears any minute.

I say: "Listen, Juanella, you tell me something—you're a very swell dish. Guys would go for you in a very big way —rich guys I mean. But I reckon you're only stuck on one man an' that would be Larvey T. Rillwater—your husband. Right?"

She says: "No." She sits down in the chair next to me. She puts her elbows on the table an' she leans forward. I can smell the perfume that she is wearin' an it's terrific.

"You sweet bastard," she says, "what d'you think you're playin' at? As if you didn't know."

"Meanin' just what?" I ask her. I take out my cigarette case. I give her a cigarette an' take one myself. I light 'em.

She blows a puff of smoke. She says: "Do you remember years ago I said something to you when you was doin' that job at Le Havre about that gas formula? Well, I gave you a hand then, didn't I?"

I say: "Yeah—so what!"

"You remember what I told you then?" she says. "You wouldn't give me a tumble, so I'd stick to home-made pastry in future. An' it still goes."

"Meanin' what?" I ask her.

"Meanin' this," she says. "I'm a two-man woman. I go for Larvey—that unfortunate husband of mine who's in the cooler—in a very big way. But maybe I wouldn't if the guy I'm really crazy about would give me a break."

I say: "That guy being . . .?"

"That guy being you," she says. "An' you know it goddam well." The joke is she looks as if she sorta means it.

I told you she was a cute baby, this Juanella. Maybe she's speakin' the truth for once, because what she says about the old days is certainly true.

I say: "All right. So you're a two-man woman an' I'm one of the two guys. So where does that get me?"

"Where do you *want* it to get you?" she asks. "You don't think you could ask me for something I wouldn't give you, do you, Lemmy?"

"Is that a fact?" I ask her.

She leans forward. I can see her breast heavin'. "That is a fact," she says. She clasps her long white fingers over mine an' the ice in the rings she is wearin' glitters.

"Well, if that's a fact," I tell her, "I'll take another whisky an' soda."

She shrugs her shoulders. Then she looks as if she'd like to cut my throat; then she mixes the drink.

I say: "Listen, honeybelle, let's get this straight. Maybe you can help me; in spite of all the funny business I don't think you'd do anythin' that would get you in bad with me, would you?"

She says: "Definitely *no*, Lemmy."

"O.K.," I tell her. "Well, when I saw you last night I told you what was breakin', didn't I? Maybe I was a mug. Maybe I ought not to have talked to you."

She says: "An' why not? You told me you'd got yourself in bad with somebody; that you'd been shootin' your mouth. Well, so what?"

"So a lot of things," I say. "First of all let me ask you a little question. You told me you was livin' at the Hotel St. Denis. O.K. Well, I went around there. I meet a *concierge* guy who tells me the number of your room. I go up there but I don't find you. I find Marta Frisler an' some Cuban guy. I have quite a tough time with them. In point of fact the Cuban unlimbers some artillery an' they try to fog me. What's the big idea?"

Her eyes are wide. She says: "Listen, Lemmy, what are you tryin' to sell me."

I say: "I'm not tryin' to sell you anythin', Juanella. I'm tellin' you the truth."

She says: "You must be nuts. Where is this Hotel St. Denis?"

"Wouldn't you know?" I ask her. "It's a dump near the Boulevard St. Michel."

She starts laughin'. She says: "Why don't you get some sense, Lemmy. That ain't the Hotel St. Denis I was talkin' about. The place I'm stayin' at is between here an' Paris. Everybody knows it. Why the hell should you think I'd stay in a dump like this place on the Boulevard St. Michel?"

I don't say anythin'. Then: "Well, life is very funny, because if what you're tellin' is the truth there is so many coincidences in this goddam business that I don't know which way I'm pointin'."

She says: "Such as what?" She leans towards me again an' I get another whiff of the perfume. "Why don't you tell me what the trouble is, Lemmy? Why don't you let me help you? I'd do anythin' for you."

I think: O.K. Here goes. I'll try anythin' once.

I say: "Look, there was gonna be a sort of enquiry on me, see—about my havin' talked to this dame called Marceline du Clos. Well, last night somebody got her outa the cooler on a forged police pass, took her over the river an' knocked her off so *she* couldn't say her piece, see? O.K. That don't matter very much because she'd said all she wanted to say to an F.B.I, man named George Ribban—a guy who was a pal of mine—a nice guy. This Ribban was the one who had reported about me talkin' to du Clos. You got that?"

She says: "Yeah, I got it." She is listenin' in a very big way. I can see she is interested.

"O.K.," I go on. "Well, after I left you I went along to see Ribban. I wanted to have a little talk with him before the enquiry started. I wanted to find out what he was supposed to have on me. Well, when I got to the dump where he was I found him on the staircase. He was dead."

She says: "You don't say, Lemmy. Say, this is a tough business. So the du Clos woman was dead an' Ribban was dead. That left you up in the air, hey?"

"You're tellin' me, Juanella!" I say. "And howl Here am I suspected of havin' shot my mouth to this woman an' all the evidence against me is dead." I grin at her. "If I hadn't some alibis," I say, "they might even have thought I'd bumped 'em off."

She says: "Hooey! It's a lotta punk."

I say: "Maybe it is. But it leaves a nasty taste m your month. But listen, I have not finished yet."

She says: "I'm listenin'. You go ahead."

I say: "Well, I got an idea that I'd come an' talk to you. I go to this dump where I think you're stayin' an' I find Marta Frisler an' this Cuban guy. Maybe it's another coincidence that she's workin' here doin' a strip-tease act. Maybe it's another coincidence that this boyo is workin' in the bar here, or says so."

She looks at me with a faraway look in her eyes. She says: "Yeah, it's sorta funny, isn't it, Lemmy? It must look goddam strange to you."

"Does it look strange to you?" I tell her. "Well, listen, here's some more coincidences. When I find this guy Ribban lyin' on the stairs he's gotta fountain pen in his hand. It's got the cap on just as if he'd taken it outa his pocket to write a letter an' hadn't had time to unscrew the cap before somebody gave it to him. This fountain pen was a part of a set of a pen an' pencil—a set that's bein' sold on the black market in Paris. I traced it. The set was bought by Ribban a few days ago."

She says: "Yeah? So what?"

I say: "Nothing much. Only I took the pencil outa the Cuban's pocket after I'd smacked him down when the shoot in' business occurred at the Hotel St. Denis. Does that stink or does it?"

She says: "So you think that this Cuban—his name's Enrique; he works in the bar here—you think he killed Ribban?"

I smile at her sweetly. I say: "No, Sweetiepie, that's what somebody *wants* me to think."

She says: "Listen, Lemmy, I'm interested. Tell me some more."

I say: "O.K. I come out here tonight because I heard you were workin' out here. I see the Frisler piece is playin' in the strip-tease act down on the dance floor. I go around to her room an' I find Enrique there. I bust him one, tie him up an' chuck him in the store-room. You got that?"

She says: "I've got it. That's the Caution technique all right. Maybe you'll do that to me one day."

I say: "Who knows?"

She says: "Maybe I'd like it, Lemmy." She throws me a very warm look.

I say: "O.K. Then I go back to the dressin' room an' I wait for Marta. When she comes off she wantsta know where Enrique is. I tell her I got a military police waggon here an' I have had him knocked off for killin' Ribban."

"Hey . . . hey . . .!" she says. She looks sorta serious. "I do not like that thing one little bit."

"An' why not, honey?" I ask her.

She shrugs her shoulders. She says: "If somebody goes inta that store-room an' finds Enrique there, there's gonna be a whole lotta trouble breakin' around here. Another thing," she goes on, "this guy Enrique is not at all a nice guy. He can be tough in a big way if he gets sorta annoyed about something."

"Maybe," I tell her. "But the bigger they come the harder they fall. Any time this Enrique bird wantsta get tough with me he don't have to buy a ticket. I'll let him in on the free list an' throw him out when I've done with him."

She puts one hand over mine. She says: "You're just the same as you usta be. Just as tough an' lovely, sweetiepie. I could die for you, Lemmy." She heaves a sigh an' I can hear her **brassière** strings creakin' with the strain.

"O.K.," she says. "So you wait for Marta an' you tell her that Enrique is knocked off an' is in the police waggon outside. Well . . . how does she like that?"

"She loves it," I say. "She says yes he did it. He did it because he had to do it. He did it because of some guy called Varley—the guy who brought those two over here, who's since made a getaway to England. So," I go on, "it looks to me like this Frisler baby is tryin' to ditch Enrique for something he didn't do." I draw a deep breathful of smoke an' give her a long look. "Listen, Gorgeous," I tell her, "I suppose you wouldn't know anythin' about this guy Varley, wouldya?"

She says: "Why should I? Who the hell is this Varley? I suppose I have not got enough trouble in front of me without havin' Mr. Varley as well. I never heard of him an' I don't want to."

"O.K.," I say. "So you don't know this Varley an' you think it's on the cards that Enrique is the guy who creased Ribban?"

She spreads her hands. She says: "But why shouldn't he have done it, Lemmy—if he'd got the pencil from the set?"

I say: "Look, honey, use your brains. This guy Enrique is no mug. We'll imagine for sake of argument that he went round to the Club Leon to kill Ribban. O.K. He goes upstairs to Ribban's room an' Ribban is writin' a letter or is gonna write something down that Enrique's told him. So Ribban takes his fountain pen out of his pocket an' is just gonna unscrew the cap when Enrique hands him a tough one an' kills him."

She says: "Yeah. That's all right."

"So then," I go on, "Enrique takes the trouble to take the propellin' pencil outa Ribban's pocket. He does not worry to take the pen. Is that sense, honey, or is it?"

She says: "No, that's not sense."

"O.K.," I tell her. "Well, if that's not sense, what is sense?"

She thinks for a bit; then she shrugs her shoulders. She says: "I wouldn't know. Me—I am not one of those brain women."

I say: "Look, beautiful, this guy Enrique has got brains, hey? He is no mug. He knows his way around?"

"Sure," she says, "Enrique knows his way around all right. That one is nobody's fool."

"All right," I say. "That bein' so we can take it for granted that Enrique would not be mug enough to take that pencil outa Ribban's pocket. You got that?"

She says: "Yeah, Lemmy, I got it." She is sittin' there with her elbows on the table, her chin restin' on her hands an' her pretty lips sorta parted. She looks good enough to eat, an' she is concentratin' on what I am sayin'. She is listenin' hard an' she does not realise that I am givin' her a first class line of dope. What I am tellin' her is hooey. Maybe you'll see why pretty soon.

I say: "O.K. So we agree that if Enrique had killed Ribban, he wouldn't have taken the pencil an' left the pen, would he? He'd have taken the pen an' the pencil, that is if he was a mug. But he's not a mug so he wouldn't have taken anythin'. He wouldn't have touched anythin' that was on Ribban. That makes you think, hey?"

She says: "Makes you think *what*?"

"Use that pretty little headpiece of yours," I tell her. "Don't you see it wasn't Enrique that killed Ribban. It was some other guy. Look, when I found Ribban he had a fountain pen in his hand. The cap was still on it, see? The mug who killed him knew that. He knew somebody was gonna see that pen. So what does he do? He takes the pencil an' he gives it to Enrique because Enrique is one of those flash guys who likes havin' pretty things stuck all around him, an' the killer knows that Enrique is gonna like that pencil. The killer knows somethin' else too. He knows there is only one set like that on the black market, an' he knows that some clever guy like me is gonna find out where it came from."

She says: "I get it, Lemmy. All you wanta find out now is the guy who gave that pencil to Enrique."

I finish my drink. I push the glass over towards her an' she gives me another one.

I say: "I reckon I *know* who it was gave that pencil to Enrique."

Her eyes pop. She says: "You don't say. Who was it, Lemmy?"

I say: "If I'm not very much mistaken it was the guy called Varley. Look, when I told Marta back in her dressin' room a little while ago that I thought it was Enrique who'd slugged Ribban she agreed good an' quick. She agreed a damned sight *too* quick. She was also in a hurry to tell me something else. She was in a hurry to tell me that Varley had made a getaway some days before; that she thought he was in England. You got it?"

"I got it," she says. "She was tryin' to alibi Varley an' hang the rap on Enrique?"

"That's right," I tell her. "It looks like this guy Varley is an influential guy. He's got friends. He's certainly got this baby Marta workin' for him."

She says: "Yeah. It looks like that. But listen, why does Varley have to kill Ribban—you tell me that one?"

I say: "There could be half a dozen reasons, Juanella. Let's make a coupla guesses. This guy Varley has got Marta an' Enrique workin' for him. He knows that Ribban has got next to this Marceline du Clos who is his other side-kicker. Well, I have been told that Varley was suspicious of du Clos. He got the idea in his head that she was gettin' scared; that she might shoot her mouth, see?"

She nods. I drink some whisky. I am watchin' her outa the corner of my eye. I can see her fingers are tremblin' a little bit.

"O.K.," I go on. "Well, Ribban sees du Clos an' du Clos talks to him. Ribban throws a scare into her. She's frightened sick she's gonna be shot or flung inside or somethin', for espionage. So what does she do? She tries to make it good for herself. First of all she probably tells Ribban about Varley an' secondly a lotta stuff about me. By tellin' them that I've been talkin' to her she's sorta doin' what she can to get in with Ribban an' anybody else so she can get a break. You got that?"

She says: "I've got it."

"All right," I go on. "Well, it's logical, isn't it? Somehow Varley finds out that she's talked to Ribban an' he wishes he'd thrown this dame overboard before, but it's too late now. So what he's gotta do is to get rid of Ribban quick *an'* the dame, but he thinks it might be a good idea to fix her first just in case she does any more talkin'. Well, maybe he's got some pals around here in Paris. He certainly seems to have because he fixes up a forged Police pass an' gets du Clos out, takes her over the river to the Rue Zacherie an' bumps her. Then he goes back an' goes up to Ribban's place an' he slugs him. An' he reckons he's sittin' pretty."

I grin. "Personally speakin'," I say, "I think he is. He did himself a good turn an' he did me a goddam bad one. Now you've got it."

She says: "Yeah, it is a tough situation. It's—" She looks over my shoulder an' her eyes widen.

I get up outa my chair an' turn around towards the door. Standin' in the doorway are two guys. They are not at all nice-lookin' guys. One of 'em has got a short snub-nosed belly gun in his right hand that's pointin' at my lower regions.

I give a big sigh because I find that practically everywhere I go some guy is followin' me around with a gun.

I say: "Look, what is this?"

One fella says in a sorta sarcastic fancy French accent: "You would not know, m'sieu, hein? A leetle while ago we find the unfortunate Enrique in the store-room. He tells us all sorts of interesting things about you." He grins. This guy—he seems sorta pleased with himself. "It would seem that Enrique is not ver' fond of you."

The other guy says: "Yeah, that's how it is, buddy."

I look at Juanella. She is lookin' scared, but she gets up an' goes inta bat. She says: "Wait a minute. I think you boys are makin' a mistake. This gentleman is Mr. Hicks—an American business man. He is here playin' the tables."

The fat man says: "Yeah, I know. He's Mr. Hicks an' I'm the King of Spain. You'd better come along with us. Mister Caution. We gotta date with you."

I say: "Hey! What goes on around here? It won't be so good for you guys if you get fresh with a Federal officer."

The French guy with the gun gives me another big grin. He says: "M'sieu, you know Paris ees in a ver' extraordinary state. The police organisation is not ver' good. People disappear every day but nobody knows where they go to. You will be just another one of those people."

I say: "Well, if that's how it is that's how it is." I am doin' a little quick thinkin', wonderin' how I'll get out of this one.

Juanella turns towards me an' gives me a big smile. She says: "Well, whatever happens, Lemmy, remember I'm for you."

I say: "Yeah, sweetheart? I hope it's gonna do me some good."

She says: "Well, you can only die once an' if you do I'll think of you. One for the road before you go. These boys won't mind waitin' a minute."

She gives me my glass. She has filled it up again.

I say: "Well, thanks a lot." Just for a minute the idea passes through my head that I might take a chance an' fling this whisky inta the eyes of the boyo with the gun, but what good is that gonna do me. I reckon the other guy is heeled too. He's got one hand in his coat pocket. Maybe I'd just be pushin' things forward a little.

I say: "Well, here it is." I drink the drink. I put the glass down on the table an' that is about all I do, because the next minute the room starts spinnin' around an' my centre of gravity is practically a hundred per cent. loss. The table comes up an' hits me a neat one on the snoot.

I go out like a lamp.

When I decide to come back to earth I do not feel so good. I am leanin' up against a stone wall an' all around me is pitch darkness. I cannot see a thing. I gotta headache like somebody has hit me over the head with an iron bar an' a taste in my mouth like I have been eatin' bird-seed.

I just lie there an' sorta relax. After a bit I begin to feel a bit better an' my head begins to clear. I start wonderin' what the hell this is all about.

I start thinkin' about Juanella. What is this baby playin' at? Why the hell just when these guys propose to knock me off does she have to hand me out some Dutch drops an' put me out? I reckon that whisky was some drink. It was about the quickest Micky Finn I have ever had in my life. Maybe I know why she did it. Maybe I got an idea about that. Maybe she is not so friendly with these guys an' she thinks if she puts me out the gentleman with the shootin' iron is not gonna get busy. In other words she wants me all in one piece. This is one idea I got.

On the other hand it is very interestin' to know why Juanella should be all ready to slip some dope inta my liquor. But perhaps she just has it around. Maybe she keeps it for the customers when they get tough. I wouldn't know. But what I do know is this—somebody went inta the store room an' found Enrique, so by this time Marta will know that I was stringin' her along. She'll know that all the stuff I told her about Enrique bein' knocked off was a lotta hooey. Well, that's O.K.

You gotta realise that in a job like this you gotta start something. It is no good just hangin' around an' lookin' for clues. The great thing to do is to throw a spanner in the works an' get everybody sorta annoyed with each other. Do this an' *somebody* is gonna talk *sometime*.

But I am wise to one thing. I am wise to the fact that Marta Frisler is prepared to sell Enrique out at any time. Didn't she try an' do it a little while ago? For some reason which I do not know my mind keeps comin' back to Juanella. What a babe she is. She certainly has got something—that one, even if I am not quite certain what it is.

I lie there in the darkness an' I start thinkin' about this guy Confucius—the boyo who has a saying for everythin'. I remember one of the things Confucius said. "Beware of the lovely with the sympathetic smile," says this Confucius. "One day she will fling herself to the tigers for you an' the next day she will be seen lurkin' in a back alley waiting with a spanner all poised to catch you a nasty smack on the bean. Beware of her O ye mugs. Because the dame without beauty, who is known as Sourpuss to all an' sundry is as faithful as a yellow dog, because once she hath got herself a man she dare not lose same. But the blonde baby with a figure like a serpent, with nerve troubles, is as restless as the jumpin' bean an' will take a run-out powder or a sock at you with an iron bar just as she would give herself a manicure. Take heed, my foolish brethren, therefore, an' start somethin' with a puff adder or a bad-tempered crocodile rather than the dame who has what it takes an' knows all the answers. Otherwise the coyote will howl around your tombstone or the alimony will be so tough that it would be cheaper for you not to have been born at all."

Which will show you mugs that this Confucius certainly knew his way around.

I am feelin' not so bad now. I search around in my pocket an' I find they have not frisked me because my cigarette lighter is still there. I snap it on an' take a look around me. I am in a sorta basement cellar. There is a door at one end. I get up, go over an' try it. It is locked an' it is a very solid door. Up in the wall just above where I have been lyin' is a gratin'. There is a little light comin' from the other side but not enough to worry about. I reckon that gratin' leads to some room on the ground floor. But I should worry. It is too high for me to get up to an' it is an iron gratin' an' closed anyway.

There is an electric light switch on one side of the door an' I switch it on. I put my hands in my pocket an' I start walkin' up an' down. I reckon that so far as I am concerned there is no next move at the moment. I just gotta wait an' see what happens.

Right in the middle of these deep ruminations I hear a little clinkin' noise. I turn around. Behind me lyin' in the middle of the stone floor is a key. It has gotta label or something attached to it. Somebody must have thrown it through the gratin'. I pick it up. It is a big key with a luggage label on it, an' written on the label is:

Aren't you the big mug? What would happen to you if I wasn't lookin' after you? If I hadn't slipped you that Micky Finn those two wolves woulda fogged you. You'd have been cat's meat by now. Just remember that, will you? Maybe you'll give me a tumble some time. And for love of Mike tear this up. Otherwise they'll probably fix me too. Just get outa here, will you?
Yours, Juanella.

I stand there with the key in my hand. I think: Well . . . well . . . well . . . Maybe this guy Confucius was not so right all the time. I wonder!

I take out my lighter an' I burn the label. Then I try the key in the door. It opens easily enough; I switch off the light, go outside. I am in a sorta stone passage, but at the end there is a little light comin' from somewhere, an' I can see some steps. I ease along, go up the steps, open a door that is half open an' I find myself in a sorta vegetable garden. I take a look around. I reckon this place is at the back of the house.

I look at my watch. It is six o'clock in the mornin' an' the air don't taste so bad either. I draw in a big breath. It looks like I oughta be grateful to Juanella.

I start walkin' along one of the paths until I come to a wicket gate. I go through it. In a coupla minutes I am on the main road. I stand there for a minute waitin' to see if I can hitch-hike a ride, but nothin' passes by. So after a bit I reckon I will do some leg work.

I start walkin' back towards Paris.

Chapter Four
WEEK-END BLUES

LIFE can be sweet. I'm tellin' you mugs an' I don't mean perhaps. It does not matter about the old dark clouds hangin' about behind the silver linin'. No, sir . . . life is what you make it, an' if you don't make it then it is your business an' it is about time to get around to wonderin' on what particular gland you are shortin'.

I am walkin' down Piccadilly an' the sun is shinin'. Me—I am feelin' good an' I am not lookin' so dusty. I am all dolled up in the uniform of a Captain of U.S. Marines. I have got my cap stuck over one eye an' creases in my pants that you could shave yourself with. I am feelin' very well groomed an' slightly handsome an' by the looks that one or two babies sling me as I wend my way I got the feelin' that I am registerin' one hundred per cent. an' no misses.

Because there is somethin' about London that gets you in a very big way. This burg has certainly got atmosphere. Last time I was here was in 1943 when I was on that Gayda Travis case with Benzey an' even if the old *ville* has been smacked about a bit by Mr. Hitler's doodle-bugs it is still the same—except that there are a helluva lot of Americans kickin' around here. Still, like the old lady said, I reckon you cannot have too much of a good thing.

I change direction right an' slip into the Rivoli Bar for a snifter. While I am dealin' with this double Scotch I am doin' a little quiet thinkin'. Because even if I am a poetic sorta cuss I am still very much concerned with this guy Varley an' his sister. An' in a very big way. The day I really get my hooks on that guy in the way I wanta is gonna be a star day with me.

I finish my drink an' scram. Outside I grab myself a cab an' tell the driver to take me around to Scotland Yard. When I get there I give my name an' say I would very much like to have a few words with Chief Detective Inspector Herrick.

I stick around for a bit an' then some cop comes along an' takes me through a lotta corridors to Herrick's room.

He still looks the same sorta guy. He is sittin' there behind his desk in the corner by the window, drawin' on the blottin' pad. He is a little bit greyer an' there are a couple more lines on his face. He is still smokin' that short chubby sorta briar pipe that smells as if he was smokin' a nice brand of carpet mixed with onions.

He gets up an' comes around the desk with his hand held out. He says: "Well . . . Lemmy . . . this is pretty good seeing you. I wondered what had happened to you. Take a chair."

I sit down an' we do a little talkin' about the old days. Then he says: "Well . . . what's the trouble?"

I give him a big grin. I say: "Of course you wouldn't know anythin' about it, wouldya?"

He grins back. He says: "I've an instruction to render you all the assistance in my power. I understand that you and a Mr. James Cleeve, who is attached to your Service, are looking for an American infantry officer named Varley, and his sister. I've already seen Cleeve. I suppose you haven't contacted him yet?"

I shake my head. "Nope . . ." I tell him. "I got balled up in Paris an' missed the 'plane. Jimmy came over here on his own an' I followed next day. I reckon I'll be seein' him pretty soon. He's stayin' at the Savoy."

I light myself a cigarette. "Would you know anythin' about this Varley proposition?" I ask him.

He shrugs his shoulders. "It's like looking for a needle in a haystack," he says. "Work it out for yourself, Lemmy. There are umpteen thousand American troops over here an' naturally there are always a few of them absent without leave or taking a mike without permission or something like that. So there are quite a few Americans in this country running around sort of spare. And they're very difficult to check on."

I say: "That don't sound so good. Did you tell Jimmy Cleeve that?"

He says yes he told him. I ask him what Jimmy said to that one.

Herrick starts fillin' his pipe. "He didn't seem to mind," he says. "I got the idea that he had something in his head. Something to work on. Perhaps he's got an idea where this Varley is. In any event he seemed very optimistic about finding him."

I nod my head. I reckon that Jimmy *has* got some idea. I reckon that is the reason why he slipped off ahead of me in an earlier plane. That boy is out after all the breaks he can get an' I reckon he is not gonna wait around for Ma Caution's little boy Lemmy. No, sir . . . he is gettin' right ahead on his own. An' why not?

I get up. I say: "O.K., Herrick. I'm stayin' at my old dump in Jermyn Street. The place I was at when I was here before. You got the telephone number?"

He says yes he's got it.

"Well . . ." I tell him, "any time somethin' breaks that you think I oughta hear about give me a call. When I got somethin' to tell you I'll come through. An' while I'm away don't do anythin' that I wouldn't like photographed."

He gives me a big grin an' a sealed envelope an' we shake hands an' I scram. A very good guy Herrick. I reckon that him an' me understand each other like we were a coupla twins —only better.

I start wanderin' down Whitehall. Right now I am a little bit undecided as to what I am gonna do because you gotta realise that so far as this Varley business is concerned I know sweet nothin' about it an' am waitin' for a lead from somebody or other. But I am not worryin'. I got an idea that Jimmy Cleeve has got one up his sleeve an' that when the time comes I am gonna get to know about it.

I go inta some bar an' get myself four fingers of whisky. I light a cigarette an' ponder on this an' that. Life—like I told you—is very sweet an' it can also be goddam funny. But me —I do not mind because I am a philosophical sorta cuss who is not given to worryin'. Because any time I get that way I sorta fall back on my old pal Confucius who, if he had been with us to-day, would surely have been an ace-high guy with the dames because he was a one hundred per cent, horse-sense guy an' hadda line, where dames was concerned, that woulda knocked your eye out. I give myself another shot of whisky for the road; then I go out inta the street an' start walkin' towards the Savoy Hotel. I get around to thinkin' about Jimmy Cleeve. I wonder what this guy's got on to; what he knows. Then I give a big grin.

Because I suddenly realise that this is the first of April. Over here they call it "All Fools' Day." Maybe somebody was thinkin' of me when they called it that because I reckon you guys will have concluded by now that I'm a little bit of a mug, an' maybe you're right. At the same time you will also allow that it is a very wise man who knows when to be a mug, if you get me.

When I get to the Savoy I ask the reception clerk if Mr. Jimmy Cleeve is in. He does a lotta phonin' an' then he tells me that Mr. Cleeve is not in; that he checked out this mornin' an' does not reckon to be back for two three days. I say thanks a lot an' scram.

I go back to my dump in Jermyn Street, take off my uniform, take a shower an' dress myself in a very nice suit of grey pin-head. I put on a light blue silk shirt an' a navy blue tie. When I take a look in the glass I do not feel too displeased. I reckon maybe if I had been issued with a better lookin' face I woulda got myself some place.

Then I open the envelope that Herrick has given me. Inside is a British police pass with an endorsement askin' all police forces in the country to render me assistance if required, two National Registration cards in different names, two licences for a motor car in the two names on the registration cards, the address of a garage near Jermyn Street with a check to get the car out an' a whole wad of petrol coupons, all folded up in a sheet of paper that has got written on it: *"Good luck, Lemmy,"* an' signed by Herrick. So it looks like I am all set to go somewhere—the only thing bein' I do not know where.

I start walkin' up an' down the room thinkin'. But this does not get me any place because as you guys will realise I have not got a great deal to think about. So I give up thinkin' an' go over to the sideboard an' pour myself out a little snifter which is a very good thing to do when you are not busy on anythin' else.

I am just in the middle of this business when the telephone jangles. I go over, yank off the receiver an' say hello.

Some voice says: "Hello, Lemmy. How's it goin', fella?"

I nearly do a coupla backfalls because this is Dombie speakin'.

I say: "Look, what goes on around here? What's cookin'? Are you talkin' to me from Paris?"

He says: "No. I'm not so far away."

I say: "I see. So it's like that. Well, what's the big idea?"

He says: "Look, there's a place about twenty odd miles from London called Reigate, an' if you go along the Reigate-Dorkin' road there is a little village called Brockham. This is one of them old-fashioned places. It is a nice sorta place an' tourists like it. You get me?"

I say: "I'm beginnin' to. What sort of tourists?"

He says: "That's just nobody's business. Well, right in the middle of this village is a green. They call it Brockham Green an' on the other side of the green away from the main road is a little country road. If you go along there you come to a pub called *The Square Bottle*. Well, I don't know what you're doin', but if you're not doin' anythin' much I reckon it's a good place to stay."

I say: "Thank you for nothin', Sourpuss. Look, what's goin' on around here? Maybe you'll talk to me sometime. I hate bein' curious."

He says: "Well, maybe I will, but right now I gotta scram. Another thing, I'm talkin' from a pay-box. I'll be seein' you."

He hangs up.

I go back to the sideboard an' finish pourin' out the whisky. Then I drink it. It looks to me like something might be gonna happen around here, because like I told you before that Dombie is certainly nobody's fool. First of all I would like to know what the hell he is doin' over here an' certainly I would like to know what he means about this Brockham business. But who am I to argue?

I give myself a cigarette, get myself a hand-grip an' throw inside a very nice line in pyjamas an' one or two other things. Then I put on my hat an' go out.

I eat some lunch at a place just off Piccadilly; then I ease around to the garage an' get the car. Me—I am all set for a little holiday in the country. An' why not?

It is five-thirty an' a lovely afternoon. The sun is shinin' an' the road is stretchin' out in front of me like a piece of string. I go for these English roads. They are all curves an' up an' down, an' you never know what's around the corner.

When I am about seven miles outa Reigate I find a side road with a sign-post on it that says "Brockham." I go down this road an' after a bit I come to a big green. There is a church on one side with a clock an' everythin' is very old-fashioned an' period if you get me. I drive the car down a side road, park it, get out an' start walkin' around. I hang around for about half an hour; then I go back across the green, down the road on the other side. About twenty-five yards down I come to a funny little inn standin' back off the road. There is a sign outside that says *The Square Bottle*.

I go inta the bar, order myself a whisky an' soda. There is nobody in the place but me, an' the dame who is servin' behind the counter is a nice-lookin' doll. I get crackin' with this baby. I tell her I am an American business man over here tryin' to start some business for after the war. Pretty soon she loosens up an' gives me a big line of local dope. After a bit I ask her if there are any visitors around here as I heard that this was a great place for tourists if they could get here. She says yes but it is very quiet because there's no petrol an' it is too far to walk from the railway station. But she says there are one or two people around here, an' they can put me up if I wanta stay there.

I say thanks a lot, I'll wander around a bit an' let her know.

I finish my drink, go outside an' start walkin' down the road. Away on my right are fields an' beyond them I can see a golf course. I told you guys before that this is pretty swell country.

I light a cigarette an' start walkin' across the fields towards the golf course. Me—I am thinkin' that it would be very nice if I had a chicken farm in some place like this an' could sorta relax an' indulge in poetic thoughts all the time instead of rushin' around chasin' guys.

I am ponderin' on these deep thoughts when all of a sudden I hear a whistle. I look behind me an' comin' along the path is nobody else but Dombie.

He looks terrific. He has got on a plus-four suit with a check cap. Slung across his shoulder is a bag full of golf clubs.

I say: "Well . . . well . . . well . . . what is this an' what is the make-up for, Dombie? First of all what're you doin' over here?"

He says: "Look, Lemmy, just sit down for a minute under this hedge an' relax. I wanta talk to you."

We sit down an' I give him a cigarette.

He says: "This is the way it goes. After you'd gone Flash got a little bit worried about something."

I say: "You don't say? So the General was worried, was he? What was he worried about? Maybe he thought I'd be talkin' to some more women. Is that it?"

He looks at me an' gives a big grin. He says: "I don't think so. You know, Lemmy, I got an idea in my head that Flash has got some ideas about Cleeve."

"Oh yeah?" I tell him. "Such as what?"

"Well," he goes on, "he sorta reckons that this guy is tryin' to make the grade. He got the idea in his head that maybe he knew a little bit more about Varley's whereabouts than he let on. He also noticed that Cleeve was very keen on makin' a quick getaway from Paris an' gettin' over here before you."

I say: "Yeah, I coulda told him that. So what?"

"So nothin'," he says. "Well, he gets the idea that Cleeve might be tryin' to run away with this job, an' Flash don't wanta see you ditched."

I say: "You don't say? You mean to say that he wants me to make a big come-back. He wants *me* to bring Varley in?"

He nods his head. "That's what I think," he says. "You gotta remember that Flash was a Federal Bureau guy before he was a soldier. He's jealous of the Department. He hates all this stuff that's been said about you. He wants you to make a killin'. He reckons that Cleeve is a bit too keen on playin' his own hand."

"I get it," I say. "So he's tryin' to even things up for me, hey?"

"That's right," says Dombie.

I say: "All right. You go on from there."

He draws a big lungful of smoke down. He says: "Well, directly you got away, he gets in touch with London. He gets somebody over here to keep tabs on Jimmy just in case he tries to ditch you when you get here."

I grin. "A wise guy, the General," I say, "because that is exactly what Cleeve has done. When I went round to the Savoy this mornin' he wasn't there. They said he'd be away for two or three days."

He says: "Yeah, that's right. He's down here. He's stayin' at Holmwood—that's a place on the other side of Dorkin'."

I say: "Well, I reckon all this is very interestin', but what's he down here for? Does he know somethin'?"

Dombie shrugs his shoulders. He says: "What would he be down here for? There's only one thing. I reckon he 's got an idea that Varley is around here somewhere. Work it out for yourself. There are lots of Canadians around here. If Varley wanted to front as a Canadian he could do it. If he had some place to hide out he'd be O.K. Nobody'd find him in a thousand years."

I say: "That could be. D'you know Cleeve's address?"

He says: "Yeah, he's at a place called Thorpe Cottage. It's between North Holmwood an' a place called Capel—practically a straight line from here."

I light myself a cigarette. I say: "Did you have any other instructions or is this the works?"

He says: "That's all. After the General got somebody to keep a line on Cleeve he sent me over here quick. I've been stoogin' around. The guy who was lookin' after Cleeve told he where he is an' scrammed this mornin'. I also got a line that you'd arrived an' were stayin' in Jermyn Street, so I called through to you. Well, where do I go from here?"

I think for a minute an' I say: "Look, Dombie, you scram back to town. First of all it's not sense for both of us to be playin' around here. Somebody might recognise us an' if there's two of us there's a double chance. Secondly, I cannot bear the sight of you in those fancy pants. You get back to London. I shall be stayin' at this *Square Bottle* dump. When you get back to town ring me through an' give me a phone number where I can get at you. You got that?"

He says he's got it. He says: "This is all very well, an' I always do what I'm told, but it's a bit hard."

I ask him why.

He says: "That dame at *The Square Bottle*—you may have noticed she is a very nice baby an' she is beginnin' to fall for me in a very big way indeed. Always, when I'm gettin' ahead with some frail I have to have my romance broken up."

I say: "Yeah! There'll be some more. You'll find another dame in London, but take care she doesn't take a sock at you with a flat iron like that French dame wanted to."

Dombie gives me a sour look. "Not so good," he says. "Always just when I am gettin' away with it in a very big way with some beautiful dame I get sent off some other place. Me . . . I never get any luck. What the hell . . . I feel sorta embarrassed."

I give him a big horse laugh. "You—embarrassed!" I tell him. "It is not possible. Anyway, what have you got to be embarrassed about?"

He says: "Listen . . . last night I see some beautiful babe. She is walkin' down one of the roads leadin' to the green in Brockham an' she is the berries. I'm tellin' you that this dame has got everything that Cleopatra ever had an' then a truckful. She is the most terrific piece of woman that I ever got my eyes on. So what do I do?"

"O.K.," I tell him. "I'll buy it. So what did you do?"

"I sling her a very hot look," says Dombie. "Believe it or not I put everything I got inta that look. An' does she react? I'm tellin' you she reacts in a very big way. She gives me one of them long,

sideways looks that woulda taken the varnish offa battleship.
You know one of them looks. But *looks*. Then she turns around
an' goes inta one of those cottages with honeysuckle around the
door just off the side road to the green. An' just when she is goin'
in the door she slings me another look. I'm tellin' you this babe
is nuts about me. All I gotta do is to wait until I see her next time
just to put the old high-sign on her. So instead I haveta go back
to London."

"Maybe I'm doin' you a good turn," I tell him. "Maybe I'm savin'
you from a lotta grief. This dame may not be very good for a guy
like you. Maybe she's got too much brains for a hick like you."

"Yeah . . ." he says. "Maybe. But I woulda liked to have found
out for myself. Listen, Lemmy . . . I'm tellin' you with my hand on
my heart that this honeypot is the definite frail to end all frails.
She is *terrific*." Dombie starts rollin' his eyes like he was dyin'
of some form of poisoning. Then he gives a big sigh that sounds
like a whale comin' up for air.

"Figure to yourself, Lemmy," he goes on. "She is a brunette.
She has got big amethyst eyes that sorta make you go funny inside.
She has got a figure that is just nobody's business. She is wearin'
a pair of jodhpur breeches an' a blue silk shirt an' little brown
shoes, an' I could have eat her without salt or pepper. Everything
about this babe is perfect—except maybe one little finger."

Something goes *click* inside my brain. I don't say anythin' for
a minute then I say sorta casual: "An' what was the matter with
her little finger?"

He shrugs his shoulders. "It don't even matter," he says. "She's
got the little finger of her left hand sorta twisted. But even that
sorta looks good to me."

I give myself a big grin inside. So it looks like I'm on to
somethin'. Maybe you will remember the description of Varley's
sister that I gave to the General. If you do then you will see why
I am beginnin' to feel good.

Dombie says: "So I reckoned that I would stick around this
evenin' an' wait until this lovely comes out for her evenin' walk.

I thought maybe I could get goin'. An' now I gotta scram. It ain't right."

"You'd be surprised how right it is," I tell him. "You get back to London, Dombie, an' give me a call like I told you so's I can get you if I want you. You get off right now. An' if I see the girl friend sorta wanderin' about spare maybe I'll keep an eye on her for you."

"Like hell you will," he says. "That's what I was afraid of. Well . . . I'll be seein' you."

He picks up the golf bag an' starts walkin' back across the fields. I watch him until he is out of sight.

A good guy, Dombie. An' just how good he has been right now he does not even know.

I light myself another cigarette an' lay back in the grass lookin' at the sky. I reckon that things are beginnin' to move a bit. Work it out for yourself. Jimmy Cleeve is down here stayin' somewhere around the place at Holmwood because he is on to somethin'. An' the only thing that is interestin' him right now is the whereabouts of Varley. Dombie—not even knowin' what he is doin'—catches a look at this beautiful dame in Brockham. He don't even know who she is. The thing is does Jimmy Cleeve know that she is there. Does he? Me—I reckon the answer to that one is no. If he knew that anybody connected with Varley was stayin' at Brockham you could bet your boots an' your best pair of pants that he would not be stickin' around at North Holmwood—which is about five, six miles away.

I lie there grinnin' at the sky. I am feelin' very good about things. Also I am very pleased that the General had that idea about puttin' Dombie on Jimmy Cleeve's tail. Because, as you guys will have seen for yourself, the General is no mug. No, sir. He has been wise to Jimmy from the start. He has been wise to the fact that just because I am in bad with one an' all about shootin' my mouth off to this Marceline du Clos dame Jimmy reckons that he can pull a coupla fast ones on me an' use me for stoogin' around while he gets crackin', collects Varley an' brings him in. An' he gets all the credit an' I get a big kick in the pants. But the way things are goin' it looks like I have got a break. It looks like

I might be able to pull one on Jimmy an' get away with it before he knows exactly what is happenin'.

Because it looks to me like this. It looks like he had an idea where Varley would make for directly he got to England. Somebody was able to slip some information to him about this. An' I will give you two guesses as to who that somebody might be. Work it out for yourself. Jimmy Cleeve brings Juanella Rillwater over to Paris after he has got Larvey Rillwater knocked off an' safe inside Alcatraz. Why does he do this? He does this because Varley used Larvey in the old days to help him. Therefore it is a stone cinch that Juanella has met Varley an' will know what he looks like. Not only that but she also probably knows where Varley has got a hide-out in England, because it is stickin' out like the old stone pier that Varley had got some place over here all ready-eyed to go to. An' Juanella knew whereabouts it was even if she didn't know the exact place.

An' that is the reason why Jimmy Cleeve is hangin' around at North Holmwood while the beautiful babe with the twisted little finger is in Brockham.

All of which will show you guys that it looks like Mrs. Caution's little boy Lemmy has got a break at last.

An' how . . .!

Somewhere away in Brockham Village I can hear a clock strike seven. It is so quiet around this dump that you can almost hear yourself breathe. Me—I feel sorta happy because I am lyin' on the bed in the best bedroom at the *Square Bottle Inn*. I have got a half a bottle of rye whisky which I packed in my bag on the table beside me. I am smokin' a cigarette an' I am ponderin' on life in general. Things are beginnin' to take shape in my mind. I'm gettin' a whole lot of ideas. I hope some of 'em are gonna be good.

I give myself a shot of rye, get off the bed, stick my head in some cold water an' change my shirt an' tie. I put on a very snappy striped silk shirt that I got from some guy in Paris an' a swell tie, after which I take a look outa the window.

The bedroom I have got in this dump is on the first floor in the corner of the house. There is a window in both walls. Outa one window I can look across Brockham Green an' see the old well that the local guys usta get their water from on the other side of the green. The other way I can look down the dirt road, which I reckon is the road that interests me. Twenty, thirty yards down this road on the other side are two cottages standin' about ten yards apart. One of 'em—the nearest one—has a lotta honeysuckle an' jasmine an' stuff round the door, an' even if it ain't flowerin' yet it still looks good.

I start walkin' up an' down the room smokin' an' keepin' an eye on both windows. I get to thinkin' about Dombie. It is a goddam funny thing but very often it is a guy like Dombie, who does not know anythin' about anythin', who is just stoogin' around the job an' doin' everything anybody tells him, who puts his finger on an important point, which I reckon he has done good an' plenty. One of these fine days I am gonna tell that boyo just how important it was, but right now I'm wonderin' how I am gonna play this along.

I do some more thinkin' an' drink a little more whisky. Then I take a look outa the window that looks down the dirt road, an' stick my nose right up against the pane an' look—an' look some more. Because the door of the cottage with the honeysuckle around it has opened an' a dame is comin' out. She walks down the little crazy path that leads to the gate an' she stands by the gate as if she is undecided which way she is goin'. After a minute she opens the gate an' starts walkin' down the road towards the *Square Bottle*.

I reckon that when Dombie said that this babe was a honeybelle that big lug certainly knew what he was talkin' about. This dame is the berries. She is the ultimate end. She is the answer to every sort of prayer that was ever put up by everybody in the Marine Corps an' every other unit. Everything that this baby has *not* got could be stuck in a thimble an' thrown away—you'd never miss it. Me—I have seen dames all over the world. I have seen dames in U.S., England, Germany, Spain, Manilla, an' anywhere you like to go on an American Express trip ticket. I have seen practically every sort of thing that gets itself around with a skirt on, but I am tellin' you mugs with my hand on my heart that I have never seen a babe like this babe.

She has got on a grey wool frock with blue collar an' cuffs. She is wearin' brown silk stockin's an' little brown brogue shoes. She has got on a tan soft felt hat pulled over one eye with a blue ribbon in it. Underneath one side of the hat I can see her hair curlin' against the side of her face an' her neck. Boy—what a picture!

She is too far away for me to see her left hand, but I reckon when I do see it I am gonna see that the little finger is twisted.

I say to myself: Well . . . well . . . well . . .! After which I take another slug at the rye bottle just for old time's sake an' to keep the germs away, an' I ease down the stairs an' scram along a passageway that has got a grandfather's clock an' a lotta antique stuff stuck all along the walls, an' I open the side door that looks out onta the dirt road. I leave the door open an' stand there leanin' against the door-post pretendin' to be lookin' across Brockham Green.

I take a cigarette outa my case an' light it sorta casual. Outa the corner of my eye I can see her comin' closer. Boy—is this dame a dame or is she? I am tellin' you mugs that if she hadn't got anythin' else except that walk she'd be terrific. Maybe you been to the Russian Ballet. Maybe you think you know what gracefulness is. Brother, I'm tellin' you don't know a thing till you've seen this baby walk.

By now she is almost opposite me on the other side of the narrow road. She looks at me—just the sorta casual look you give to anybody you pass in the street. Then she looks away.

I say sorta quiet: "Hey, sister!"

She stops. She looks over her shoulder. Then she says in a soft Virginian accent: "Did you say something?"

I am still leanin' up against the door-post. I say: "Yeah. I said 'Hey, sister,' an' I wasn't too far wrong either, was I?"

She stands there on the other side of the road lookin' at me. Now I can see her left hand. Now I can see that the little finger is twisted. My heart beats a little bit faster.

She says: "Meanin' exactly what?"

"Meanin' that you're American," I tell her. "When I saw you walkin' along the road I thought you looked good enough to eat. I thought that dame is an American. Well, you are, hey?"

She gives me a little smile. I believe I sorta suggested to you guys that this dame has got a lovely face, but when she smiles it lights up. She shows a very nice set of teeth.

She says: "That's very nice of you. I take it you're American too."

I say: "You bet. Me—I'm a Marine—Captain Clauson, 71st Battalion. I gotta little leave so I thought I'd kid myself I was a civilian an' come down here an' take the country air."

She says: "And do you think you'll like it?"

I give her a big smile. I say: "I think it's gonna be very good. Maybe you an' I could go a walk some time?"

She tilts her nose a little at that one. She says: "Possibly. But why? Do you want to go walking with every woman you meet?"

I say: "No. Believe it or not, lady, I am a very selective guy. I only wanta go for walks with some dames. But Gee . . . I would like to go for a walk with you. To look at you takes years off my age."

She smiles again. Even in spite of herself I think she is rather goin' for the line I am givin' her, but all the time I am talkin' to her I am watchin' her. I know exactly what she is thinkin'.

I say: "You know, it's a funny thing, but the world is a very small place. But maybe they told you about that?"

She says sorta casual: "Yes? And why?"

I say: "Well, just now I was lookin' at your left hand. I see you had an accident with that little finger of yours. I thought I met you before some time."

She thinks for a minute; then she raises her eyebrows a little as if she was curious. Then she moves a coupla paces across the road. This road is not very much more than a track. She is standin' in the middle of it sorta relaxed lookin' at me.

She says: "So you think you've seen me before. I think you've made a mistake. I don't ever remember seeing you before."

I shrug my shoulders. "I can be wrong," I tell her, "but I gotta good memory. An' anyway how could I forget anybody like you?"

She says: "Well, nothing's impossible." She gives me another little smile but I can see she is thinkin' hard, bein' sorta careful. I think underneath she is a very cautious dame. Then she asks: "And where did you think you'd seen me before?"

I throw my cigarette stub down on the ground an' put my foot on it. I take another cigarette outa my case an' light it. I draw the smoke down inta my lungs an' blow it out again. I take a long time about this.

Then I say: "Well, some time ago when I was back in the States I went to a party. A big guy threw it. His name's General Flash. He usta be in the F.B.I. or something like that. Now he's in charge of Intelligence some place. I had an idea that I met you there."

She doesn't say anythin' but when I say the name Flash her face alters. It sorta tautens up.

She says: "I think you're wrong. I never knew anybody called by that name. Well, good-day to you." She gives me a little cool nod. She turns around an' starts walkin' towards the green.

I give a little grin. I say to myself: Well, so long, Miss Varley. I think I'll be seein' you sometime.

It is dark at nine o'clock. Maybe it is a little lucky for me that it is All Fools' Day an' the 1st April, because double summer time comes in later to-night an' that sticks another hour of daylight on. For what I wanta do this evenin' I'd like a little dark. I have been eatin' dinner an' talkin' to some of the guys who come inta the bar at this *Square Bottle*. Nice guys, these guys. They play darts, drink beer an' nothin' seems to disturb 'em. Anyway, I think it would take a helluva lot to disturb the English.

I walk around to the back of the inn where I have got the car parked in a yard; start her up. I drive down to the main Reigate-Dorkin' road an' ease along it. I go past Betchworth, through Dorkin'. When I get out the other side I see a sign that says: "South Holmwood," so I slow down. I roll along at about fifteen miles an hour up the hill an' down on the other side. A coupla miles farther along the road I am in North Holmwood. I see some guy comin' along by the side of the road—a farmer I reckon. I pull up the car an' ask this boyo if he knows a place called Thorpe Cottage. He says yes he knows it. It's a big white cottage standin' back from the road between North Holmwood an' the next place—Capel. He says you can't mistake it because it's got a red roof.

I say thanks a lot. I drive along the road for another coupla miles. Then I run the car through a gate inta a field an' stop behind a hedge. I take out the rotor cap an' start walkin' along the road. It is quite dark, but there is a little bit of a moon, an' pretty soon I see the white walls of this cottage. It stands way back from the road maybe fifty or sixty yards. There is thick shrubbery an' coppice around it on three sides. I get off the road, walk across the fields an' come on this place from the back. I walk through the trees an' bracken bein' very careful not to make any noise.

There is a little white palin' around the back of the cottage an' inside the palin' is a flower garden. It is a swell lookin' place, but the blinds are all drawn an' beyond the fact that there is a little smoke comin' outa the chimney I cannot see a goddam thing. I get behind a tree an' light a cigarette. I hide the lighted end of the cigarette in the palm of my hand, lean up against the tree an' smoke. Maybe something will happen an' maybe it won't, but all I can do is to wait.

This guy Confucius has got somethin' to say about this waitin' business. "All things are for him who hath the patience," says Confucius. "All the things that the other guys have forgotten about. Because the boyo who is prepared to stick around an' wait whiles his pal is makin' a big play for his girl friend is like the hamburger that was left over from the Christmas celebrations—no goddam good to anybody. At the same time," he goes on, "at the same time the guy who sticks around an' does nothin' at all is liable to save himself a lotta grief through not gettin' entangled with beautiful babies through sheer inertia; which is a good thing in its way because it stops you from doin' anythin' an' you are therefore practically assured of bein' entirely unconscious all your life. An' no worries at all."

Anyhow that will teach you guys that patience is a great virtue. You gotta have it anyway because somebody else once said all things come to him who waits, an' even if the thing that comes is only a smack on the kisser that it still something even if you can't look forward to it.

I am just gettin' myself immersed in some more great thoughts about Confucius when I hear a noise. I look around the tree. The back door of the cottage is openin' an' somebody is comin' out. I can hear the sound of a woman's high heels on the stones of the path. Then I see her openin' a little white gate that is in the middle of the palin's. A little path runs from this gate just past the clump of trees where I am standin'. I reckon she is gonna come this way. I drop the cigarette an' put my foot on it.

Pretty soon I can hear that this dame is singin'. She is pleased about something an' in a minute I can recognise the tune. She is singin' a number that usta be popular seven or eight years ago—*As Time Goes By*.

I stiffen up. I got an idea in my head but I'm tellin' myself that it just can't be possible. It would be too good.

Well, it is possible an' it is not too good, because when this dame gets just opposite me takin' the bit of the path that goes round my clump of trees, the moon comes out an' I get a good look at her, an' it is nobody else but who do you think?

I step outa the trees. I say: "Just a minute, babe. Look, you're not gonna give your old friend Lemmy the frozen mitt? You wouldn't do a thing like that, would you, Juanella?"

She turns round an' looks at me. An' she says: "Jeez . . . of course it would *have* to be you!"

She stands there lookin' at me like she has been pole-axed. I lean up against the tree an' grin at her. I reckon she is not feelin' so good.

"Right, honey," I tell her. "It looks to me like you was singin' the wrong song. Instead of *As Time Goes By* you oughta been singin' *It Had To Be You*." I give her another big grin. "Larvey is the guy who should be singin' *As Time Goes By*, but I guess that it is not goin' so fast as that guy would like it."

She looks down at the ground an' I can see that she has got tears in her eyes. Maybe I told you guys before that this baby is a looker. Well, right now—standin' there lookin' sad—she looks good enough to eat without any sugar. She says: "It's a goddam shame about Larvey. It's a goddam shame I'm tellin' *you*!"

"An' why, Sweetiepie?" I ask her. "Why is it a goddam shame because the law caught up with Larvey an' smacked him in the cooler? Surely you ain't gonna tell me that old bed-time story that he was framed. I reckon that if Larvey got what was really comin' to him he woulda spent about four hundred an' twenty years in the can an' then got himself fried when he came out. That boy has been so lucky that it positively creaks."

She says: "That's as maybe, Lemmy. An' you might be right to say that he's been lucky. But he certainly has not been lucky this time."

"All right, Gorgeous," I say. "So that's fine. An' you an' me are havin' this little meetin' under the trees right here outside North Holmwood just to have a heart-to-heart talk about Larvey." I give her another outsize grin. "Maybe you have not got anythin' else to tell me, Beautiful," I tell her. "Maybe you have not got any other confessions to make."

She don't say a goddam word. She stands there lookin' at her shoes with a sorta sad expression on her face that woulda frozen the whiskers offa coupla brass monkeys. Then suddenly she takes a step towards me an' flings her arms around my neck an' starts kissin' me like it was her last night on this earth an' I was the guy who gave that mug Casanova his first correspondence course in how to get on Nice Terms with a Blonde in Six Easy Lessons in a plain envelope.

I don't do a thing. I just take it easy an' get what is comin' to me. By now she is cryin' like a waterfall an' sobbin' like she really meant it.

"Lemmy," she says, "I'm in bad. I'm in it up to my neck. I've never been in such a spot in my life. I'm in about the worst jam that a girl ever got into an' I can't see my way out anyhow. An' so is poor old Larvey. I reckon that guy is gonna stay in Alcatraz until he rots an' nobody is gonna give a damn. They won't even let me write to the poor sap. An' you are the only guy that can help me because you are a good guy an' you got a big heart as well as bein' the most handsome thing in pants. So for the love of Mike *have* a heart an' do somethin' about it."

"O.K.," I tell her. I take her arms from around my neck an' start cleanin' some of the lipstick offa my mouth with my handkerchief. She is still standin' near to me an' I get another whiff of that perfume she is wearin'. I get to thinkin' that this Juanella is practically in a class by herself an' that if this mug Confucius hadda met up with her I reckon he woulda invented a coupla thousand more sayin's about dames bein' dangerous.

"O.K., Sweetiepie," I say. "But I would like to tell you that I do not consider that is the time or the place for heart-to-heart talks. Still, if you want me to give you a hand over this business that is O.K. by me except that you gotta come clean. You gotta give me the whole goddam works from the start an' no nonsense. An' if you try any more funny business with me I am gonna get so tough with you that you will have to eat your lunch offa the mantelpiece for about three months. An' after that I am goin' to fix it so that Larvey gets another sentence—after he's finished the one he's doin'—a sentence of about four thousand years just so it's a cinch that you never see the guy again. Well, are you gonna do business?"

She takes outa little lace-edged handkerchief an' she starts dryin' her eyes. When she has finished I can see that the dame has *really* been cryin', an' I get around to thinkin' that possibly for the first time since she was about two she has been tellin' the truth.

She says: "Lemmy . . . I'm gonna play ball with you. I'm gonna give you the works if it's the last thing I do. But it's a helluva long story an' you got to believe it. You got to believe every word of it even if it sounds as phoney as hell. Whatever you think you *got* to believe it."

I give her a reassuring grin. After all there is no reason why this baby—if she is scared enough—should not tell the truth—if it suits her.

"Look, honeypot," I tell her. "Where are you livin'?"

She says: "I'm livin' at some dump in South Holmwood—a little cottage called Mayleaf. It's just at the bottom of the hill near the church."

"O.K.," I tell her. I look at my strap-watch. It is now nearly half-past ten. "You come along an' see me to-night, round about twelve o'clock. You come along to the *Square Bottle Inn* at Brockham. I'll be waitin' for you at the side door. But you gotta give me the genuine stuff an' no nonsense."

She says: "I'll be there, Lemmy . . . I'll give you the whole goddam shootin' gallery. I'll tell you everythin'. I don't give a hell what happens I'm gonna spill it all."

I grin at her. "That's the stuff, Juanella," I tell her.

She says: "An' there's another thing you might remember, *Mister* Caution. If it was not for me you would be a stiff at the present moment. Those two guys at that dump in Auteuil were all set to iron you out an' I slipped you a Mickey Finn an' told 'em that you would be out cold for ten hours an' that it would not be a good thing to bump you whiles there was people around the place. You gotta remember that I practically saved your life."

"O.K.," I tell her. "I'm rememberin'. Maybe I'll save yours one day. Anyhow, you come around an' see me at twelve to-night an' say your piece."

Her face changes an' she gives me one of them sideways smiles. She says: "Of course it's a bit late to go callin' on a guy like you, but," she gives me a big sigh, "a girl has gotta take a chance sometimes." She turns away an' starts walkin' along the path, across the fields. When she is a few steps off she looks at me over her shoulder an' I can see she is still smilin'.

"So long, Lemmy," she says. "I'll be there on the dot. There's nothin' on earth is gonna stop me."

She scrams. As she goes off I can hear her start hummin' to herself. An' this time it is *It Had To Be You*.

I think well . . . well . . . well . . .! An' I wonder what Confucius woulda done about Juanella.

I light myself a cigarette an' stick around leanin' up against the tree thinkin' about this an' that, but especially about Juanella. Maybe if you guys can put two an' two together without makin' twelve out of it you will see the way my brain is workin' an' if you don't what does it matter?

By the time I have finished the cigarette I feel I sorta got things sorted out just about as far as I can. I walk outa the little wood towards the cottage. I open the little white gate in the palin', walk up the stone path an' bang on the knocker. I wait a bit an' nothin' happens. I knock again because I have got an idea that there is somebody in this dump.

I am right. After a coupla minutes the door opens. There is a light on in the hallway an' standin' there with a surprised expression on his face is Jimmy Cleeve.

I say: "Well . . . how's it goin', Jimmy? I wonder if you expected to see me quite so soon." I stand there grinnin' at him.

He shrugs his shoulders. Then he laughs. He says: "Well, Lemmy, I'm not *really* surprised. You're no mug, but I hoped I'd get a few days more start on you. I'd hoped I'd get this job sewn up an' in the bag before you even got wise to where I was. Come on in. I gotta bottle of whisky in the livin'-room."

I go in an' he shuts the door. We go inta the sittin'-room. It is a nice comfortable old-fashioned cottage an' Jimmy has certainly got himself well fixed. There are two bottles of Haig whisky on the table, some syphons an' glasses. He pours out a couple stiff ones.

Then he says: "Well, so what?"

I hold up the glass. I say: "Here it is, Jimmy! An' I'm *very* glad to see you again."

I sit down in the big chair on one side of the fireplace an' he sits down opposite me.

He says: "Look, Lemmy, you don't have to be sore at me. You know how it is. You're a big time guy. Everybody knows you. You're a hundred per cent. You're ace high in the F.B.I. You gotta reputation. An' what am I—just a small-time private dick tryin' to make the grade. You can see how I figured it out. I reckoned if I could get my hooks on this Varley an' take him in without you I'd be in line for a job with the Federal Service, an' I want it goddam bad. This war's taught me a coupla things an' I reckon I'd rather work for Uncle Sam than a private agency any time."

"Jimmy, that is O.K. by me," I tell him. "I'm not feelin' sore because for one thing I gotta good memory. I haven't forgotten that good turn you did me over Ribban. If it hadn't been for that story you put up to the General it might not have been so good for me. I might not have been here at all."

He says: "Aw, hell, forget it!"

I say: "All right. Let's forget it an' let's get down to hard tacks. Listen, fella, it is no good you an' me workin' against each other. We gotta do this job together. Let's pool our information an' make a start. What are you doin' down here, Jimmy? Maybe you got something?"

He says: "Yeah, I got something all right. Lemmy, I been holdin' out on you. Before I came over from New York to join up with the General in Paris I had an idea in my head that this guy Varley would slip over here to England if things got a bit hot for him on the other side of the Channel. See?"

I nod my head.

He goes on: "I pulled a coupla strings. I gotta guy detailed to work with me over here. He's a Lieutenant in a Canadian Infantry Regiment, but he used to work for the Agency in the old days. He's a good dick. He's got brains, he's young an' he's keen."

"An' he's been stuck over here keepin' things warm for you, hey?" I ask him. "I'm beginnin' to think you got brains, Jimmy."

He shrugs his shoulders. "I'm tryin' every goddam thing I can," he says. "An' do you blame me? O.K. Well, this guy—his name is Sammy Maynes—knows Varley. He came up against him once before in the old days when Maynes was workin' for the Agency. You'll like Sammy."

I nod my head. "I reckon we can use everybody," I tell him.

"Another thing," he goes on, "*I* had a line about this Varley. Varley was over here in England before he went to New York to start that interior decoratin' business. He had a cottage down here—usta like this part of the country."

I say: "Yeah? An' where is the cottage?"

He grins. "This is it," he says. "I'm stayin' here waitin' for him."

"I get it," I say. "So you think the big boy is gonna come back here?"

"That's what I think," he says. "As a matter of fact I don't think about it. I sorta know."

I ask: "How come? You got some very good lines, Jimmy. You know a goddam sight more about this bezusus than I do."

He grins at me. He says: "Well, maybe I've had the breaks, Lemmy. Look, I'm gonna tell you something. When Varley was operatin' in New York he knocked off a lotta documents—Government stuff. See? An' it was a neat job. But Varley didn't knock 'em off himself. He got somebody else to do it for him."

I say: "No? Who did he use?"

He says: "A guy called Larvey Rillwater—an ace safe-blower. Maybe you heard of him?"

I say: "You'd be surprised. An' how I've heard of him!"

He says: "Well, Larvey got himself knocked off. I suppose they wanted to keep him safe for the war, so they slung him into Alcatraz. He's in the cooler now an' he's likely to stay there."

I say: "Yeah? What did they charge him with?"

He says: "I wouldn't know, but it was a Federal charge—something to do with bein' accessory to espionage or something like that."

I say: "I get it. Go ahead, pal."

He says: "Well, I was goin' around New York. I was on leave from Illinois where I was workin' with the State Police. While I was down there the Federal Bureau got at me. They got the idea that I could help 'em with this Varley business. They asked me what I knew. I told 'em I knew very little about it which wasn't the truth, because I thought if I told 'em that an' found something out they'd think I was a bigger shot than I really am." He gives me a sorta self-deprecatin' grin. "It is the old story, Lemmy," he says. "A small time guy tryin' to pretend he's a big one."

"Aw, shucks," I tell him. "You're not doin' so bad. Well, go on from there."

He says: "Well, I have a bit of luck. Who do I run into one day on Fifth Avenue but Juanella Rillwater—Larvey's wife. You know, she's nuts about that husband of hers. When they flung him inta the can she was good an' steamed up. She was like a ship without any rudder—like a cat without a tail. She didn't know which way she was pointin'."

"I get it," I say. "So you thought you could use Juanella?"

He says: "Sure. Sure I did. You see, Juanella knows Varley. She had to know him. She knew him when Larvey was workin' with him. So she talked. She told me that Varley lived over here before he went to New York. She told me she thought it was on the cards he'd come back here if it got too hot for him in Paris."

I say: "It looks like this dame was pretty useful to you, Jimmy."

He says: "You're tellin' me. Maybe she's gonna be of some more use before I'm through."

I grin to myself. I say: "You're tellin' me. But," I go on, "I think it was pretty goddam smart of you to bring her over to this country."

His eyes widen. He says: "Are you the clever bastard or are you the clever bastard? So you've seen her?"

I say: "You bet I've seen her. I saw her walkin' down the street in South Holmwood this afternoon. There's only one figure like that in England an' that belongs to Juanella. An' there's only one figure that's better than that one."

He says: "No, you don't say, Lemmy?"

I say: "Look, fella, this is where we get crackin' because I had a bit of luck too."

He says: "Yeah? What?" I can see he's interested. I say: "Jimmy, you remember when I was talkin' to General Flash about Varley's sister?"

He says: "Yeah, you knew something about her."

"Yeah," I say, "I knew something about her all right. I knew what Marceline du Clos told me. But that isn't all. I reckon you're right about Varley bein' somewhere around this district, Jimmy. In fact you're goddam right an' I know it."

He leans forward. He gets hold of the bottle an' gives me another shot. He says: "Look, I'm gettin' excited. What's goin' on around here?"

"Just this," I say. "I saw Varley's sister this afternoon. An' how d'you like that?"

He says: "Jeez, Lemmy! Then I was right. Then he is here."

"You're tellin' me," I say. "It looks as if the whole goddam Varley family is around here." I give him a big grin. "Just a nice little quiet spot in the English countryside," I say, "just full of everything that opens an' shuts."

He says: "Well, what do we do?"

I say: "I'll tell you what we do, Jimmy. The first thing we don't do is to take each other for a ride. Let's stop this competition business. Let's clean this job up. You'll make the grade in the F.B.I. all right an' maybe I'll get my record cleaned up. Maybe they'll forget about this Marceline du Clos thing an' the talkin' I was supposed to do."

He says: "Aw hell, they've forgotten that already."

"That's as maybe," I tell him, "but this is how we play it. Each of us lets the other one know everythin' that's goin' on. You stick around here. You wait for this Varley guy to show up. You know what he looks like—I don't. So you look after this end of the stick. Directly you set eyes on that palooka you get in touch with me an' let me know. I'm stayin' at the *Square Bottle* in Brockham."

"O.K., Lemmy," he says. "That's how it's gonna be. I'll look out for Varley an' directly I see him I'll let you know."

"Fine," I say. "An' I'll look after the sister. She's stayin' in my part of the world. I'm gonna stick closer than the plaster on the wall to that baby. Another thing," I say, "I think it would be a very good thing if Juanella was to lie low for a bit. We don't want her to be seen walkin' around this district. If Varley saw her maybe he'd get a little bit suspicious."

He says: "O.K. I'll let her know about that."

I finish my drink. I get up. I say: "Look, the other thing is this. You an' I had better not be seen too much together. Let's play this thing nice an' quiet. If I get anythin' I'll get in touch with you. You got a phone here?"

He says: "Yeah." He gives me the number.

"O.K.," I tell him. "Here's the number of the *Square Bottle*." I write it down for him. "We don't want any meetin's until somebody has got something to report. If you get something call through. I'll do the same. Well, so long, Jimmy. I'll be gettin' along."

"So long, Lemmy," he says. "You're a good guy. I hope you don't think I was tryin' to pull a fast one on you."

I give him a big grin. "Don't worry your head, Jimmy," I tell him. "You're O.K. with me. There's just one other little thing. Give me a call some time to-morrow evenin' an' send this guy Sammy Maynes up to see me. I reckon I can use that guy. Maybe we can put the screws on that sister of Varley's. Maybe that babe can be made to talk."

He says: "That's a helluva idea. So long as she don't talk to Varley. It would be a goddam shame if she wised him up to the fact that we're stickin' around waitin' for him. If he got wise he's gonna ditch those documents that Larvey Rillwater pinched for him. Remember we gotta get those back whatever happens."

"I'm rememberin'," I tell him. "But I'll look after that end, an' you can bet that Varley's sister is not gonna talk to anybody. I'll look after that end of the stick. Say . . . did this guy Maynes ever meet up with her?"

He shakes his head. "Nope," he says. "Varley was a close guy. He never talked about his family, an' always kept on his own." He thinks for a minute. "Maybe this dame is not his sister," he says. "Maybe she's some other baby he's got playin' in with him an' she's frontin' as his sister because that's the easiest way. Varley was always keen on blondes."

"If he was he altered his mind this time," I tell him. "She's a brunette an' she's *some* oil paintin' I'm tellin' you."

I open the door an' stand on the little path lookin' towards the back of the house. It is a swell night an' I feel very good. Things are beginnin' to shape up.

"Good-night, Jimmy," I tell him. "Keep your nose clean an' send that guy Maynes up to see me to-morrow after you've called through. An' don't show around too much. I got an idea that things are comin' to a head."

"You're the boss, Lemmy," he says. "An' remember I'm not tryin' to steal anythin' on you from now on. We play this together."

I say O.K. an' scram. I walk across the fields to where I left the car an' start her up. I drive along the quiet road towards South Holmwood.

Me . . . I am as happy as the birds in May even if it is only April an' the first of April at that.

CHAPTER FIVE
SOME MORE JUANELLA

MAYBE you guys are aware of the fact that the English are great on sayin's, proverbs, an' what-have-you-got generally. Any time some English bozo finds that he is at a loss for words an' cannot explain somethin' that he probably does not know anythin' about anyway, then you will find that the said bozo will quote some proverb at you. By the time that you have worked this proverb out—that is supposin' you ever get around to workin' it out—then the English guy has either disappeared or has thought up somethin' else.

This is the reason why the English are a very great people. Because anythin' they do not wish to understand they just let ride good an' plenty. Like maybe you heard about James Second or some such mug who, bein' told that his latest girl friend had been seen havin' fun an' games with Lord High Admiral, says *"We are not amused,"* an' sends the Lord High Admiral off to discover some new country hopin' that this palooka will be well an' truly masticated by man-eatin' cannibals while he is on the job.

Instead of which the guy goes off an' *does* discover some place, comes back an' says: "And how do you like that, Kingsie-Wingsie?" After which James Second bein' by this time slightly wearied by the contour map of the dame in question, gives three hearty cheers, starts knightin' everybody in sight an' celebrates by puttin' a tax on beer-spigots.

This is the reason why the English have got such a helluva big Empire an' it will also show you that the old-time Kings around here musta had a tough time with their girl friends, an' is also responsible for the proverb that says "Love makes the world go round."

Anyway this proverb is all hooey because Love does *not* make the world go round. It only *seems* to make it go round. An' the same sensations can be experienced much cheaper by drinkin' a lot of bootleg liquor on an empty stomach.

All of which great thoughts come crowdin' around on me because it is nearly twelve o'clock midnight an' I am standin' by the side door of the *Square Bottle* waitin' for Juanella to show up an' wonderin' whether that babe is really gonna do her stuff an' report for duty or whether she is gonna take a run-out powder on me an' scram before I start somethin'.

It is a lovely night an' there is a moon an' there are shadows an' moonbeams all over the place. I am feelin' so goddam poetic that it nearly makes me feel sick an' I get around to thinkin' about all the lovelies that I have met up with in different parts of the globe an' also about that sister of Varley's who believe it or not is definitely a queen woman if ever I saw one.

An' the guy who said that this was the witchin' hour of midnight certainly knew his vermicelli—at least I reckon he did—but I did not rightly know what the mug meant by "witchin'". Maybe this is a misprint an' he really meant ditchin' because this maybe is the time when girls around this part of the world make dates an' then stand their boy friends up an' do not appear. But whether this guy meant this or that does not really matter an' is only just one of those things the English say when they are at a loss for words. Like "Rome was not built in a day" an' "Fair words butter no parsnips"; two things that are so goddam obvious that you would think the English would sorta take 'em for granted. Instead of which the only two things they do take for granted are beer an' the idea that a guy who does not play darts regularly at the local hop shop is qualifyin' for a nut-house.

Just at this moment I take a look towards Brockham Green. The green is bright with moonlight an' comin' across the pathway in the centre is Juanella. I give a little grin to myself because I am very relieved to know that this baby has turned up an' I also see that she is dressed to make a killin'. When she gets close to me I see that she has got on a green coat an' skirt under a short beaver coat. She is wearin' a beige silk shirt blouse an' she has got one of those turban things around her head to match the blouse. In front of this turban is stuck a little diamond question mark.

She stops a coupla paces from me an' gives me a long look. Then she smiles sadly—a sorta piteous attempt to be brave if you get me. I give a sniff when I get another whiff of her perfume.

I say: "Look, Juanella, that is *some* perfume you got. That never came out of any drug store."

She says: "No, Lemmy, I got it in Paris. It's good, hey? It's called Imprudence."

I say: "Yeah? Well, you oughta know. So you've come over to do your stuff. I was wonderin' whether you was gonna turn up or not."

She says: "Listen, Lemmy, an' you listen good because I'm tellin' you I'm on the up an' up from now on. I'm not takin' any more chances on you. Even if I do haveta play a bedroom scene with you, well, I'm doin' it."

I say: "Don't worry, my sweetiepie, there are no bedroom scenes in this act because I gotta sittin'-room hired here. Come on in."

We go in an' I take her up to my sittin'-room on the first floor. I pull a big chair up for her an' give her a whisky an' soda. She puts her handbag down on the table. It is a large crocodile bag—dyed green to match her coat an' skirt.

I say: "Now, honey, get crackin' an' make it good."

She says: "Well, I'm not gonna try an' make anythin' good. I'm just gonna tell you the truth. You're gonna be surprised."

She sits there lookin' sorta demure.

I say: "Nothin' would surprise me, Juanella. Maybe I know a goddam sight more than you think, an' maybe what I don't know I can guess."

She says: "Yeah? But you'll never guess this one."

"No?" I tell her. "All right. I'll do a little talkin'. Maybe I know very nearly as much as you do."

She looks at me. Her eyes are wide. She says: "You couldn't, Lemmy. It's not possible."

I grin at her. I say: "You know, Juanella, I was always a good guesser, an' the trouble with you is you are not a very good liar. Your lies are so goddam thin they creak."

She says: "Oh yeah? Such as what?"

I go on: "Such as that stuff you told me in Paris the first time I met you. You remember? You told me that Jimmy Cleeve had found you kickin' around New York; that you weren't feelin' so good so he got you that job in Paris. Remember that?"

She says: "Yeah, I remember."

"You didn't tell me that Jimmy Cleeve was in Paris at the time," I go on. "But you knew it, didn't you?"

She says: "What do you mean, Lemmy. Why should I know it?" I can see her brain workin'. She is tryin' to gain time. Maybe she wants to do a little more inventin'.

I say: "Look, you been workin' for Cleeve all along. Why don't you come clean, Juanella? Mind you I don't blame you an' I don't blame him. Both of you got motives an' maybe they're not bad ones."

She takes a drink of whisky. I pour myself out a slug an' drink it, but all the time I am drinkin' I am watchin' her over the top of the glass.

I say: "Look, how does this go for guessin'? You know goddam well that Jimmy Cleeve wants to get himself in the F.B.I. You know what he was—a small time dick playin' around some private agency in New York. O.K. Well, he gets a break. He gets loaned to the Illinois State police because they want extra help while the war's on, an' while he's there he hears that there is a drag net out for Varley. So what does he do?"

She says: "Yeah?" She is lookin' at me sorta strange. "Well, what does he do?" she repeats.

"He takes a chance," I go on. "He wants to get himself in good with the Federal Authorities, so he say that he knows Varley. He says he knows all about him. They fall for this an' Jimmy begins to think he is all set for a big job."

She says: "Well, why not, Lemmy? What's the matter with that?"

I say: "Listen, baby, you know goddam well that Jimmy Cleeve has never set eyes on Varley in his life. That's why he's usin' you. Well, is that the truth or is it?"

She don't say anythin'. She looks at her fingernails.

"This is the way it goes," I go on. "Jimmy Cleeve does not know Varley, but he knows this: He knows that Larvey T. Rillwater— your lovin' husband—has been thrown in the cooler an' he knows the reason why. The reason why is because the said Larvey was concerned with Varley in pinchin' some documents. I reckon I'm a bit sorry for Larvey. I reckon he didn't know what those documents were. Maybe he thought they were just bonds or bank securities or something like that. That poor mug probably didn't know they were State documents—important stuff about this war. But I reckon Jimmy Cleeve had an idea about that, so he knew one thing. He knew that Larvey T. Rillwater knew Varley an' it was a stone certainly that if Larvey knew him you knew him as well. Is that right?"

She nods her head. She looks dumbfounded. She says: "Lemmy, you're a good guesser. That's O.K."

"All right," I say, "let's go on from there. So Jimmy Cleeve tells the Federal Authorities that he knows Varley an' he's got an idea where he can put his hooks on him. He reckons that Varley has already got outa the United States an' got over to Paris, so Cleeve gets himself sent to Paris attached to General Flash's staff an' he takes you with him. He takes you with him because you're the little girl who's gonna identify Varley when they catch up him. An' I said *when*. An' there is something else you know too," I go on—"something that's important. And you know what that is, don't you?"

She shrugs her shoulders. She says: "It looks to me as if you know all the answers, Lemmy."

"Well," I say, "this is how I figure it out. I reckon that Varley had told Larvey some time or other that he got a hide-out here in England in case things got too hot for him. I reckon that Larvey had told you about it. O.K. When you an' Cleeve got to Paris he looks round an' there is no sign of Varley. He reckons by this time that Varley has got out of it; that he's over here. Then you played your trump card. You made a deal with Jimmy, didn't you?"

She nods her head. She says in a funny sorta voice: "That's right, Lemmy. I made a deal. Well, what would you have done?"

I shrug my shoulders. "Maybe I'd have done the same," I say. "I reckon you figured it out like this: Larvey had got a fifteen year sentence. He'd got a fifteen year sentence because he was charged with stealin' Federal documents which is a pretty bum offence in war-time. But Larvey hadn't got any previous convictions an' you knew goddam well that if you could prove that Larvey pinched those documents with the idea in his head that they were only bank securities or something like that, that sentence could be reduced considerably—maybe to a coupla years. Well, there was one guy who might pull that for you—Jimmy Cleeve. So I reckon you made a deal with Jimmy. The deal was that you'd tell him where Varley had got a hide-out in England if he'd guarantee to get Larvey's sentence reduced on the grounds I just mentioned after he'd got his hooks on Varley. Well, am I right or am I right?"

She says: "Yeah, Lemmy, you're terrific. You're a hundred per cent. right."

She finishes her drink. I pour her out another one an' give myself another shot. As I put her glass down I knock her handbag off the table. It bursts open an' everything spills out onta the floor. I bend down an' pick up a .38 colt automatic. I pull out the clip. There are ten shells in it.

I say: "Hey . . . hey . . . what's goin' on around here? Maybe you haven't heard these English guys don't like people who tote a gun in this country—not unless you gotta police permit. How come?"

She says: "Well, I thought I oughta have one. I thought it might not be so safe stickin' around here with the guy Varley about the place."

I throw the gun back in her handbag. I put the handbag back on the table. I say: "Well, there's an old proverb which says that the dame who carries a gun is always the dame who gets shot. Also," I tell her, "with the way you're lookin' an' that perfume you don't need a gun, baby. Just throw 'em one hot look an' you'll slay 'em anyway."

She looks at me sorta old-fashioned. She says: "Just the same old Lemmy, aren't you? Just a big laughin' guy. That's why you bring the mother out in me. That's why I feel like a sister to you, Lemmy."

"Maybe," I tell her. "But after that stranglehold you put on me last time I got the idea you was feelin' like somethin' else. At the same time," I go on, "are you the little mug or are you?"

She says: "Maybe, Lemmy." She looks sorta miserable. "But what the hell was a girl to do? You know, I'm so stuck on Larvey that I don't know what to do about it. At least . . ."

"At least what?" I ask her.

She says: "Well, when I'm away from Larvey I'm nuts about him. When I've got him with me I'm nuts about you. What's a girl to do?"

I say: "I wouldn't know. But you're still a mug."

She says: "Maybe. But why?" She is lookin' at me. I can see she is interested.

I say: "Listen, why don't you use your brains? Jimmy Cleeve is a guy who is out for himself. All he wants to do is to get himself a job with the F.B.I. To do that he'd ditch you; he'd ditch me. He'd ditch anybody." I give her a grin. "He has already tried to ditch me," I tell her.

Her eyes pop. She says: "What! He's tried something funny with *you*?"

I nod my head. "Jimmy is nobody's fool," I tell her. "So far as you're concerned he's playin' you along. He's gotta have you around so's you can identify Varley an' when you've done it he'll be through with you." I give her another grin. "Do you seriously think," I say, "that after he's got his hooks on Varley, Jimmy Cleeve is gonna worry about Larvey? You bet he won't."

She says: "Well, I had to take a chance on it. He told me the day he got Varley he'd get in touch with the Federal Authorities an' try an' get Larvey's case re-heard. He said he reckoned he could get that sentence reduced to a coupla years—three at the outside."

"Yeah, I know," I tell her, "an' he probably told you he'd get him paroled even before then." I shrug my shoulders. "Maybe he mighta tried," I say. "But tryin' is one thing an' doin' it is another." I look at her sideways. "Now if it had been me"

She says sorta soft: "Yes, Lemmy, if it had been *you* . . ."

I say: "That woulda been a different matter, wouldn't it, Gorgeous? Me—I am a Federal guy. I've been in the Federal Service for years. I am a 'G' man with a good record. I reckon if I wanted to get Larvey out I'd get him out, an' you know it."

She says sorta doubtful: "Yeah, I reckon you could have in the old days, Lemmy, but—"

"But what?" I ask her.

She says: "Well, there was a sorta rumour flyin' around in Paris that you'd slipped a bit."

I give myself a cigarette. I say: "Yeah, *I* told you about that. Maybe you heard it from somewhere else too. Maybe Jimmy Cleeve told you?"

She says: "Well, maybe he did." She gives a big sigh. "What was I to do? Jimmy told me he didn't think you'd be able to do anythin' for Larvey. He said right then you were in bad; that you were workin' like hell on this case tryin' to make a come-back; that General Flash was tryin' to give you a break."

I say: "Juanella, why don't you be your age. Look, aren't you wise to this Jimmy Cleeve yet? I've told you a dozen times before he's just playin' it off the cuff himself. He does not give a damn so long as he makes a big killin'—at least that's how it *was*."

She says: "What d'you mean—that's how it *was*?"

I say: "I stuck a pin in that balloon. I've seen Cleeve to-night. I knew goddam well he'd be stickin' around that cottage somewhere, so after you'd gone I went an' had a few words with him. Well, he's not a bad guy. He told me that most of my guesses were O.K. He's agreed on one thing from now on. He an' I are workin' on this job on the up an' up. Nobody is tryin' to take anybody, see?"

She says: "I see. What do I do?"

I grin. I say: "You're all right. Maybe if there's anythin' else I should know you'll tell me. Maybe I haven't guessed the lot. Maybe you got one or two small points that'd help me a little, Juanella. Well, what about it?"

There is a silence for a little while. Nobody says anythin'. I can see she is thinkin' like hell.

Then she says: "I reckon you've got the lot, Lemmy. I reckon you've guessed it all. You always was a brain guy. You've got it on 'em all."

I say: "Yeah, sometimes—maybe not always. Tell me something, Juanella. What does this Varley look like? I reckon you saw him around plenty with Larvey. You oughta be able to give me an exact description of him. Get crackin', sweetie. How does he look?"

She says: "Well, I'll tell you." She pauses; then she begins to speak, but I interrupt her.

I lean across the table. I say: "Look, Juanella, are you the brown snake in the grass? Are you the little complete heel? Do you think I'm such a mug as to stand for a line like this from you? You're tryin' to make up a description of Varley, an' why? Why are you doin' that?"

She says: "Well, I was thinkin'. I had to think about it."

I say: "Baby girl, you are one goddam liar. *You* never had to think about anythin'—not with a brain as quick as yours. An' shall I tell you why you didn't haveta think? *You've never seen Varley in your life.*"

She sits back an' she gives a gasp. "An' how d'you like that, Gorgeous?" I ask her.

She does not say anythin'. She sits there lookin' at the table fingerin' her glass of whisky an' soda.

"You're the complete little nut," I tell her. "First of all, I know enough about Larvey T. Rillwater to know that if he was in any funny business with Varley—anythin' that was even likely to land him in the cooler—there is one person he wouldn't have told anythin' about it. There's one person he'd never have let meet Varley an' that person would be you."

Her shoulders sorta drop. I reckon I have put my finger on the spot.

"Larvey T. Rillwater was a very smart guy," I go on. "Also he is probably the finest safe blower in the United States, but there is one thing about him that is not so bad. He's stuck on you. He's stuck on you like hell, an' Larvey would never do anythin' that woulda got you up against the Federal Authorities such as introducin' you an' Varley, lettin' you be seen by Varley or generally gettin' mixed up with the business they were in, an' you know that's the truth."

She says: "Yeah, you got it, Lemmy. I reckon that is the truth."

"So," I tell her, "you take Jimmy Cleeve for a ride. He thought he was bein' clever with you. Instead of which you were bein' clever with him. You told him that you could identify Varley. Maybe you had an idea, an' maybe it was right, that Varley would come over here to this place. Maybe Larvey let something fall by accident or you found an address or something, so you saw a way of gettin' Larvey's sentence reduced by doin' a deal with Jimmy. An' Jimmy Cleeve believed you—the poor sap!"

She spreads her hands. She says: "Well, Lemmy, what the hell was I to do?"

I stub out my cigarette. "I wouldn't know," I say. "I reckon you did what you thought was best for you an' Larvey. The thing is what are you gonna do now?"

She shrugs her shoulders. "I don't know," she says. "I don't feel so good about it. I reckoned that if Cleeve got Varley, or somebody he thought was Varley, there'd be a showdown, but I thought maybe by that time he mighta done something about Larvey. I was hopin' against hope, playin' it any way I could."

I say: "Well, maybe there's another angle. Maybe Cleeve has got some other means of identifyin' Varley when he gets him. Maybe he wanted you for sorta corroborative evidence because you gotta realise that this Cleeve is a clever guy. Me—I like him."

I light myself a fresh cigarette. "Listen, honeybelle," I tell her. "You go back to Mayleaf Cottage, an' you stick around there. Just behave yourself. If Jimmy Cleeve asks you to do anythin' for him just do it. You play ball with that guy as far as you can an' maybe when we get this job cleared up I'll do my best for you. Maybe I might even get Larvey's sentence reduced—who knows?"

She says: "Lemmy, you've always been a swell guy. I've always been for you one hundred per cent."

She takes a dive at me, flings her arms around my neck an' starts kissin' me as if I was her long lost husband. I'm tellin' you guys that at close range Juanella is a little bit overpowerin'. I put her back in her chair.

I say: "Look, honey, you relax. You're too temperamental for this sorta business. Take a nice cool walk back to the cottage, take your hair down, smoke a cigarette an' just think things out. When you've done it come to a conclusion an' you can go on from there."

She says: "Yeah, Lemmy, an' what conclusion am I gonna come to?"

I grin at her. "I think you'll conclude that Mr. Lemuel H. Caution is not such a mug as he looks," I tell her. "Anyway, that will be a very wise thing for you to think. Now finish your drink an' scram."

She gets up. She heaves a big sigh. She says: "Me—I am always havin' a tough time. The trouble with me is that I'm a two-man woman. It would be O.K. if I just stuck on Larvey, but bein' stuck on you too makes life very difficult." She gives another sigh. "Maybe you're right," she says. "Maybe it's my temperament. Well, so long, Lemmy."

She goes down the stairs. I go after her an' open the side door for her. She gives me a look over her shoulder.

She says: "So long, I'll be seein' you."

I see her walkin' towards Brockham Green. I stand in the doorway. There is still a suggestion of the scent she is wearin' hangin' about the place. Some perfume—Imprudence!

You're tellin' me!

I stand at the doorway watchin' Juanella as she goes across the path that runs through the centre of the green. Me . . . I am very undecided about that baby. Maybe you guys have met people like Juanella yourselves. If you have not you do not know a thing. Because it is dames like Juanella who throw a spanner inta the works the whole time. The reason bein' that they have always got some sorta man trouble. *If* you get me.

An' I reckon that what she says about Larvey is one hundred per cent. O.K. I reckon that just because Larvey is well an' truly stuck in the cooler at Alcatraz that guy is the only guy in the world for Juanella. I reckon that she would do any goddam thing to get him out. An' when she's got him out she won't even want the mug. That is the sort of babe Juanella Rillwater is.

An' she is very cute an' very cunnin' an' very sweet. Some guys do not let their left hand know what their right hand is doin'. But she goes one better. She does not even let her *right* hand know what her right hand is doin'. Her only failin' is that she is so goddam smart sometimes that she is liable to double-cross herself outa existence outa sheer exuberance.

An' she is clever enough to tell you just enough of the truth to make it sound like *all* the truth. I guess that is the technique she has been usin' on me. She has told me a bit of the truth an' she is still keepin' somethin' up her sleeve against a rainy day—as they say over here. Though why anybody would wanta save up for the times when it rains I wouldn't know.

Because dames—as maybe I have told you guys before—are *very* peculiar things. They are very fascinatin', very cute an' very smart. Sometimes they are *too* goddam smart. I remember some honey blonde I met up with in Saratoga. This babe was the answer to a G.I.'s prayer. She had practically everythin' that anythin' in pants has ever dreamed about. She was so allurin' that you positively needed dark glasses to look at her.

Well, one evenin' I go around to this baby's apartment an' she opens the door an' stands there smilin' at me, showin' her pretty teeth. I put my arms around her neck an' give her such a helluva kiss that when I break away it sounds like tearin' the porous plaster offa grandfather's chest.

Then she steps back an' she says: "Justa minute, Lemmy. There is a blonde hair on your coat—a short one. The dame who had that hair originally was a dame who wore her hair bobbed."

I say: "Sweetheart, you are wrong, I would not kiss any dame but you."

She says: "No . . . not even my sister who is my twin an' looks exactly like me?"

I say: "Well . . . if she is your twin an' looks exactly like you I might kiss her some time for that very reason—supposin' I ever met up with her."

She says: "Well . . . she wears her hair bobbed an' I am gonna take it that if you *had* met her you woulda kissed her. Which is bein' unfaithful an' you have just admitted same."

After which she socks me on the dome with an ice-pick that she has got for the cocktails. An' when I come to I find her bathin' my head an' cryin' like hell. Then she says that she feels terrible for takin' a sock at me an' that any time I meet up with her sister I can kiss her as much as I like.

I then tell her not to feel so bad because I *did* meet up with her sister just around the corner an' I *did* kiss her.

After which she busts me another one with the ice-pick so that I haveta have four stitches put in my head.

All of which will prove to you guys that logic is not one of a dame's strong points an' that any time you are gonna be frank with a dame just see that there is not an ice-pick around the place. An' at the same time you might also remember to be very careful when you are dealin' with twins because twins—when they are good-lookin' babes—are always very distrustful of each other an' are always askin' you if there is *any* difference at all between them as far as you know.

So if you *do* know my advice to you is to keep your trap shut an' your fingers crossed.

By now Juanella is outa sight. I light myself a fresh cigarette an' stand there by the doorway lookin' at the moonlight an' thinkin' poetic thoughts about one an' all. But mainly I am thinkin' about what is gonna be the next move in the game.

So far as I am concerned I reckon that there is not gonna be any next move. I guess that the next move is gonna come from Jimmy Cleeve an' it will come when he has got some idea as to the whereabouts of this Varley. After which he will probably let me know *after* he has informed Headquarters of the fact that he has got his hooks on the guy.

I turn away inta the passage an' am makin' for the stairs when the telephone bell along in the bar parlour starts janglin'. I dive in, grab off the receiver.

Some voice that I do not know says: "Is that the *Square Bottle Inn*?" an' when I say yes they say they wanta speak to the American gentleman who is stayin' there.

I say: "Yeah? Well, I am that American gentleman an' what can I do for you?"

There is a little pause; then the voice says: "Say, is that you, Mr. Caution?" When I say yes, he goes on: "Look, you don't know me, but maybe you've heard a little about me. My name's Sammy Maynes. I usta work in the same agency as Jimmy Cleeve. Maybe he told you that. Well, I've been over here workin' for him an' the F.B.I. on this job that you're on. I been around here for three or four months."

I say: "Yeah? All this is very interestin' an' so what?"

He says: "Well, I think you an' me oughta have a little talk—just on our own—sorta nice an' quiet—you know, with nobody around."

I say: "What is the idea in havin' nobody around? You mean not even havin' Cleeve there?"

He says: "I certainly mean not havin' Cleeve there. Maybe you haven't guessed that he's sorta stringin' you along."

I say: "Yeah. I guessed that all right. So you wanta talk to me. Would you call this urgent?"

He says: "I call it goddam urgent. It's dynamite. Another thing," he goes on, "it's gonna be a very bad thing if we meet anywhere around here. But I wanta see you pretty soon."

I say: "O.K. Where are you?"

"Right now I'm at Leatherhead, but I gotta car an' I can get practically any place you like."

"O.K., Sammy," I tell him. "Well, I tell you what to do. You drive up to town—go to 177a Jermyn Street. It's an apartment block. My apartment's on the first floor. Tell the night porter to let you in an' give yourself a drink. I reckon I'll be along there within an hour."

He says: "O.K., Mr. Caution, I'll be seein' you. I'll go right away."

I hang up the receiver. I stick around for a minute, listenin' to see if anybody in the inn has been disturbed by the telephone bell, but everything is nice an' quiet.

I stand there smokin' in the darkness an' wonderin' what is breakin' now. I wonder what this guy wantsta talk to me about. Maybe I have got an idea. Maybe this guy Jimmy Cleeve is one of those guys who is so smart that maybe he is a little bit too smart. Just as he has tried to pinch all the kudos in this business offa me maybe he is tryin' to pull the same stuff on this guy Maynes. If this is so an' the Maynes bozo gets sore maybe he's gonna do some talkin' too. All of which shows you that in my business it is sometimes good not to be too selfish.

I go upstairs, give myself a little shot of whisky, fill up my cigarette case, grab my hat. Then I come down, shut the side door of the inn quietly behind me an' make for the lock-up shed where I got the car. I got an idea in my head that something is gonna develop. Maybe this guy Maynes knows something that matters.

I get the car out, drive around the edge of the green an' down the main road that leads towards the Reigate-Dorking road. It is a lovely night an' quiet, an' I get around to thinkin' about that chicken farm that I reckon I'd like to settle down on.

The road is a long piece of road an' when I am halfway along it I come to a little stone bridge crossin' a stream. On the other side of this bridge is a bunch of trees. I slow down to go over the bridge an' just when I get the other side something smacks hard against the nickel edgin' of my windshield. It hits so goddam hard that it makes a sorta squeal; then I hear something fall in the bottom of the car by my foot.

I pull over to the side of the road, snap on my cigarette lighter an' have a look. My guess was right. It is a bullet an' by the look of it the slug came out of a .38 automatic.

I remember the gun that Juanella had in her handbag.

I get outa the car, take a run for the shadows at the side of the road, ease along the hedge an' start lookin' around me. I cannot see a goddam thing. Me—I am gettin' a little bored with this business because I am not a guy who likes bein' shot at on a moonlight night like this. It sorta breaks up my poetic feelin's if you get me. I stand there in the shadow of the hedge listenin'. It is so quiet that I reckon I could hear anybody movin' around, but I cannot hear a thing.

After a bit I get back inta the car an' drive on down the road. I am wonderin' who it was took that shot at me. I'm wonderin' if it was Juanella. Supposin' that baby has stuffed me up with a lot of hooey. Supposin' the story she told me was absolutely phoney an' she has got the idea in her head that I'm gonna find out an' make it tough for her. Well, maybe she'd think it would be easier if I was outa the way.

An' if it was her it means she has been hangin' around in that bunch of trees on the other side of the little bridge. She walked over from this Mayleaf Cottage because Juanella would not have a car. She would haveta walk, an' unless she'd got up to some nonsense she oughta be a long way further along the road than this.

I get a bright idea. When I swing around on to the Reigate-Dorking road I put my foot down on the gas an' accelerate up to sixty. I miss Dorking an' go around on the by-pass road. I hit South Holmwood on the other side of the town, turn the car inta a field near the church an' start lookin' around for Mayleaf Cottage. There are not a lotta places around here an' pretty soon I find it—a little white cottage on the left, halfway up South Holmwood Hill. It has got the name written on the gate.

I push open the gate, walk up the path an' knock on the door. Nothing happens. I wait two, three minutes; then I go round the back. There is a kitchen window which is easy. I have this window open in next to no time, get my leg through an' get inta the kitchen. I pull the window blind behind me, switch on my lighter, find the electric light switch, snap it on.

I get outa the kitchen, along a little passage an' find two doors left an' right. The one on the right is a sorta sittin'-room an' the left hand one is a bedroom. Beyond these two rooms an' the kitchen there is only a bathroom in the cottage.

I go inta the bedroom, pull the window curtains an' put the light on. It is Juanella's bedroom all right. I stand there sniffin'. I can still get a sorta suggestion of that perfume Imprudence that she was wearin'. Maybe that baby is wearin' the right sorta scent. I reckon she's bein' *very* imprudent.

I take a look round the bedroom. I open the chest of drawers. They are stuck full of pretties an' all sorts of stuff. Me—I always thought Juanella would go for a rather good line in lingerie. I go through everything, lookin' for somethin' I'm not quite certain what, but there isn't a thing. I straighten the room up, put the light out, go inta the sittin'-room. Over in the corner is a little writin' desk. I go over to it an' take a look around. There are just one or two bills an' receipts from local tradesmen in Dorkin'. There is a blotter on the desk an' I take off the top sheet of blottin' paper because I have noticed that dames who wanta hide something always stick it under the top sheet in a blotter because for some reason they think nobody is ever gonna look there.

O.K. Well, I am dead right, because there is a sheet of notepaper there an' it looks like the second page of a letter that somebody has written to Juanella. I take it up an' read it. It says:

"And another thing, if you play ball with me over this Federal business you don't have to worry about a thing. I'm telling you!

You asked me why I was so certain that I could get Larvey's sentence reduced to a short term even if I couldn't get him out. Well, Juanella, you're entitled to ask that and I'll tell you. When Larvey pinched that stuff for Varley he didn't even know what he was pinching. Varley had told him that the stuff he wanted was

*some counterfeit State bonds that Varley had deposited at the
Bank to get a loan on. Varley said he was afraid that somebody
was going to find that they were counterfeit; that he wanted
them moved. So as far as Larvey was concerned he wasn't even
stealing anythin' that mattered. He was just pinching a block of
counterfeit stock. What he didn't know was that that stuff was
important Federal documents having a direct bearing on the
conduct of the war.*

*When he got knocked off he played ball by Varley and kept his
trap shut, so he took a nasty rap. He got himself fifteen years on
an espionage charge. But I can prove that he didn't know what
he was pinching. And as he'd got a clean record before, if I tell
my story, that sentence is going to be well and truly reduced.*

*Another thing is this; when I get Varley I'm going to tell the
Authorities that I have been able to get him because you've helped
me one hundred per cent. Well, you're Larvey Rillwater's wife,
aren't you, and they're going to take that fact into consideration.
If when they hear the whole story they don't let him out on parole
then I'm a Dutchman.*

*So you do what I've told you—lie low and say nothing. When
I want you to do the identification I'll let you know. You've seen
Varley. You know him. You can swear to who he is and that's
all I want.*

All the best, kid,

Yours,

Jimmy Cleeve.
P.S. I'll get in touch with you during the next day or two."

So there you are! I stand there in the middle of the little sittin'-
room with the note in my hand. It looks like I was right. It looks
as if Juanella has told me a certain amount of hooey. It looks as
if she agreed with everything I said when she knew goddam well I
was talkin' a lotta guess work. She was prepared to let me believe
that she didn't even know Varley; hadn't seen him. But here in
this letter Cleeve says she does know him. He says she can make
the identification, an' you can't do that unless you know a guy.

I put the sheet of notepaper back under the blotter, put out the light, go back to the kitchen an' get outa the window. I walk back to the car. One of these days I'm gonna tell these two—Jimmy an' Juanella—just where they get off.

It is nearly a quarter to two when I stop the heap outside my apartment block in Jermyn Street. I go in an' the night-porter tells me there is a gentleman waitin' to see me. I go up to the flat. In my sittin'-room is a guy sittin' in the big armchair in front of the fireplace smokin' a cigarette. He has gotta large glass of whisky balanced on the arm.

I say: "Well, good-mornin'. I'm glad to meet you, Sammy."

He gets up. "I'm even more glad to meet you, Mr. Caution," he says. "Gee, I've been worryin' plenty."

I say: "Yeah? Well, sit down. Maybe you haven't got so much to worry about as you think."

He looks at me hard. He says: "You don't know the half of it."

I throw my hat in the corner, go over to the sideboard an' pour myself a drink. I like the look of this guy Maynes. He is a short guy with good shoulders an' a thin humorous face. He has got nice eyes an' wavy brown hair. His hands are short an' practical. I see there are good-humoured lines about the corners of his eyes an' his mouth is sorta shaped into a permanent half smile. I reckon it would take a lot to disturb this guy.

I take my drink an' I sit down in the chair opposite to him. I say: "You know, Sammy, I reckon this is one of the funniest cases I have ever been on. Most of the time I seem to be chasin' myself around in circles. It's just one of those pieces of business where nothin' practical emerges. Nobody ever does anythin' but talk an' just what they mean when they talk I wouldn't know."

He finishes his drink. He says: "Can I have another piece of this?"

"Sure," I tell him. "The bottle's on the sideboard an' there's another one inside. Help yourself."

He goes to the sideboard an' pours himself a stiff one. He comes back an' he stands in front of the fireplace lookin' down at me.

He says: "Mr. Caution, I heard a lot about you. I heard a lot about you in the old days when I was a small-time dick, just after I got my job with the Alliance Agency. I thought you were a terrific guy."

I give him a big grin. "That's very nice of you, Sammy," I say. "Maybe you're thinkin' I'm not so hot these days."

He says: "Look, bein' a good investigator is just one of those things. You don't always get the breaks an' there's something worse than that. It's bad enough not gettin' the breaks, but when you're workin' with guys who're throwin' a spanner in the works all the time it can be very difficult for the cleverest guy."

I say: "Meanin' what an' or meanin' who?"

He says: "Meanin' Jimmy Cleeve. Surely you've guessed."

I say: "Well, maybe I had a coupla ideas, but why don't you start from the beginnin'? Take your weight off your feet. Give yourself a cigarette an' let's hear the story, because I reckon you didn't ask me to meet up with you at this time of the mornin' just to discuss the weather."

He laughs. When he laughs he shows a very nice set of strong white teeth. I think this guy is one of the nicest lookin' guys I've ever seen in my life.

He says: "You're tellin' me. Well, I've got three people to talk about. One of 'em's Varley—the guy you wanta get your hooks on, who believe me is pure poison. The second one is Jimmy Cleeve an' the third one is that honeybelle called Juanella Rillwater. What a trio!"

I say: "Yeah? You sound as if you don't like 'em."

He says: "Well, the amount of like or dislike I've got for each one is inclined to vary a bit. But I think directly or indirectly, either meanin' it or not meanin' it, they are bein' very nice to each other."

I say: "No, you don't say, Sammy. So it's like that?"

He says: "That's what I think. Look, here is the story. I was workin' for the Alliance Agency. I just got the job." He gives me a big grin. "I was pretty small-time in the agency. The big shot in the Alliance Agency was Jimmy Cleeve. Well, I reckon that guy's got one little failin'."

I grin at him. "That's interestin'. An' what is the failin', Sammy?"

He says: "He's got too much ambition. He wants to get some place an' he reckons nothin' is gonna stand in the way of him gettin' there—nothin' or nobody."

"Not ever Mr. Lemmy Caution," I say.

He laughs. "That's right," he says. "He does not give a damn who goes out so long as he's in."

"Well, we'll take that as read," I tell him. "Let's go on from there."

He goes on: "But I had a bit of luck. There was some small-time job came through to the Alliance—chicken-feed stuff. It was so unimportant they put me on it. Well, I cleaned it up. It was my first successful case. I got a bonus an' I felt like a king. But the important thing that had happened—the really important thing—was something I didn't even notice at the time."

"Yeah?" I ask. "Which was what?"

"Which was Varley," he says. "During that case I met Varley. During that case I got to know him. The actual case was a small-time steal. It didn't matter a damn but the fella who pulled this job—it was a jewellery steal—was put inside by a guy who wanted him outa the way an' was prepared to find the evidence to put him in the cooler. That guy was Varley. I reckon he got it in for this other bozo. I met Varley. I took down his statements. I got the evidence from him that we got this mug convicted on. There was only one thing I had to do an' I did it. I kept Varley in the background. But that was O.K. by me. Nobody had anythin' on him. He was simply a guy givin' evidence. You got it?"

I say: "Yeah, I got that."

He goes on: "That's why I was valuable to Cleeve. That's why he got me fixed up over here. That's why I'm hangin' around in this Canadian uniform stoogin' for Mm."

I get it. I say: "The reason bein' that you know Varley. Is that it?"

"That's it," he says. "The reason bein' *I* know Varley *an' Cleeve does not*. He's never set eyes on Varley in his life. He wouldn't know what he looked like if he met him to-morrow. An' what do you know about that one?"

I don't say anythin'. Now I am beginnin' to see daylight. Now I understand a lotta things I did not understand before. Now I reckon I got the idea as to why Cleeve wants Juanella Rillwater hangin' around.

I say: "Well, it looks as if this guy Jimmy Cleeve is a pretty fast worker. So that's why you were brought inta this case?"

He nods his head. "There's some more to this story yet," he says. "When the war started the Illinois State Police came down to borrow some responsible dicks from good agencies in New York. They were short-handed up there an' they got a lotta trouble on their hands. One of the guys they borrowed was Jimmy. I remember goin' out with him the night he went up there. He was tickled stiff. He thought he was gonna get into the big time. He reckoned from the Illinois State Police to the F.B.I. was just another jump, an' he was lookin' for some way to make it."

I say: "Well, there is nothing wrong with that, Sammy. An' it looks to me, if he goes on the way he's goin', he's gonna make it."

He gives me another grin. He says: "Maybe. But I personally think that the boy has got too much brains." He goes on: "O.K. Well, he goes up to the Illinois State Police an' he sticks around there. Then something breaks. The F.B.I. get a line on this guy Varley an' this is what they get on him. Varley has been workin' for some time in connection with the Hitler Bund. He's been gettin' information to the enemy; first of all the Japanese an' afterwards the Germans. He's found a swell way of makin' big money. So he arranges around him a little organisation—very small but very good.

"Now this Varley is no mug. The three or four crooks big an' small-time that he's got workin' for him don't know what he's playin' at. He don't let 'em know, see? But he pays 'em plenty an' everybody's happy."

"I'm ahead of you," I tell him. "I take it that one of these guys workin' for Varley is Larvey T. Rillwater—our safe-blowin' friend?"

He nods his head. "That's right," he says. "O.K. There are some Federal documents stuck away in some bank. They are waitin' to be moved to Headquarters in Washington. They're important. They're something to do with what was gonna happen after the invasion. All sorts of top Government stuff was in these documents an' Varley wants to get his hooks on 'em." He grins. "He did get his hooks on 'em," he says. "He's got 'em now. That's why they want him so badly."

I say: "I got it, Sammy. These are the things that Larvey knocked off for him?"

"That's right," he says. "Varley tells Rillwater that those documents are just a lot of counterfeit bonds in big sealed envelopes. He tells Rillwater they are certificates an' stuff he's had forged an' on which he got a loan from the bank. He reckons that now the bank are gonna start askin' questions about the repayment of the loan that there's gonna be a check-up an' that they are gonna find these documents are phoney. He knows that the bank vault is an easy job for Larvey. Larvey falls for the line, blows the vault, gets the stuff an' hands it over to Varley. But he doesn't know what he's pinched, because I reckon," says Sammy, takin' a big pull on his cigarette, "that Larvey T. Rillwater may be a crook but he wouldn't have sold his country out for money. If he'd known that the stuff he was pinchin' was dynamite, if he'd known it was Federal stuff, he'd have left it alone. But he didn't know."

I say: "I get it. An' after the stuff disappeared there was a lot of noise about it. The F.B.I. got steamed up, so somebody had to take the rap an' the guy that Varley intended to take the rap for that job was Larvey Rillwater, an' he took it. Very interestin'. An' how was it the F.B.I. knew that Larvey was the guy who had actually pinched the stuff?"

He knocks the ash off his cigarette. He says: "I'll give you two guesses. They got the information through an anonymous letter. It's stickin' out a foot that the anonymous letter was written by Varley because he got the idea in his head that once the Authorities got their hooks on the man who had actually pinched the stuff they'd be satisfied. They wouldn't go lookin' any further."

"That's all right, Sammy," I say, "but why did Varley think that Larvey wouldn't open his trap when he found out what the truth was? Why didn't he do that? You tell me. You say he wouldn't have pinched that stuff if he'd known what it was. I bet the F.B.I. told him, didn't they?"

He nods his head. "I reckon they did," he says. "Well, there's an explanation for that. This is where Jimmy Cleeve comes in again."

I go to the sideboard, get the bottle, fill up his glass an' my own.

"Sammy," I tell him, "this is a very interestin' story. It's intriguing me one hundred per cent. Go right ahead."

He says: "I will. O.K. Well, Jimmy Cleeve is one of the guys who were put on this job. He's put on the job after the F.B.I. have talked to Larvey Rillwater. Larvey doesn't say anythin' about Varley for reasons which I'll tell you in a minute, but as you know the F.B.I. are no mugs. They checked up on the people Larvey had been gettin' around with just before this business happened, an' one of 'em was Varley. Well, there was nothing much on him an' there were six or seven other people that mighta been the ones too.

"But after a bit there were more indications that Varley was behind this. Well, nobody knows anythin' about Varley. He's got no record an' nobody knows where he is, see? The F.B.I. are just for a minute in a little bit of a jam until the guy comes forward who knows all about Varley an' who says he reckons if he's given the chance he can pull him in. That guy was Jimmy Cleeve. You got that?"

I drink a little whisky. I say: "Yeah, I got it. An' why is he able to say this if he never met Varley?"

"That's easy," he says. "When the drag-net went out, when the F.B.I. sent the information round to all State Police Forces that they wanted Varley, Jimmy remembered the name. He remembered that this Varley was the guy I had contacted over the little case I was handlin' for the Alliance Agency. So what does he do? He gets himself attached to the F.B.I. on the strength of the fact that he knows Varley. Then he comes scrammin' along to New York an' sees me. He tells me he is gonna turn me inta a big shot if I work with him. He tells me that he will probably get me on the F.B.I. He tells me a whole lotta fairy stories an' I fall for 'em because in those days I was believin' in Jimmy Cleeve."

I say: "Right, fella. You were public sucker No. 2. I reckon I was public sucker No. 1. An' he promised you all those things because you knew Varley. You were the guy who could really do the job."

He says: "That's right. Cleeve told me," he goes on, "that all I've gotta do is to play it off the cuff, get as much information as I can about Varley an' let him know, an' he will look after me. So I get crackin'. I find that Varley was operatin' an interior decoratin' business in New York with a woman called Marceline du Clos. The business was just a front. Then I found out that they had it all laid on to make a getaway to France. I found something else out too. I found that for a long time this guy Varley has had a cottage laid on near North Holmwood, England, an' it is stickin' outa foot that this is his third line of retreat if France gets too hot for him."

"I get it," I say. "So you told all this to Cleeve?"

"Yeah," he says. He gives me a big grin. "Then," he says, "he proceeds to get me pushed outa the way. He fixes with the F.B.I. an' the Alliance Agency that I shall work with him. I suppose he fixed some story to cover that an' before I know where I am I am sent over here an' stuck around here in England, leavin' him behind to be the big shot." He laughs. He says: "You told me I was public sucker No. 2. I think I rate the top grade. I think I'm No. 1."

I say: "Wait a minute, Sammy. This business is not over yet, fella, an' anyway Jimmy Cleeve hasn't done any harm. Now you an' I have got together we know as much as he does. It would be funny if we got there first, wouldn't it?"

He says: "It would be a goddam treat. I'd give a coupla month's pay to get in front of that bozo. I got an idea in my head I'm not very fond of him, because I reckon he will ditch me an' you just as soon as he can."

I say: "Yeah? You sound as if you meant that. You got something else in your mind?"

He says: "Yes, I got two things in my mind. One of the things is this. When I was talkin' to him way back in the States, when I was bein' the mug an' shootin' my mouth about everything I knew,

I told him I reckoned one of the best bets in this business was gonna be Juanella Rillwater. You know, that baby is really stuck on that husband of hers. I told Cleeve that if he got permission for Juanella to see Rillwater in the cooler, and if she told him that she's seen Varley an' that if Rillwater would keep his mouth shut to the Federal Authorities about Varley's part in the game she would skewer out of Varley where the documents were; that when those documents turned up Cleeve would get him out on parole. You got that?"

I say: "Now I've got it. Now I know why Larvey kept his trap shut. You know, that was a clever idea."

He says: "It was clever all right, but it's done me a lotta good, hasn't it?"

I say: "So that's why he sent Juanella over to France, an' that's why she's over here in England now?"

He says: "That's it, because you can see what's in his head now, can't you?"

I say: "No, you tell me, Sammy."

He says: "Work it out for yourself, Mr. Caution. Varley is gonna make a bee-line for that North Holmwood Cottage. He's got to. He knows goddam well that when he got outa Paris everybody in this country would be lookin' for him. You know how hard it is for a guy to get along these days without proper identity cards an' ration cards an' this an' that. That's why he's goin' to North Holmwood because he was known there—a sorta respected citizen. I bet he's got identity cards, ration cards an' everything laid on. He's gotta get back there because that gives him a background an' he's safe."

I say: "Well, that's O.K. When he gets back there, Sammy, we knock him off."

"Yeah," he says. "That's what I'm afraid of."

I say: "What the hell do you mean? Why should you be afraid of that, Sammy?"

He says: "You know what I think? All Jimmy Cleeve wants to do is to get his hooks on those documents. Once he's got those he'll take a run-out powder on you an' me. He'll scram back to headquarters in France with the documents an' he'll be the big shot." He grins. "You an' I'll knock off Varley all right. Maybe he'll let us have *him*, but who'll worry about him once they got those papers?"

I say: "Well, you might be right. But forewarned is forearmed as the old lady said. Maybe we can get goin' from there. Maybe we can do something. We might even pull a fast one on Mr. Cleeve."

He says: "Yeah." His voice is sorta dubious. "There's another thing, Mr. Caution, that I don't like so much."

"Which is what?" I ask him.

"Which is this," he says. "I reckon Jimmy knew that you were gonna be assigned to this job. Well, he told me all that stuff about you bein' supposed to talk to that du Clos woman—the Marceline baby who was killed by somebody in Paris. I reckon that he didn't dislike that idea a bit. I reckon he didn't dislike the idea of you bein' under a sorta cloud."

I grin at him. "I get that one too," I say. I think for a moment. "Look," I tell him, "you wouldn't mean this, would you? You wouldn't mean that Jimmy Cleeve might be waitin' around there to get Varley before you an' I get a chance to see him. You wouldn't mean that he might make a deal with Varley; that he might tell Varley he was gonna give him a break provided he'd hand over the documents. You wouldn't mean *that*, would you?"

"That's precisely what I mean," he says. "If he gets away with the documents an' Varley makes a break, who's the guy in charge of this case; who's the guy who's gonna be suspected? Certainly not Jimmy Cleeve who cashes in with the papers, but Lemmy Caution who is already under a certain amount of suspicion. Well, am I wrong or am I wrong?"

I go over to the sideboard an' give myself a short one. I turn around. I say to him: "Sammy, it looks to me as if you are one hundred per cent, right. It looks to me as if Mrs. Caution's little boy Lemmy has to look after himself, which he is gonna do from now on. An' you're gonna help, Sammy."

He says: "You bet your life I will." He gets up. He says: "Mr. Caution, I'd do anythin' for you for two reasons. One is I like you, an' the other is I hate Cleeve's guts. So where do we go from here?"

I say: "Look, I'll tell you something that maybe you don't know—something that's gonna give you a big surprise."

He says: "*Nothing* would surprise me."

I say: "Wait a minute. What would you say if I told you that Varley's sister was down livin' at some place near the Inn where I am stayin' at Brockham—not five or six miles from Varley's cottage in North Holmwood?"

He raises his eyebrows. He says: "What! What the hell does that mean? Say, this is a new one on me. I never knew this guy Varley had a sister."

"Well," I tell him, "I was told he had. She was pointed out to me in New York. She's a swell dish—a lovely piece of frail that one. She's got a twisted little finger on her left hand."

He says: "Well, it could be true. Varley was a funny sorta guy. He was always mixed up with a lotta women. Maybe she wasn't his sister. Maybe he just said she was."

I say: "Does that matter? It does not matter if she is his sister or his grandmother. You can bet your sweet an' holy life she's not down there just for fun. Maybe she's in on this racket. I got an idea."

He says: "Such as what?"

"Such as this," I say. "I think we'll go an' see that baby. I think we'll go an' see her now. I got a car outside. Maybe we can put the screw on her. Maybe we can pulla fast one on Mister Cleeve."

He gets up. He says: "*Now* I'm really interested. I'm with you one hundred per cent."

I say: "O.K. Here we go."

We have one for the road, get downstairs, into the car. I start her up. It is a lovely night. I start singin' to myself. Me—I am feelin' *very* happy an' more goddam poetic than ever.

CHAPTER SIX
THE DAME IS TOUGH

I TAKE the by-pass road around Leatherhead. I am thinkin' of the old days, years ago, when I was kickin' around these parts tryin' to get my hooks on Max Schribner. I reckon that was a good time. Maybe I'm gonna have a good time some more. Maybe not. But I'm gonna know pretty soon.

Sammy is sittin' beside me in the passenger seat smokin' a cigarette. He is relaxed an' easy. When he is not smokin' he is hummin' to himself. I reckon the boy is feelin' good that he has got all that stuff offa his chest an' that I am takin' notice of it.

On the other side of Leatherhead, where the road curves around the hill towards Burford Bridge, I cut the motor an' pull the car inta the side of the road. I pull it up in the shadows an' get out my cigarette case. I light a cigarette, open the carrier under the windscreen an' grab out half a bottle of Scotch which is there. I take a swig an' hand the bottle to Sammy.

He says: "Yeah? You just thought of something, didn't you?"

I nod my head. "I just thought of this one," I tell him. "I been thinkin' about this Varley dame. Maybe I got an idea."

"Which is what?" he asks me.

"Look, Sammy," I tell him, "you said something back in my apartment that got me thinkin'. You said that you'd never heard that Varley had a sister. Well, supposin' this baby at Brockham is *not* his sister. Supposin' she is not even related to him but is just callin' herself Varley. What about that one?"

He says: "I don't get it. What's in your head?"

"Only this," I say. "Supposin' this dame is wise to this business or some of it. Supposin' she knows that Varley has got those documents an' is comin' to Holmwood to lie up. Maybe she is playin' in with him. Maybe he arranged that when he was on the point of comin' back to Holmwood she should stick around at Brockham. Maybe she could act as a sorta post office for him."

He says: "What good's that gonna do him?"

I shrug my shoulders. "It might do him a helluva lot of good," I say. "You know they got a very good postal service in this country. Nothin' ever gets lost or goes astray. Maybe Varley is not such a mug as you think. Maybe that boyo is not gonna go round this part of the world with those documents on him. Maybe he's gonna send 'em on to her, which would be a very wise thing to do because if he gets knocked off he reckons he's got somethin' left to bargain with."

He thinks for a bit. Then he says: "You might be right, Mr. Caution. You might be goddam right at that. This Varley is no pushover. He's never been knocked off yet. I always heard that he was a guy who always sorta left the back door open in case he had to get out that way. It could be that he's got an idea like you say."

"Why not?" I say. "Maybe he thinks he'd still be sittin' pretty. An' maybe he'd be goddam right. He knows that the Federal Authorities want those documents a damn sight more than they want him. Mind you, they want him *and* the documents if they can get 'em both but if they gotta make a choice. . . ."

He says: "I believe you got something. I believe you put your finger on it. It looks like this Varley dame is playin' in with him. What are we gonna do about it?"

I switch on the engine an' start the car up. "We'll still have a little talk with the girl friend," I tell him. "Maybe she'll be sort of surprised to see us at this time in the mornin'. Maybe she'll be good an' surprised. So surprised that she won't have time to make up anythin' nice an' phoney an' good enough to sound like the truth."

He says: "O.K. I think you're right."

"Me too," I tell him. "Anyway, let's try it."

I put my foot on the accelerator. Two, three minutes afterwards we are swingin' around at the intersection outside Dorking. We get on to the Reigate road. Beside me Sammy is still hummin' a song. I draw in a deep breath of air. It is one of those lovely nights you read about in books—moonlight an' just a little soft breeze an' everything hunky dory.

I start thinkin' about this Varley baby. I reckon quite a lot depends on this puss. I hope she is not one of those too clever dames. I hope she is intelligent enough to play this thing the way I want it played, but you never know with dames.

I say: "Sammy, there is one thing we're takin' a chance about, my bucko."

He says: "Yeah, what is it?"

I say: "Supposin' this dame is *not* Varley's sister, or his cousin or any relation; supposin' she is his girl friend; supposin' she's really and truly stuck on him. It's not gonna be so good for us, is it? We're gonna give our hand away."

He says: "You mean she's gonna agree with everything we say an' then wise Varley up."

"That is exactly what I mean," I tell him.

He says: "Well, what are you gonna do about it?"

I give him a grin. "It's just one of those things," I say. "An' I reckon you've gotta take a chance sometimes."

Six minutes later I drive the car around the side of Brockham Green. I ease very quietly around the back of the *Square Bottle* so as not to make a noise. I pull the car up outside my lock-up.

I say: "Listen, Sammy, stick around here an' smoke a cigarette for a minute. I wanta see if anythin' has been goin' on while I been away."

He says: "O.K."

I scram across to the side door of the *Square Bottle*, open it with a key they have lent me an' gumshoe up to my room. When I switch on the electric light I can see there is a sheet of paper on the table. Somebody has put an inkpot on it so as I shall notice it. It is a note from the landlord. It says:

Dear Captain Clauson,

It is just half-past two and a gentleman by the name of Dombie has telephoned through from London to tell you that his telephone number is Mayfair 63261; but that he does not wish to be disturbed as—and these are his own words—"he is all tied up with a Duchess who is so goddam crazy about him that every time he leaves her she starts doin' backfalls through pique."

He also said that "this Duchess is extremely high-life and she is so easy to Look at that she would have made Desdemona look like the girl who comes around to do the mangling every second Thursday."

Under these circumstances he does not wish to be sent off to any place unless it is absolutely necessary.

I do not know what he means by all this but that's what he said.

John Shaw.

So Dombie has come through an' even if he had to get the landlord of this place outa bed to take that phone message I reckon it was worth while.

I throw the note in the waste-basket, ease downstairs an' along to the bar parlour an' grab off the telephone. I ring Dombie's number. I stick around for a bit an' then his voice comes on the line.

I say: "Hello, Unconscious! How's the Duchess?"

He says: "Not so loud, you big low-life. I don't want her to hear you."

I say: "Do you mean to tell me she's not asleep outa sheer boredom?"

He says: "Say, listen, Lemmy, why don't you lay off my love life? Where's your soul, fella?"

I say: "Look, I don't wanta touch your love life, but do you mind gettin' yourself outa that scented boudoir or wherever you are, gettin' a heap from somewhere an' gettin' down here good an' quick?"

He says: "I knew it. Directly I get interested in some smashin' bit of cracklin' in a big way you haveta hand me out some lousy job. Well, what's the new thing?"

I say: "Listen, I got an idea that something is gonna pop around here in a minute. You get down here good an' quick. You oughta be down here in forty minutes. Just start operatin' on the road between South Holmwood an' North Holmwood. Keep one eye on Mayleaf Cottage in South Holmwood an' keep the other on Thorpe Cottage between North Holmwood an' Capel where Jimmy Cleeve is expectin' Varley to turn up."

He says: "Jeez . . . what an assignment. I suppose I have to run up an' down the road all night."

I say: "Listen, you big sap, there are practically no houses between those two places an' the road's deserted. All you gotta do is to sit under a tree an' pretend you're an owl."

He says: "I got it. An' what do I do after that?"

I say: "Stick around until I pick you up. I'll be seein' you, fella." I hang up.

Outside, Sammy Maynes is sittin' in the car still hummin' to himself.

I say: "Everything is O.K. I just been through to London in case we need any more assistance some time. Now let's go an' see the girl friend."

He gets outa the car an' we walk around to the front of the *Square Bottle* an' down the dirt road. The cottage with the honeysuckle around the door is lookin' very attractive. The moonlight is shinin' on the red tiles an' the white walls show up like it was some fairy place. All the time I am tryin' to keep these poetic thoughts outa my mind an' concentrate on the business in hand.

We go through the gate an' I bang on the door. We stick around for a bit an' then a paned window above the front door opens. The Varley dame's head comes out an' I'm tellin' you it's a very swell head. She is lookin' down at me an' her brunette hair tied with a ribbon is hangin' over one shoulder. I am tellin' you mugs she makes a picture. But a *picture*.

I say: "Good-mornin', Miss Varley. This is my friend Mr. Maynes. We'd like to have a little talk with you."

She heaves a big sigh. She says in that soft Virginian accent: "Really, Captain Clauson, you're a most amazing person. The last time I saw you, which was the first time I'd ever spoken to you in my life, you wanted to come for a walk with me. Now for some reason best known to yourself you bring your friends to visit me at some unearthly hour in the morning. You don't really think I'm going to let you in, do you?"

I say: "Gorgeous, I don't think anythin' about it at all. I'm goddam certain you're gonna let us in."

She raises her eyebrows. She says: "Yes? May I be permitted to ask why you're so certain?"

I say: "Look, lady, will you tell me something?"

She asks: "What?"

"I would give a lot to know what your first name is."

"Captain Clauson," she says, sorta ice cold, "it won't cost you anythin'. My first name as you call it is Lana, although I fail to see what that has to do with the question under discussion at the moment."

I say: "Look, Lana—an' I'd like to tell you here an' now that that is a most lovely name. I would also like you to know that I am a guy who is very fond of pretty names, an' when a dame has a pretty name like you have got it is a stone cinch that she is also intelligent. Now personally I reckon you are an extremely intelligent baby. That bein' so, when I tell you my name is not Captain Clauson, but that I am Special Agent Lemuel H. Caution of the Federal Bureau of Investigation, an' that this is my assistant Mr. Sammy Maynes, maybe you, being a good American citizen with—I hope—a passport stuck around somewhere in that cottage, you will have sufficient horse-sense to come down here an' open the door."

She says sorta demure: "Oh yes, and what happens if I don't?"

I give her a big grin. "If you don't I shall be under the painful necessity of bustin' the front door down," I tell her, "which I would not like one little bit."

She says: "Neither would I. I'll come down and open the door. But I hope what you say is correct."

I say: "Lady, you'd be surprised!"

We stick around for a minute or two; then she comes down an' opens the door. We stand there lookin' at her, an' I hear Sammy give a sorta little gasp. She has put the electric light on in the hall behind her an' I'm tellin' you guys that this babe is some oil-paintin'. She has put on a long aquamarine velvet housecoat with pillarbox-red silk facin's. She is wearin' a wide red sash an' little blue velvet mules with high heels. She stands there as cool as a cucumber.

I do not wish to go inta any rhapsodies about this baby. I do not wish to say anythin' that is gonna sorta excite you guys an' make you take a long sweepin' glance at your girl friend an' wonder why you thought she was good. No, sir. . . . I do not wish to tell you anythin' like that. I will just state the simple truth an' say with my hand on my heart that this piece of honeypot has got such a lotta allure that she is dynamite.

She has got this, that an' the other, in a very big way, an' I am tellin' you here an' now that if King Solomon hadda taken one look at this Lana Varley he woulda turned a coupla somersaults, transferred the harem to the Army Reserve, got himself a box of gland tablets an' took up Ludo.

What I mean is this baby has got plenty, an' when they was issuin' sex-appeal somebody left the key in the cupboard door an' she just helped herself.

She says: "Well?"

I say: "Just a minute while I get my breath. It is a long time since I have seen a sight like you. This oughta be a very pleasant meetin'."

She steps back a little. We go inta the hall. The place is bigger inside than you would think an' is very nicely furnished.

She says: "I hope so too. But first of all I would like to see some sort of authority or identification, Mr. . . . ."

"Caution is the name," I tell her.

I bring out my Federal Bureau identity an' my English police pass. She looks at 'em; then she looks at me. She is smilin' a little.

She says: "I've got an idea that I've heard of you some time before, Mr. Caution. I believe you're one of those rather super cops that have become so fashionable in the United States during the last ten years. Well, if I can tell you anythin' that you're entitled to know I suppose it's my duty as a good American citizen to do so. Won't you come in?"

We follow her inta some sittin'-room on the right of the hall. This baby is so cool she almost takes my breath away. She sorta gives you the impression that she is not at all surprised at being visited at half-past three o'clock in the mornin'. She shows us a coupla chintz-covered chairs an' puts some cigarettes on a little table. She takes one of 'em an' I light it for her.

Then she says: "Well, what is it? Don't tell me I'm suspected of murdering somebody." She gives a little yawn. "Although that at least would be interesting."

I say: "Look, lady, supposin' you take your weight off your pretty feet for a minute an' sit down. Let me do a little talkin' because," I go on, "I would hate to see you get inta any sort of jam an' it looks to me at the present moment like you are standin' just on the edge of one."

She raises her eyebrows. She sits down in a big chair on the other side of the room an' looks at us. She looks from one to another; then she crosses her legs. I oughta tell you guys that this dame's ankles match up with the rest of her.

She says: "Really, how very interesting. I believe the correct expression is that I'm in a spot. So you think I'm very nearly in a bad jam, Mr. Caution? May I be curious and ask why?"

I say: "Yeah, I'll tell you why. The thing is this: We are after a guy called Varley. You remember, Miss Varley, that when I saw you before in the dirt road yesterday, I said I thought I'd seen you sometime before. Well, whether I've seen you or not I had a description of you. The little finger on your left hand's twisted a bit, isn't it? O.K. Well, if you're not Varley's sister you're some relation of his, an' you know who I'm talkin' about."

She says: "Do I?" She shrugs her shoulders. She goes on: "My name being Varley I'm going to have relatives of the same name. I believe there are quite a few male members of my family called Varley."

"Maybe there are," I tell her, "but I'm only interested in one of 'em. I'm only interested in the guy called Varley who owns a cottage at North Holmwood called Thorpe Cottage. I'm just interested in one bozo who's been on the run from New York over the last year—a fella who got inta France, had a hand in two murders there an' skipped over here with a bunch of important state documents in his pocket. That's the Varley I'm interested in."

She says: "How very exciting. How amusing if I had a relative as romantic as that. Do tell me, who did he kill in France? I hope it was somebody who ought to have been killed."

This dame is beginnin' to give me the needle. I say: "Look, you wouldn't have a passport anywhere around the place, would you? If you have I'd like to see it. It might save a lotta confusion."

She gets up. She says: "Of course I have a passport. I'll show it to you with pleasure." She goes over to a writing desk in the corner of the room, opens a drawer, takes out a document case. She unlocks it; then she comes over to me with a passport in her hand. She gives it to me. I open it, look at the photograph. It is hers all right an' the passport is O.K. It is made out in the name of Lana Geraldine Varley. She is a citizen of the United States all right an' she comes from Richmond, Virginia.

I give her back the passport. I say: "That looks O.K. to me." She puts the passport back in the drawer. She goes back to her chair an' sits down.

She says: "Well, gentlemen, having established my identity where do we go from there?"

I do not say anythin'. I reckon if one of those English guys that I've been talkin' about was here he'd say we was on a bad wicket. I do not know what this means but when anythin' smells an Englishman says he is on a bad wicket an' I reckon this situation smells good an' plenty.

This baby looks as if she is right on top of the job. She is just sayin' what she likes an' doin' what she wants an' nobody is gonna shake her.

I take a look at Sammy. He has gotta sorta amused expression on his face an' when he sees me lookin' at him he cocks one eyebrow as much as to say we've had it, which is a thing that the R.A.F. say when they haven't.

I say: "Well, it looks as if we are not goin' any place from there except that I thought I oughta tell you that you're takin' a bit of a chance because it is not a very good thing to play funny games with Uncle Sam which is what I think you are doin'."

She gives another little sigh. She says: "Mr. Caution, believe it or not you amuse and intrigue me very much. You come round here with your friend to my cottage at half-past three in the morning. You tell me all sorts of amusing stories and seem vaguely surprised that I don't even know what you're talking about."

I say: "O.K. O.K. I have got it. Maybe you're a believer in coincidences, Miss Varley, or may I call you Lana?" I slip her a big grin. "But me I am not a guy who believes in coincidences at all because I think it is a very odd an' peculiar thing that this Varley we are lookin' for should have arranged just about this time to come to this part of the world. I think it is a big coincidence that you, just about this time, should be hangin' around here. I think it is right on the cards that this Varley has possibly arranged to slip you those documents he's got just so as he could do a deal with us in case we caught up with him."

Her eyes widen. She draws a deep breath of cigarette smoke an' blows it out through a very pretty pair of lips.

She says: "Mr. Caution, supposin' all that were true what good would it do me and what good would it do this Varley? How could he do a deal—supposin' for the sake of argument that I had those documents?"

"Be your age, baby," I tell her. "You know goddam well that we want Varley an' the documents if we can get 'em both, but you know we gotta have the documents. O.K. Well, supposin' we got Varley with no documents; supposin' somebody else like you has got 'em stuck away some place. Maybe Mr. Varley thinks we should *have* to do a deal, but that if we let him scram off sometime you might hand over the documents."

She says: "I see. Now I'm beginnin' to see daylight. That really might be a very clever scheme, mightn't it, Mr. Caution?"

I say: "It's not particularly clever but it's common sense, and it is what a smart alec like Varley might think of, especially if he had a sister, a cousin or a girl friend, as close, as beautiful an' as goddam cunnin' as you are."

She purses her lips at me. She says: "Dear . . . dear . . . dear . . .! Do you know, Mr. Caution, I've been told before that I was beautiful but nobody has ever told me I was goddam cunnin'. You are very forthright, aren't you?"

I say: "Whether I would like to be forthright with you is just nobody's business." I get up. "Look, baby," I go on, "I am not a guy who is gonna waste his time especially at this hour of the mornin'. Think it over. Maybe to-morrow you'll have thought somethin' up. Maybe you'd like to talk."

She looks at me. She gives me a bewitchin' smile. She says: "But I like talking, Mr. Caution. I must say I'd rather talk in the morning than at this time of night and I daresay we might find a lot of interesting things to talk about. *I* think you're most amusing."

She gets up. Sammy gets on his feet too.

She says: "Well, I am awfully sorry you must go. This has been very nice. You must come in and see me sometime. Come in and have tea one day."

I take a sideways look at Sammy. He is almost grinnin'.

I say: "O.K., Miss Varley. You have it your way. Maybe I'll be meetin' up with you again sometime. In the meantime I'm sorry we got you outa bed."

She says: "Not at all. It's been a great pleasure, I assure you."

She leads the way out inta the hallway, opens the door. We go out. When we are in the road she says: "Good-night, Mr. Caution. It's been so nice meeting you." Then the door shuts with a bang.

We walk down the road round the back of the *Square Bottle* to where the car is. Sammy takes a coupla cigarettes outa his pocket an' gives me one. We light 'em an' stand there on opposite sides of the car leanin' on it lookin' at each other.

He says: "It doesn't look so good, does it?"

I shrug my shoulders. "Did you think she was gonna come across right away?" I say. "Look, I reckon when she saw me yesterday she knew something was crackin'. She didn't believe that I was any Marine Captain down here on leave. She knows goddam well somebody's after Varley. Well, that bein' so you didn't expect her to make a confession an' sign it, did you?"

Sammy says: "I see. You think she was playin' for time?"

I say: "Maybe."

There is a silence for a little while. We stand there smokin' our cigarettes; then I say: "Look, Sammy, I got an idea. I got an idea that dame doesn't like my face a helluva lot."

He grins. He says: "Well, it looked that way to me."

I say: "But she might like *yours* a little better. Listen, I reckon that dame is not goin' back to bed. I reckon she is gonna smoke a cigarette an' do a little quiet thinkin' for a few minutes. Either she does not know anythin' at all about this business, which would be too much of a coincidence to be true, or else she is gonna do some very heavy thinkin'. You got that?"

He says he's got it.

"O.K.," I go on, "I'm goin' back to bed. You wait five or six minutes; then work around the back of that cottage. Get down to the other end of the road an' come to the cottage from the opposite direction. Knock quietly on the door. Go in an' see her."

He is lookin' at me pop-eyed. "What the hell for?" he says. "What d'you think I can do?"

"You'd be surprised," I tell him. I grin at him. "Listen, tell her the truth," I say. "Tell her that you're a private dick workin' for the Alliance Agency; that you're sorta stoogin' around with me because you got to; because there's a war on. Give her the idea that you don't like my face very much. Then tell her somethin' that I didn't tell her. Tell her this: Say that supposin' by some chance my guess is right an' Varley does send her or post her those documents somehow; tell her that directly she's got those papers in her possession she becomes a Federal outlaw. If we get her she's liable to them back to the Federal Authorities. You got *that*?"

He says: "Yeah, I got it." I can see he is wonderin' what's comin'.

"Then tell her this," I go on. "Tell her that if she was workin' in with you she'd be all right even if she got those documents providin' she got 'em for the purpose of handin' them bask to the Federal Authorities. You got *that*?"

He nods his head.

"O.K.," I say. "When you get that inta her head tell her that there is a reward issued by the Federal Authorities of one hundred thousand dollars for the return of those papers. Now ask her which she'd like to have—the first proposition or the second."

He says: "Jeez, Mr. Caution, that's a damned clever idea. If this baby is a girl friend of Varley's I reckon she's gettin' good an' scared right now. I reckon if she can see a way out like this an' some money on the end of it, she'll play ball. You know what they're like these frails. They play along with a guy like Varley till things get a bit too hot; then if they get a chance to sell him out they'll do it."

I say: "That's what I'm countin' on."

He says: "All right. I'll try it. When do I see you?"

I say: "Don't bother. Give me a ring some time to-morrow mornin'. I'll make a date with you. Now get crackin', Sammy. Maybe we'll still be able to handle this honeybabe."

He says: "O.K." He throws his cigarette away an' he scrams.

I stick around for a few minutes an' finish my cigarette. I leave the car outside the lock-up. I got an idea I'm gonna need it sometime. Then I get inta the *Square Bottle*, up the stairs to my room. I throw my hat in the corner an' give myself a slug of Scotch. I sit there waitin'.

Half an hour goes by an' nothin' happens, but I am not an impatient sorta cuss because this guy Confucius says it is the impatient cuss that is in such a hurry to get something that he never gets anythin' except heebie-jeebies. I got an idea in my head that I am gonna hear somethin' from Dombie before very long.

An' I am not wrong because at a quarter past four the phone downstairs starts janglin'. I make a dive for the stairway an' get to it before it wakes the whole place up. It is that mug all right.

He says: "Say, listen, Lemmy, I don't know if this means anythin' to you but about ten minutes ago when I'm watchin' this Thorpe Cottage place, some dame comes out. She starts walkin' down the road towards South Holmwood. She passes quite close to where I am standin' an' who d'you think it is? I'll give you two guesses."

I say: "I don't even wanta make one guess. Who was it?"

He says: "Nobody else but Juanella Rillwater. What d'you know about that one? Me—I didn't know what to do. I didn't know whether to stick around here or go after her. So I stuck around."

I say: "That's all right, Dombie. Look, you can take a powder now. Go an' fix yourself up some place in the vicinity. Get some sleep an' to-morrow keep an eye on Thorpe Cottage. I'll be seein' you."

He says: "O.K."

I hang up the receiver. I think this is gonna be a very interestin' night. I think maybe that all sorts of things are gonna happen, but right now I know one thing that is gonna happen.

I give a big sigh when I think of all the sleep I do not get, after which I take one little swig from a half bottle of rye I got stuck away in a cupboard, put on my hat, scram outa the side door an' get in the car. When I look at my watch I see it is just after four. I wonder what sorta luck Sammy Maynes is havin' with that babe Lana Varley, that is if he is havin' *any* luck.

I light a cigarette, drive away round the edge of the green, down the Brockham road. I drive through Dorkin' an' park the car at the bottom of the hill at South Holmwood. I put it behind some trees where nobody is gonna see it; then I walk along to Mayleaf Cottage. The place is in darkness. I give two, three hard raps on the door an' stick around. A few minutes go by an' then Juanella's voice says: "Who's there and what do you want?"

I say: "This is Mrs. Caution's little boy, Lemmy, an' I wanta talk to you, sweet puss. So you better open the door."

She says: "Look, what the hell is all this? Anybody would think this dump was a railroad enquiry office."

I give a big horse-laugh. I say: "Well if it was, Cantankerous, you'd know all the answers."

"You're just the clever guy," she says. "You know everything. I reckon your Ma musta been pleased with your Pa when you was born—that is if she knew who he was."

I say: "Do not get steamed up, Sugarpot. An' do not make any tough cracks about my old mother. She was married six weeks before I was born because I have seen the Marriage Licence."

"Yeah?" she says. "Well, I hope it was one. Because any dame who was nuts enough to marry your father probably could not read anyway, an' I am prepared to take six to four that what she thought was a Marriage Licence was probably the Saratoga Race Card."

"Which makes me a horse," I crack back at her. "Anyway, Gorgeous, maybe you have not heard that there is no rest for the wicked. Get crackin' now."

She says: "All right. Wait till I put a dressing-gown on."

I light myself a cigarette an' stand there leanin' up against the rustic porch sniffin' the night air which is very nice an' soft. I am just startin' to get all filled up again with poetic thoughts, an' I pull myself back to the realities of the moment with a bit of a struggle. I reckon I am a guy who shoulda been writin' books about flowers an' dames, but mostly dames, in a very big way, instead of which I am rushin' about the countryside at all hours of the night an' mornin'.

Right now the door opens an' Juanella is standin' inside. The two or three minutes she has kept me waitin' she has used to very good effect because she looks very nice. She is all dolled up in a black crepe-de-chine robe with a gold girdle. Her hair is sorta hangin' loose but very attractive. She has got on black crepe-de-chine slippers with four-inch red heels. Under the hem of the robe are two, three inches of very attractive apricot silk nightgown.

I say: "Juanella, during the day you are a honey; at night you are even better."

She says: "Oh yeah?" She looks at me sideways. "What's goin' on around here?" she goes on. "What're you gonna pull now? Come in. I expect you wanta drink, don't you?"

I say: "Yeah, I'd like one."

I close the door behind me an' we go inta the sittin'-room. She brings out a bottle of Scotch an' pours out two shots. She mixes some soda water with it an' gets some ice out of a refrigerator in the kitchen.

She says: "Well, what's on your mind?"

I am standin' in front of the fireplace. I say: "Look, honeybunch, just sit down. I am gonna talk turkey to you."

She says: "Yeah, you haven't ever done anythin' but talk turkey to me. It would be a nice change if you got around to talkin' something else."

I grin at her. "What I am gonna talk to you about is interestin' enough," I say. "Incidentally," I go on, "it wouldn't be you, would it, that took a shot at me over at Brockham bridge earlier to-night, soon after you left the *Square Bottle*?"

She looks at me with her eyes poppin'. She says: "What the hell d'you mean by that one? Why should I wanta take a shot at you?"

I say: "Well, you might have a reason. You might have a lotta reasons, but I know one goddam good one."

She says: "An' what is that?" She is lookin' at me with a very grave expression in her eyes.

I say: "The best reason I can thing of is Larvey T. Rillwater."

She takes a sip at her whisky. "O.K.," she says. "So I am gonna bump you because of Larvey. I cannot make any sense out of that."

"No?" I tell her. "Well, I can. It looks to me like you got a little arrangement all fixed up between you an' my associate, Mr. Jimmy Cleeve that when this an' that happens, that is if this an' that does happen," I go on sorta sarcastic, "he is gonna maybe have Larvey's case tried again. He is maybe gonna have the sentence reduced to a coupla years, an' even better than that because of the services that Mrs. Juanella Rillwater has rendered to him, Mr. Jimmy Cleeve, maybe he is gonna get Larvey out on parole without servin' any time at all. An' how d'you like that?"

She says: "You know the whole bag, don'tya?"

I say: "You're tellin' me! Why shouldn't I? I read the second page of the letter you got stuck under the blotter—a sorta agreement, wasn't it, between you an' Jimmy Cleeve?"

She says: "Well, for cryin' out loud. You yellow-bellied heel! So you been crawlin' around here while I've been out?"

"That's right, baby," I tell her. "Just that thing. An' now all you gotta do is just take yourself back inta the bedroom an' get some clothes on."

She says: "What the hell do you mean? What do I have to put clothes on for? But maybe you don't like me like I am."

I say: "Juanella, you look terrific, but I would not like to take you up to London in your nightgown. So go an' put some clothes on, an' get crackin'."

She says: "Listen, Lemmy, I am not leavin' here."

I say: "Sweetheart, you are leavin' here an' you're leavin' here within ten minutes—clothes or no clothes."

She gets up from the chair. She stands there lookin' at me. I can see her eyes are filled with tears.

I say: "Look, there is no necessity to turn on any cryin' act. I know what all the trouble's about, Juanella, but don't you worry. You got the idea in your head that if I take you up to town you're not gonna be able to play this thing along the way Jimmy Cleeve wants it played. You got the idea in your head that if you aren't around here shall we say to-morrow Jimmy Cleeve is gonna be slightly annoyed with you, an' you think if he gets annoyed with you, old man Larvey is gonna be stuck in the cooler to serve that fifteen year sentence. An' that is why you don't wanta go up to town. Well, am I right or am I?"

She gives a little sob. Just for a moment I think this baby is really stuck on Larvey.

She says: "That's the truth, Lemmy, an' you know it."

"O.K.," I tell her. "I'm not arguin' about it. Now you listen to me. The thing is who do you wanta believe in—Mr. Cleeve or Mr. Caution—because I'm tellin' you this—you get some clothes on, come up to town with me an' keep outa the way to-morrow. You do what I tell you an' I give you my word—an' you've never known me to break it yet—that when I get this job cleaned up the way I want it maybe I'll spring Larvey an' if I say I'm gonna spring a guy I spring him."

Her eyes light up. She says: "Say, listen, Lemmy, do you really mean that?"

I say: "Yeah, that's a fact."

She takes one of her well-known dives at me, slings her arm around my neck an' gives me one helluva kiss. When she breaks away that scent she is wearin' seems to be stuck all over the lapels of my coat.

She says: "I won't be a minute. Give yourself another drink. An' I hope you choke!"

It is a quarter to five when we pull up at my apartment block on Jermyn Street. Me—I am goddam tired an' Juanella looks as if she could use a little sleep. We go inta the sittin'-room an' I tell her to sit down in one of the big chairs. I pour out a coupla drinks. Then I give her a cigarette.

I say: "Now, listen, babe, just relax because I've only got a few minutes to spend here an' I have gotta get crackin'. When I leave here just take yourself to bed. You'll find some pyjamas an' stuff out there an' there's a bathroom next door to the bedroom. You stick around in this apartment an' don't put that little nose of yours outside till I come back for you. Have you got that?"

She says: "I've got it, Lemmy. You know how it is. I'm trustin' you a hundred per cent."

"That's all right," I tell her. "You're trustin' me because you got to. Now you tell me something. I got an idea in my head an' I mean it—that you've never seen Varley in your life. Is that right? Now don't give me any funny business."

She says: "That's right, Lemmy. Larvey never let me meet him. I've never seen him. Larvey talked to me about him but I've never set eyes on him."

I say: "That's fine. So here's rather a swell situation. Jimmy Cleeve has never seen this guy Varley in his life, an' you've never seen Varley, but you're gonna identify him, an' you make a deal with Jimmy Cleeve to do it."

She says: "Say, listen, what is this? How d'you know that Cleeve has never seen Varley?"

I say: "I know goddam well he hasn't because the guy who's been workin' for him over here—Sammy Maynes—who is now workin' for me has told me the whole works. Cleeve got you over here in order that you might legally be able to identify Varley when he got him. All right. You've never seen Varley. So you were prepared to do a thing like that—a pretty tough sorta thing."

She shrugs her shoulders. She says: "Why should it be tough? All I have to say is that the guy is Varley. That was the only way I could get Larvey outa the can."

I say: "Sister, you don't know the half of it. One of these fine days I'm gonna open your little eyes for you. Now there's another thing," I say. "You tell me this: When Larvey was talkin' to you about Varley did he ever mention any relatives—sisters, cousins, nieces or girl friends of his—anybody who mighta been workin' in along with him. For instance, did you ever hear Larvey talk about a girl who usta play along with Varley called Lana Varley?"

She says: "Yes, he talked plenty about her—a very cute piece. She's all brains that girl an' pretty too."

I say: "O.K. Just relax for a minute an' have your drink. I'll be with you shortly."

I go outa the room an' I go inta my bedroom. I get my big trunk open an' I take out the bunch of pictures an' reports that I got stuck away in the bottom drawer. I start goin' through the photographs. After a bit I find what I want. It is a picture of Lana Varley—a picture of that swell an' beautiful dame with the twisted little finger who right now is livin' down in the cottage at Brockham. There is some writin' on the back of it. I read it through, take another look at the picture.

Then I go back to Juanella with the photograph in my hand. I hold it out to her.

I say: "Well, does that dame look like the Lana Varley that Larvey talked to you about?"

She says right away: "No, because this girl is a real peach. I remember Larvey tellin' me that the Lana Varley he was talkin' about was a good-lookin' girl but with a mouth like a chasm. This dame's mouth is the sweetest thing, so she can't be the one."

I say: "You're dead right. That's all I wanted to know."

She looks at the photograph. She says: "Gee . . . she is a lovely dame. Who the hell is this one, Lemmy? Does she matter in this business or is she just another one of your harem?"

I say: "If you wanta see who she is turn it over an' read what's on the back." She turns it over. She reads out:

Amanda Carelli (Federal Bureau Research No. 6587654)
Finger Prints and Latent Finger Print on Record. Brunette.
Fair skin type. Usual pose that of well-born girl of good Southern
parentage. Suspect White Slave operator with Venny-Kravavics
Mob 1938. Come-on girl Lyle Venzura 'con' organisation. Wanted
for suspected accessory safe blowing Periera Bank 1939.

She says: "So I get it. This is another of Varley's girl friends. He had a lot of 'em."

I give her a grin. I say: "That's what I thought." I take the photograph from her. I put it in an envelope, stick it in the breast pocket of my jacket. I say: "Well, Juanella, I'll be on my way. Now don't forget what I told you. If you want any food, ring downstairs. I'll talk to the night porter about you on my way out. You'll find everything you want in this flat. There are even some books if you feel like read- in'." I give her a grin.

She says: "That's O.K., Lemmy. I'll stay put. I reckon the best thing for me to do is to do what I'm told."

"That sounds like sense to me, honey," I tell her.

She says: "There is only one thing. How long do I haveta stick around here?"

I shrug my shoulders. "I wouldn't know," I say. "But not very long. Maybe I'll be seein' you to-morrow; maybe the next day, but it won't be longer than that."

She says: "O.K. I don't know what's breakin' but I reckon something's comin' to a head." She gives me a big smile. She says: "You know, you're a cunnin' so-an'-so. I reckon you're the brain guy. I reckon you got 'em all beaten in the long ran. Mr Caution always comes out on top."

I put on a very modest look. I say: "Yeah, well, I wouldn't go so far as to say that, but I don't like comin' out bottom. I'll be seein' you."

I pick up my hat an' scram. I go downstairs, have a word with the night porter about Juanella, get inta the car, start her up. I start drivin' back to Brockham. Me—I seem to spend all my life on this London-Brockham road, but it is a nice road an' it is a nice night an' it's what the English call good clean fun.

As I go rollin' down St. James' Street I start thinkin' of this guy Confucius. I remember a thing he said:

"Never give up," says this Confucius. "Any time it looks like you have got a kick in the pants comin' to you all you got to do is to present the other cheek. Because he that desireth to sip the nectar from the lips of the beloved who awaiteth him in the heart of the forest must also be prepared to take a smack at a coupla man-eatin' rattlesnakes who are lurkin' along the bridle path. For the guy who sayeth that what the eye hath not seen the heart doth not grieve for was just another sucker in mental blinkers with no hope an' a girl friend who has not ever got any best friends to tell her."

Which sounds pretty good if you cometa think it out. An' even if you don't.

CHAPTER SEVEN
CAUTION—CONFUCIUS INCORPORATED

IT IS twelve o'clock in the mornin' when I wake up. The sun is comin' through the window an' I lie in bed lookin' at the ceilin' with my hands behind my head thinkin' about Confucius. Maybe you guys remember what this guy said about the tiger waitin' for his prey?

"The tiger waitin' in the bull rushes," says this here Confucius, with a smile upon his pan, "is one who licketh his lips already against the thought of a juicy hamburger. An' he springeth suddenly plenty quick smackin' some guy down good an' hard an' sayin' unto himself 'Oh boy, am I good!' And this is O.K. or is it?

"But," the philosophical old cuss goes on, "what a goddam piker this here tiger appears to one an' all when he discovers that instead of springin' upon a juicy maiden he has elected to take a sock at the local witch who is about four hundred an' fifty years old an' who is so unpopular around here that she would be glad for even a tiger to make a pass at her for breakfast.

"Therefore," says Confucius, "therefore, all ye impatient cusses, just take a quick look before you start leapin' around the place seekin' whom you may devour, otherwise you will find yourself stuck with a proposition that is so goddam tough that it would have been better for you to have jumped in the lake."

An' I reckon right here an' now that I cannot do better than listen to this Confucius who, even if he was an elderly sorta guy about two thousand years old certainly knew his spring greens— an' how!

I get up, have my bath, grab some breakfast an' just three fingers of rye, after which I dress myself, put on a snappy shirt an' tie because I think this is gonna be a sorta day of celebrations. I am just lookin' in the glass an' thinkin' that if I had a better sorta nose I would be a very nice-lookin' guy when I hear the telephone janglin' downstairs. I take a runnin' dive down the stairs inta the bar parlour before anybody else gets there.

Like I thought it is Sammy Maynes. He says: "Well, Mr. Caution, how's it goin'?"

I say: "It's goin' very well, thank you, Sammy. An' how are things with you? How did you get on with the girl friend?"

He says: "It is O K.—I *think*! Can I talk on the telephone?"

I say: "Yeah, if you're some safe place. Where are, you?"

He says: "I'm at the railway station at Leatherhead. I gotta room over here but no telephone. This is safe enough."

I say: "O.K. Go ahead. What happened?"

He says: "Well, I went to see little Lana an' I handed her out the line like you said. I made out I wasn't too stuck on your attitude when you was there; that I thought you was a too clever cuss just playin' your own hand."

I say: "Yeah? What did she say to that one?"

He says: "She was sorta careful about it. She said that was a funny attitude for me—your assistant—to take. So I told her I wasn't really your assistant. I told her I was just a private dick workin' for the Alliance an' had been pushed inta this business;

that I was just stoogin' around with you because I had to. I sorta
gave her the idea that I wasn't too stuck on the F.B.I. She seemed to
soften up a little bit at that one. Then I told her this. I said maybe
she wasn't bein' too wise about this thing. I said that maybe your
guess about her was right; that she was hangin' around Brockham
hopin' she'd get her hooks on the documents Varley had; that
she thought she'd be sittin' pretty if she got 'em. I told her that
between her an' me an' the doorpost she was a mug; that there
was a very much better way to play it than that."

I say: "Yeah? And what did she say to that one, Sammy?"

He goes on: "Well, now she was definitely sorta interested, if
you get me. She says she does not know what I am talkin' about
but exactly what do I mean? I say I am just as keen on gettin' my
hooks on some dough as she is an' I can see a way in this business
where we can both make a bundle—an' legitimately—an' keep
our noses clean."

I say: "Very nice, Sammy. Your technique sounds swell to me."

He says: "Well, thanks, Mr. Caution. Well, this time it looks
like I have hit the bull's eye. She says she will be very glad to make
some money; that she is very fond of jack, especially if she can
make it legitimately. She says maybe I can explain a little more,
so I tell her. I say if she takes those documents from Varley, or
if he sends them to her, an' she tries to hold 'em up or keep 'em
away from the Federal Authorities, that makes her an accessory
with Varley; that she can rate ten, fifteen years in Alcatraz for a
job like that because it is a Federal offence. But, I go on, maybe
she does not know that there is one hundred thousand dollars
reward for those documents."

"I bet she liked that one," I tell him.

He says: "Are you right? She liked it plenty. She sat there
lookin' at me with those big eyes of hers gleamin'. I say here is
the proposition an' I would like her first of all to answer me one
question—does Varley know she is down there waitin' for him
an' when he comes around is he gonna try an' give her those
documents somehow. She just looks at me an' smiles," he goes
on. "She does not say a word. After a minute she says she'd like

to hear some more about how this reward can be got, so I tell her this. I say: 'Look, Miss Varley—if that is your name, at the present moment I am workin' with the Federal Authorities (a) to get those documents back, and (b) to get Varley if possible.' I tell her that if she makes an arrangement with me in retrieving those documents then she is performin' an act of good citizenship an' it is stickin' out a foot that she is entitled to some of the reward—if not the whole of it. In fact I tell her as I am not a Federal Officer an' as she is just a private citizen I do not see any reason why the reward shouldn't be split between the pair of us. I ask her how she likes that one."

"An' very nice too," I say. "An' how does Sweetiepie react to that?"

He says: "Well, she was a bit disappointin'. She didn't say anythin' at all. She just asked me if I'd like to have a drink. When I'd had it she said she'd think things over. Maybe she'd be meetin' me again some time."

I say: "Well, that looks all right to me because if she had not liked the proposition she'd have told you so."

He says: "O.K. Well, where do I go from there?"

"You don't go anywhere," I tell him. "You just go to the lounge of the King's Hotel in Leatherhead an' wait there for me. I'm comin' over to see you, after which you can go an' see Miss Varley again an' fix the job."

He says: "Yeah So it's like that. You got something?"

"I got plenty," I tell him. "I've got something that is gonna make that babe wanta play ball. If you stick around I'll be seein' you."

I hang up, go around to the back an' get the car out. Then I get an idea. I go back to my bedroom an' open up my suitcase. I got an extra gun inside—a .38 Mauser—a nice gun. I stick an ammunition clip in the gun, put on the safety catch, stick the gun in my pocket. I go back to the car. I start her up an' drive over to Leatherhead.

When I get there Sammy is sittin' down in the hotel lounge with some soda water, two glasses an' a flask of his own whisky. He pours a drink.

I say: "Listen, fella. Me—I am very tired an' would like to get some sleep, so I am gonna make it short. Take a look at that." I take the picture of Lana Varley outa my pocket an' give it to him. I say: "Well, do you recognise that?"

He says: "Sure, that's the girl friend. That's Lana Varley."

"Like hell it is," I tell him. "You turn over an' have a look on the back. That babe is nobody else but Amanda Carelli—a dame with a police record as long as your arm. Look, use your brains. If you read those notes on the back of the picture you will see that this baby was suspected as being accessory to a safe blowin' job in Periera."

He says: "Yeah?"

"All right," I tell him, "I got an idea about that. I got an idea that the Periera bank job was done by Larvey Rillwater. I got an idea that our friend Amanda Carelli—alias Lana Varley—helped him do the job. Now have you got it?"

He says: "Gee . . . I get it. Your idea is that when Larvey Rillwater was knocked off for this thing he was in with Varley and he got word to this Carelli baby what the job was. He gave had the tip-off that it might be a good thing for her to wait for Varley an' blackmail him for those documents."

I say: "You have put your finger right on it. That is what I thought. Look, you scram outa here. You get back to Brockham an' you see the girl friend again. Show her that picture. Show her what's on the back an' tell her she can do just what she likes. She is either gonna play ball an' hand those documents over to us if she gets her hooks on 'em or I am gonna knock her off an' have her slammed in the cooler here pendin' extradition. An' if I do that she's gonna spend a long time inside."

He says: "O.K., Lemmy. This sounds pretty good to me. An' there's another thing. If this babe was gonna stand up Varley for the documents when he got down to this district it is a stone cinch that she's gonna know when he's comin' down."

I say: "Fella, you got the wrong surname. They oughta have christened you Sherlock." Then I ask him: "Have you gotta gun?"

"No," he says. "I had a regulation British Army pistol but I lent it to Jimmy Cleeve. I don't think I'm gonna need a gun but I reckon he might. This guy Varley can be poison."

"That was a nice thought," I tell him. "All the same you better have one." I take out the Mauser an' give it to him. "You got ten shots in there—nine in the clip an' one in the barrel—an' the safety catch is on. Maybe there's gonna be a little shootin' before this job is over."

He says: "Thanks a lot, Mr. Caution." He puts the gun in his pocket.

I do not know it right now, but I am gonna be goddam glad that I gave him that gun.

"O.K., Sammy," I say, "now beat it."

He finishes his drink, grabs his hat, throws me a big grin. He says: "You know, Mr. Caution, it's a treat to work with you. I think we're goin' places."

"You bet we are," I tell him. "An' another thing we are goin' places in such a way that Mr. Cleeve will find himself left holding the can."

He laughs. He says: "Yeah, an' I reckon it's gonna be a nice big empty one."

I say: "Listen, Sammy, when you've seen this babe, she's gonna say yes because she's gotta say yes. After you leave her go back to the Square Bottle—the place I am stayin' at at Brockham—an' wait for me. Keep under cover an' do not show your nose."

He says: "I got it, Mr. Caution. So long."

He scrams.

I hang around Leatherhead for half an hour; then I buy myself a large whisky at one of the local inns, get in the heap, go back to the Square Bottle.

I eat lunch an' stick around. At half-past two the telephone goes. It is Jimmy Cleeve. He sounds plenty excited.

He says: "Look, Lemmy, some big news—Varley is comin' down to-night."

I say: "Yeah? Pretty good! I thought he would be around here sometime soon."

He says: "He's in London. I got a contact there who's been keepin' an eye on him. He'll be comin' down here sometime to-day, an' my guess is he'll come down this evening."

I say: "Well, what are you proposin' to do about it, Jimmy?"

"When he gets down here it's a stone cinch he's goin' to Thorpe Cottage," he says. "I'm gettin' out but I'm stickin' around an' am gonna keep my eye on that place. Directly he arrives I'll give you a tinkle on the telephone from the call box on the Capel Road. Then you'd better come over right away. I'll go inta Thorpe Cottage an' have a few words with the boyo while you're on your way."

I say: "Well, I would be careful, Jimmy. I reckon he is not likely to be very good-tempered when he sees the game is up."

He says: "Look, let me play it my way, Lemmy, because that is what I think. Varley knows goddam well that I'm not a Federal Officer. Maybe he thinks he'll be able to do some sorta deal with me. We got *him* where we want him. The thing is to get those documents. Maybe if I tell him that if he hands 'em over to me I'm gonna make things a bit easier for him he's gonna listen."

I say: "That's O.K. by me. Directly he gets there give me a tinkle. Go an' see him. If he thinks he can make a deal with you let him have it. All right. I'll stick around, Jimmy. I'll wait till I hear from you. Good luck, pal."

I hang up. It is stickin' out that this boy is still playin' his own hand. He is still tryin' to get ahead of me. Well, so what!

At three o'clock Sammy Maynes arrives. The bar parlour is empty. I give him a big drink. He is lookin' plenty excited.

He says: "Listen, Mr. Caution, you're the brain guy. You were dead right about this babe. She's thrown her hand in."

I give him a big grin. I say: "Now you're talkin', fella. What happened?"

He says: "Well, I went around there an' I gave it to her straight. I chucked the picture down in front of her an' told her to read what was on the back of it. I said we had her record, an' you'd sent your compliments an' said that unless she played ball you were gonna knock her off to-day, an' how did she like that?"

I say: "An' how did she like it?"

He laughs. He says: "She didn't like it a bit. But what could she do? It's a funny thing," he goes on, "directly she had a look at the back of that picture; directly she knew the game was up she became quite different. She dropped that high-falutin' Southern American accent an' started talkin' real Brooklyn. She's Amanda Carelli all right. Well, then I ask her how she knew about Varley havin' those documents, an' how she knows when he's comin' down here.

"Well," says Sammy, "you were right again. She tells me that she got the tip-off about those documents through a friend of Larvey Rillwater's. She was told that Varley had a hide-out down here; that the idea was for her to come down here an' hang around until he arrived. There was some guy in London who usta work with Varley who they knew he would go to when he got to England. This guy who was gonna take a cut in the money, is tippin' off Amanda when Varley arrives. An' she expects him down pretty soon."

I say: "Nice work, Sammy. So it's all fixed up?"

"Well, Mr. Caution, I told her this," he says. "I told her the thing for her to do was to stick around, see Varley like she'd arranged when he comes down, get the documents off him; that she was to hand 'em over to you when the time came an' that she'd get a cut in the reward. So everything's on ice."

"I reckon you've done a helluva good job, Sammy," I tell him, "an' you will not lose anythin' over it."

He says: "Thanks a lot, Mr. Caution. I think it's a lotta fun. What do I do now?"

I say: "Look, you get back to that King's Hotel in Leatherhead an' stick around. I've had a word from Cleeve to-day that Varley is expected down to-night. Cleeve's had a tip-off." I grin at him. "He's gonna give me a tinkle when the boy friend arrives," I say, "but he's gonna see him first, hopin' to do a deal an' get those papers."

Sammy laughs. He says: "Cleeve must be a mug if he thinks Varley's comin' down here with those papers on him."

"You're tellin' me," I say. "But he's sorta hopeful. Maybe he thinks he's still gonna pull a fast one on Mr. Caution."

"Like hell he will!" says Sammy. "My money's on you. I'll be seein' you."

He scrams.

I go up to my sittin'-room, give myself one short one, outa the rye bottle, after which I go to bed, because bed is a very good place if you have got some thinkin' to do, besides which I reckon I owe myself a little sleep.

Me—I am not at all dissatisfied with the way things are pointin'. I reckon I have just been playin' along on this job with that guy Confucius advisin' me. I reckon him an' me would make a good Corporation.

It is gettin' dark an' a balmy breeze—I do not know what a balmy breeze is but I read the word some place an' it sounds sorta poetic so I might as well use it—is blowin' up from Betchworth. It is a swell evenin'.

Me—I think there is something sorta electric in the air—just like you feel there is gonna be a thunderstorm only I do not think there is gonna be a thunderstorm around here—not *that* sort anyway. Also the palm of my left hand is tinglin' an' this always means something even if it only means that it wants scratchin'.

I remember some dame I usta know a long time ago. The babe's name was Marianna de Cuba. I reckon this honeybelle looked just like that too. Her mother was Irish an' her father was Spanish an' what she had not got in the way of temperament you coulda rolled in a cigarette, smoked it, an' you wouldn'ta even noticed it. That frail was certainly some Spanish bombshell.

An' she was stuck on me good. She thought that every time I looked at her the sun had come out. But she was sorta jealous. She told me one evenin' on the *hacienda* back porch that if ever she caught me neckin' around with any other *femme* she was gonna carve me up in little pieces.

So one evenin' I am on my way to meet up with this Marianna an' I get caught up with her cousin. Her cousin has also got everything it takes in the way of allure an' after a bit I find myself in a huddle with this babe an' do not realise that Marianna is watchin' me outa the back window.

After a bit I go on my way an' suddenly my left hand starts itchin'. I stop to scratch it an' at the same time a bullet misses me by about two inches—Marianna havin' opened fire with a piece of her old man's artillery from the bedroom window. After which I took a powder, the first train outa Santa Fe, an' a course in "How to keep on the Right Side of a Dame" or "Are You Usin' Your Personality?" In Six Easy Lessons with a chart showin' how to get outa the back window without catchin' your pants on a nail.

Then the telephone in the bar parlour jangles. It is a funny thing—I have been waitin' for the sound of that bell but when I hear it I nearly jump outa my skin. I ease along the passage inta the bar an' grab off the receiver.

It is Jimmy Cleeve. His voice sounds sorta funny because it's packed with excitement. He says: "Listen, Lemmy— he's here! Varley just drove up along the Dorkin' road in a high-powered car. He drove it round the back of Thorpe Cottage. He's parked it off the road where it can't be seen. I reckon he's goin' in the back way, so I'm goin' over. An'," he concludes, "don't be too long. This guy is tough, you know."

I say: "Don't you worry, Jimmy, you'll be able to handle him. I reckon I'll be with you in twenty minutes."

I hang up. I stand there for a minute lookin' at the telephone wonderin' whether I shall scram or whether I oughta wait for a call from Dombie. Just when I have made up my mind to go the telephone bell rings again. It is Dombie.

He says: "Hello, Lemmy. Look, I hadta wait to telephone to you because some guy has been usin' this phone box an' I kept outa the way because I didn't want him to see me."

I say: "That's all right, Dombie. The guy usin' the phone box was Cleeve. What's new?"

He says: "Well, somebody just shot past here in a car. From where I was—I was in a clump of trees just on the top of Holmwood Common—I could just see this palooka pull round by Thorpe

Cottage. He's parked around there somewhere. Where do I go from there?"

I say: "Look, you don't go anywhere. Just stay there behind that tree of yours. I'll pick you up very shortly."

He says: "O.K. I'll be seein' you."

I hang up, go up to my room, take a little swig at the rye bottle an' get my hat. I get out the Luger, load it up, put it in a shoulder holster. Then I go down, get inta the car an' get goin'. When I get on to the Reigate road I put my foot down. I got the hood off the car an' the evenin' wind in my face feels good.

I take the by-pass around Dorkin' so as not to lose speed an' come out the other side below South Holmwood. I race up the hill, drive the car off the road on to a grass verge, get out an' look around for Dombie. After a bit I see him. He's up in a little clump of trees leanin' over a fence. When I get close to him I get the idea that this guy has gone nuts an' is talkin' to himself, but when I get a bit closer I get quite a different idea.

"Yeah," he is sayin' sorta modest, "I served in practically every big battle. I reckon I was one of the first guys ashore at Dieppe."

Some dame whom I cannot see on the other side of the fence says: "I bet you've got a lot of medals."

"Yeah," says Dombie sorta airily, "I got practically everything, but medals don't mean a goddam thing to me. I just like fightin'. I reckon if I had a pound for every Jerry I've killed in this war I'd be a rich man. I'll tell you another thing . . ." he goes on.

I tap him on the shoulder. "Look," I tell him, "I just come from Buckingham Palace to inform you that the King has got about forty-six more medals for you. I thought you'd like to know. So you can add 'em to your collection."

There is a squeal from the other side of the fence an' some girl eases off into the darkness.

Dombie says: "For cryin' out loud. Whenever I start makin' an impression on some baby what happens? You turn up!"

I say: "Look, sourpuss, this is no time to make impressions on dames. Me—I think there's gonna be a little trouble in a minute."

He says: "Such as what?"

"Such as our friend Varley has at last arrived," I say. "He was the guy you saw in the car."

"Jeez!" says Dombie. "Now there's gonna be a whole lotta fun. What's happened?"

"Cleeve called through an' told me about it," I say. "He's gone over to the cottage. He's tryin' to pull one on Varley to see if he can get those papers outa him. I don't think he's gonna succeed. Come on, let's get goin'."

We get inta the car. I start her up an' roll down the hill good an' fast towards North Holmwood. When I get near Thorpe Cottage I swing the car on to the track that runs across the field, run her under a hedge, turn out the lights an' get out.

We ease across the field an' round to the front door of the cottage. I give it a push an' it opens. We go inside. There is a light in the sittin'-room, an' as I go in through the doorway, with Dombie at my heels, Cleeve comes along the passage from the back of the cottage. He has got a .45 regular service Army revolver in his hand. His face looks a bit strained.

I say: "So what, fella? Did he try somethin' funny?"

"Yeah," he says. "It's too bad, Lemmy, but I hadta fog him."

I say: "What happened?"

"Just after I phoned you," he says, "I came over here an' came in the front way. I reckon he musta been playin' around with the car or something because as I came in through the front of the cottage he came in through the back door.

"I said: 'Good-evenin', Varley. I wanta talk to you.' He went for a gun an' that guy is pretty quick on the draw because he had it out an' took a shot at me before I could get my hand on this one. Then he turned an' scrammed. I waited a minute because I thought he might be waitin' outside to take another crack at me, but when I heard the noise of the engine start I gotta move on. Then I saw what his idea was. It was to make a getaway. I scrammed outa the back door, took a quick shot an' got him through the head. He's in the car. He don't look so good."

I say: "Well, it can happen. You'd better give yourself a drink, fella. I'll go an' have a look at him. When I come back I'll have one too. Dombie, you stick around."

Dombie says: "O.K." an' he an' Cleeve go into the livin'-room.

I walk down the passage, out the back door, down the little pathway an' through the gate. Just outside the gate is a big tourin' car. The drivin' door is opened an' a guy is slumped over the wheel.

I reckon Cleeve was right when he said that he is not a pretty sight. This guy was shot with a .45 service pistol at close range. Cleeve hit him in the back of the head an' there is practically no head or face left.

I take out my cigarette lighter, snap it on an' take a look inside the car. Lyin' on the floor just by the gear lever where it has fallen outa his hand is an automatic pistol. I take a look at the dead guy's clothes. They are good smart clothes. Then I pull open the lapel of his coat between my finger an' thumb. By the flame of the cigarette lighter I can see a pencil—a propellin' pencil—in his left hand breast pocket. I take it out. Then I close the car door an' go back inta the cottage.

Cleeve an' Dombie are sittin' down in the livin'-room. There is some whisky an' glasses on the table. I pour myself out one.

Cleeve says: "Well, this is not quite so good. We got Varley but it looks as if we haven't got those documents."

I drink some of the whisky; then I put my hand across the table an' I pick up the gun. I throw it across to Dombie.

I say: "You look after that, pal." I finish my drink; then I say to Cleeve: "Listen, what makes you think that that guy you've just shot was Varley?"

He looks at me, his eyes poppin'. He says: "What the hell do you mean? Of course it was Varley."

I say: "Yeah? How would you know? You've never seen Varley in your life."

He looks at me. His face is sorta strained an' white. He says: "Well, we can soon settle that. I'm goddam certain that's Varley but there's somebody around here who can say whether he's Varley or not, an' you know her."

I say: "You mean Juanella Rillwater?"

He says: "Yeah, that's who I mean."

I say: "Jimmy, you're a goddam liar because Juanella Rillwater never saw Varley in her life either, which is exactly the reason you got her over here so as she could identify him."

He jumps up on to his feet. He says: "Listen. . . ."

I say: "Shut up an' sit down. Let me tell you something, fella. I been wise to you from the start. What d'you think we are in the F.B.I.—a lotta mugs to be kicked around by guys like you? Your trouble is you're too clever an' you like killin' people too much."

He says: "Caution, you must be nuts. Why the hell should I kill anybody? I hadta kill this guy in self-defence an' this guy was Varley."

I say: "Yeah?" I take out the fancy propellin' pencil. I put it on the table. I say: "Have you ever seen that before?"

He looks at it. He says: "What the hell are you talkin' about? Why should I have seen that before?"

I say: "I'll tell you why. That pencil was part of a fountain pen an' pencil set that George Ribban gave you on your birthday in Paris. Maybe you're gonna tell me he didn't. I *know* he did. He bought it off a black-market guy called Le Fevre. He went to your birthday party an' he gave it to you.

"So all right. When you killed George Ribban I reckon he had time just to have a word or two with you before you slugged him. Maybe he saw what you were gonna do an' took a grab at you. He grabbed the fountain pen outa your pocket. That's why the cap was still on it. When you moved him down an' laid him on the stairway where you knew I was gonna find him you saw the pen in his hand, but you left it there. You left it there because nobody had seen him give it to you at the party. Nobody knew about it an' you had a big idea. You gave the pencil to Enrique—the guy who was workin' with that strip-tease baby Marta Frisler—because you knew I was goin' around to see him. You knew I was goin' around to see him because you knew that Juanella Rillwater had already met me that evenin' an' given me the address at the Hotel St. Denis near the Boulevard St. Michel.

"You knew I'd go around there. You knew I'd see Enrique an' you knew he was a guy who liked showy things; that he'd wear that pencil in his waistcoat pocket where I'd see it, an' you knew then that I'd think he'd killed Ribban." I give him a grin. "Nice work if you can get it!"

He says: "You're talkin' hooey." His voice is sorta low an' hoarse. I can see his hands are tremblin'. He repeats: "You're talkin' hooey." He stands there lookin' from me to Dombie.

I say: "I'm not talkin' hooey, pal. What the hell is the good of you puttin' up a front like this when you know you're on your way to the electric chair? They're gonna fry you, pal."

He says: "What do I wanta do all this for? You must be nuts."

I say: "You're askin' me what you wanted to do it for. Look, when you heard the F.B.I, was gettin' around lookin' for Varley you got yourself tied on to the job, didn't you? You got yourself tied on the job an' you told them that you knew Varley. Well, I reckon that was the only true thing that you did say. You've been in with Varley on this thing from the start. That's why you thought you'd get me in bad."

He gives a weak sorta grin. He says: "So I did that too."

"You bet you did it," I say. "I'll tell you why you did it. Varley had already left for England. Marceline du Clos who usta work with him was in Paris. She was gettin' good an' scared. George Ribban—an' this was a little idea on the part of General Flash an' myself—was put in to get next to her—to scare her still more. Well, she talked to George Ribban an' what did she tell him? You know what she told him. She told him that Varley had already left for England. She told him that she was scared stiff *an' she told him that she suspected you was workin in with him.* So you got to work! You gotta get rid of two people—one of them is the Marceline du Clos dame an' the other is George Ribban. An' you gotta do it before either of them can talk.

"In the meantime you have been mixin' a little poison about me with the General. You told him that Marceline du Clos has told Ribban that I have been shootin' my mouth. You told him that a report was comin' from Ribban. You fake this report an' you give it to the General. An' then what do you do? Remember the night that you an' I had that conference with Flash? Well, you were the guy who got that forged pass an' got du Clos outa the 14th Police Post in Paris, an' it was easy for you to do it. You were the guy who took her over the river to the Rue Zacherie an' bumped her. You weren't worryin' about me because you knew that Juanella Rillwater was on my tail. She didn't know why she was doin' it but maybe you told her that she was to keep me busy for a little while. When I went into Wilkie's Bar on my way to see Ribban to get myself a drink she slipped in on my heels an' sat down at a table. She knew I'd see her. She knew I'd go an' talk to her."

He says: "Yeah? So she's doin' all this for me. Why?"

"Don't be a goddam fool," I tell him. "She told me why. You were gonna get Larvey Rillwater's sentence reduced, weren't you? You were gonna get him out on parole if she did what she was told. Well, I'll say this for Juanella—she'd do a lot for that husband of hers but she wouldn't make herself accessory to murder. But the poor mug didn't know. She thought you were on the up an' up. You told her the same story you told everyone else; that you were keen to get Varley; that you were keen to get yourself transferred to the F.B.I, an' be a big shot; that you were keen to get in ahead of me on the job."

Dombie yawns. He says: "You know, Lemmy, this guy is not a nice guy. Another thing I've been wonderin' what had happened to you. I thought you was losin' your grip. I reckon you're still the same Lemmy Caution—still the guy on top of the heap. You had this thing beat all along."

I say: "Thanks, Dombie."

He says: "I get it. Somebody is killed. Juanella Rillwater is gonna identify the body as Varley. In the meantime the real Varley gets away with the documents. I reckon the guy is nowhere near here—probably stoogin' around in London."

"Maybe," I say.

Dombie feels in his pocket with his free hand for a cigarette. He lights it. He says: "Say, listen, who is this dead guy in the car anyway?"

"That's easy," I say. "The dead guy in the car is the guy who had the fancy propellin' pencil—the poor mug Enrique. Here was another pair of guys—Enrique an' Marta Frisler—who was workin' in with this boy. Maybe he got somethin' on them too. But he's not a very nice guy to work for. When things get tough he just kills you so's people will think you're somebody else. He tried to iron me out too. He took a shot at me on Brockham Bridge."

I turn to Cleeve. I say: "Well, Jimmy, what have you gotta say?"

He says: "I'm not sayin' anythin'. I wanta lawyer."

Dombie gives a big horse laugh. He says: "Fella, you'll need a goddam sight more than a lawyer to see you through this."

I pour myself out a little shot of whisky an' drink it.

I say: "Dombie, take this mug out to the car outside. Take the stiff out of the drivin' seat an' sling him in the back. Stick Cleeve in the drivin' seat an' make him drive the car down to Dorkin' Police Station. Then hand him over. You can tell the Inspector in charge that he'll have a call from Chief Detective Inspector Herrick of the C.I.D. London that'll make things pretty easy for him. An' just so's he'll know you're O.K. you can show him this."

I give him the British Police pass that Herrick has given to me.

Dombie gets up. He has still got the service pistol in his right hand. He says: "I wonder why a guy should wanta use a small cannon like this to shoot a fella with. I suppose he just hadta blow most of his face off so's nobody could recognise him?"

"That's right, Sherlock," I tell him. "Well, I'll be seein' you."

He says: "Just a minute, Lemmy, when I've done this an' handed this mug in what do I do?"

I give him a big smile. I say: "Look, you gorgeous beast. You remember that Duchess you was with in London. You should remember I interrupted a little love scene of yours when you were handin' out your usual line of hooey to that poor defenceless woman?"

He says: "Yeah, I remember. She was crazy about me. She said I was just another Casanova only with more appeal."

"Like hell," I tell him. "If you're like Casanova then I got brass eyeballs. Anyway, when you hand this thug over you can go back to the Duchess. Maybe she'd like to hear the end of that bedtime story you was tellin' her."

He says: "O.K. O.K. Go on . . . make a lotta fun of my love life. The trouble with you is you have not got any delicate feelin's. But what would you do without me?"

I say: "Sometimes I know exactly what I'd like to do *with* you. So long, pal."

I get outa the cottage, ease across the road. I ring up the hotel at Leatherhead an' ask for Mr. Maynes. After a minute or two he comes on the line. He says: "Well, Mr. Caution, how's it goin'?"

I say: "It looks to me like it's not goin'. There's a whole lot of funny business over here. Cleeve has shot some guy, an' the thing that's worryin' me now is gettin' my hooks on those papers."

He says: "Yeah? What're you gonna do?"

I say: "I got an idea in my head that our little friend Lana Varley—alias Amanda Carelli—will have those documents by now. I think they've been passed to her or sent to her. I think we'll go an' see that babe. Can you get a car?"

He says: "Yeah, I can hire one."

I say: "All right. You get one. Come along to the *Square Bottle* right now. I'll be waitin' for you. Get a rustle on, fella."

He says: "O.K., I'm on my way. So long, Mr. Caution."

I hang up. I go back to where I left the car, start her up, get on to the road. I drive back nice an' easy towards Brockham.

Things maybe are not so good but they could be a darn sight worse an' who am I to grumble anyway?

The moon has come out. The night is good an' the soft breeze is blowin' an' I am feelin' so goddam poetic an' near to nature an' beauty an' all that sort of stuff that I start thinkin' about that chicken farm that I'm gonna start some time when I have finally decided to throw over this business of chasin' thugs all around the world for Uncle Sam.

I am standin' at the side door of the *Square Bottle*, leanin' against the doorpost.

Then I hear the car an' after a minute a hired heap from Leatherhead comes up an' Sammy Maynes gets out. He pays off the car an' comes over to me.

He says: "Well, Mr. Caution, it looks like things have started poppin'. What's goin' on?"

"Plenty," I tell him. "Come upstairs. I got a drink an' some sandwiches."

"That suits me," he says. "I'm goddam curious. What happened to Cleeve?"

We go up the stairs to my room. On the table is a plate of sandwiches, a bottle of rye an' some soda. I pour out the drinks.

"You sit down an' listen to me," I tell him. "Because this is a very funny story. Maybe you are gonna be good an' surprised to hear that Cleeve was a phoney."

"What!" he says. "A phoney . . . what the hell?"

"Keep cool, Sammy," I tell him. "This guy took you for a mug like he tried to take me, like he tried to take everybody. But it didn't come off. It did with you because you naturally trusted the guy. You trusted him because he usta work for the Alliance Agency where you was workin' an' you trusted him because he hadda good story.

"Work it out for yourself," I go on. "Here is this guy stoogin' around with the State Police in Illinois—where he has been lent. Well . . . the mug knew Varley. He knew him goddam well. Probably he met up with him first of all before America came into the war an' he knew goddam well what Varley was at. You got that?"

He says: "Well . . . it could be . . . but . . ."

"But nothin'," I tell him. "That's how it was. An' I reckon that when Varley planned to pinch those Federal documents Cleeve was in it from the start. Now you gotta realise that these two have got an open an' shut idea. It's terrific. First of all this guy Varley tells Larvey Rillwater that he wants some counterfeit bonds pinched from a bank. The mug Rillwater does it. Directly the documents are missed the Federal Bureau are called in. Rillwater gets pinched. He gets pinched because probably this Varley, *workin' in conjunction with Cleeve,* sends an anonymous note to the F.B.I, sayin' that Rillwater was the guy who pinched 'em.

"So Rillwater gets knocked off by the F.B.I, who are now very busy lookin' for Varley who, they have an idea, is behind the job. So then when the drag-net goes out Cleeve says that he knows about this guy Varley, that he met him when he was with the Alliance an' he gets himself transferred to the job.

"He then gets at Juanella Rillwater an' tells her to go an' see Larvey in the cooler an' tell him to keep his trap shut an' not say anythin' about Varley. He tells her to say that if Larvey Rillwater plays ball everythin' will be O.K. an' that Cleeve will get him out on parole because Juanella is helpin' to pull in Varley. He tells her to say that if Larvey does *not* play ball it is a stone cinch that Varley will get his own back by bumpin' Juanella. You got that?"

"I got it," he says. "This Cleeve is a clever bastard."

"*Was,*" I say. "Because he is not gonna be clever any more."

"Go on, Mr. Caution," he says. "This is one helluva story."

"You're tellin' me," I say. "O.K. Cleeve then tips the wink to Varley to scram out an' go to Paris. He probably makes this easy for him. He fixes it. Varley an' Marceline du Clos—his girl friend—get over to Paris, an' Varley has got the documents with him. Probably these two are met an' looked after when they get there by Enrique and Marta Frisler who are also workin' for Cleeve an' who he has got over there some time before.

"All right. Then Cleeve goes over to Paris. He gets himself sent over on the Varley job which is goddam clever because this means that he is gonna know everything that is goin' on. But what he does not know is that the F.B.I, have got George Ribban an' me workin' on the job as well an' we are not sayin' a goddam thing to anybody."

"Yeah," he says. "That's where that boy musta gone wrong. He did not know that."

"It didn't matter whether he knew or not," I say. "Anyhow, Marceline du Clos gets scared. She meets George Ribban an' she tells him that she is scared of Varley *an' Cleeve.* So George Ribbans starts to try an' get next to Cleeve. He buys him a fountain pen set an' he goes to his birthday party. Remember that Ribban has not had a chance to talk to me.

"Right then Cleeve tells General Flash, the big boy at Intelligence, that I have been talkin' to Marceline. He is tryin' to get me suspect, knowin' that he is gonna knock off Ribban before he gets a chance to say anythin' at all.

"All right. Well, Cleeve killed Marceline du Clos in Paris an' he killed George Ribban in Paris an' he has just done his third job to-night. He has killed some guy, an' we cannot tell who this guy is because he has got the pan shot off him. But Cleve says it is Varley an' personally speakin' I do not give one goddam whether it is or not."

He scratches his head. He says: "Why . . . why don't you care?"

"Look," I tell him, "why does Cleeve select to-night to kill this guy whoever he may be? Why does he do it? He does it because he wants to take the heat off Varley. He wants Varley to have a free run because he knows he's handlin' those documents. In other words, if Varley was gonna hand over those documents—or send 'em—to our little friend Lana Varley *alias* Amanda Carelli across the way in the honeysuckle cottage, then I reckon to-night is the time when the job was gonna be done."

His eyes pop. He says: "Jeez . . . Mr. Caution. Maybe you're right. Maybe she's sittin' on those documents right now."

I grin at him. "We'll find out," I tell him. "Maybe we'll go across soon an' have a little talk with Amanda. Maybe she'd like to have a little party to-night."

He pours out some drinks.

"You gotta hand it to that guy Cleeve," he says. "I reckon he's played it pretty well from the start. He's double-crossed everybody includin' me. The boy was smart while it lasted."

"Well, it didn't do him any good," I say. "Because it is always the thing that people don't know about—the *little* thing—that gets 'em in the long run. I reckon Cleeve was gonna keep you kickin' around here until the time came when Varley arrived. Directly Varley arrived Cleeve woulda sent you off on some wild-goose chase. He sends you over to see me because it suits his book. It makes it look as if he is doin' everythin' he can on this job, but what he does not know is that you are comin' to me behind his back to tell me that he is tryin' to pull a fast one on me an' get in ahead of me. He thought it was sorta artistic to make you think he was just good an' keen. Well . . . you took it the right way an' you told me what you knew an' so there we are."

He says: "Yeah . . . maybe. But we still have not got those documents."

"I reckon we'll get 'em," I say. "What I mean is I hope we will." I look at my watch. "We'll have one little drink for the road," I tell him, "an' then I think we will go an' visit with the girl friend. An' we will not be too late because I would not like to disturb the baby's rest."

He pours out the drinks an' we sink 'em.

"Get your hat, fella," I tell him. "Let's go see Amanda."

Chapter Eight
YOU'VE HAD IT

WE START walkin' down the road towards the cottage.

Sammy says: "You know, I'm sorta excited about all this. I'm on edge to know whether she's got those papers or not. I wish I could be as cool as you are. You don't seem to give a goddam about it."

"You're wrong," I tell him. "I'm just as interested as you are, fella, but I got beyond the time when I get excited about anythin' except dames an' the beauties of nature. Any thin' else is just one of those things. The guy who does not get excited is the guy who eventually gets what is comin' to him—even if it is only a smack in the puss."

By now it is about half an hour after midnight. It is a helluva night an' the front of the cottage is bathed in moonbeams. I push open the gate an' we go along the little path an' I give the knocker a good smack. We stand there waitin'.

The door opens. This time it opens good an' quick, an' honeypot is standin' in the hall lookin' at us outa those big eyes of hers.

She looks terrific. She is wearin' a cherry coloured corduroy dress with shoes to match an' she sorta looks at us as if butter would not melt in her mouth.

I say: "Hello, Gorgeous. It is such a helluva lovely night that Mr. Maynes here an' me came to the conclusion that we oughta come visitin' with you. An' how do you like that?"

She looks at me. I can see her eyes twinklin' as she steps back for us to pass.

"I like it quite a lot, Mr. Caution," she says. "I'm beginning to get used to the rather strange visiting hours used by you and Mr. Maynes. Come in and have a drink. I'm sure you've got something interesting to tell me."

I say: "And how . . .!" Beside me I can see Sammy grinnin' like what the English call a Cheshire Cat. Although why the hell a cat that comes from Cheshire should grin all the time . . . well, search me!

We go inta the sittin'-room. She puts a bottle of whisky an' a syphon an' glasses on the table, an' some cigarettes. We all sit down lookin' at each other.

She says sorta softly: "You know this is rather like a *seance*. Everybody sitting round waiting for someone else to start the talking." She looks from Sammy to me and back again. I can see her eyes sparklin'. I think that this Lana or Amanda or whatever you like is a saucy monkey . . . an' I'm tellin' you!

I say: "O.K. Well, I will start the talkin'. First of all," I tell her, "I think you oughta know that when Sammy came back the other evenin' to see you an' talk turkey to you—well, that was entirely my idea. I should also tell you," I go on, "that it was me dug up that picture an' your police record, Amanda, an' I sent him back with that to sorta get things straight between all of us. See?"

She says: "Yes . . . I see. I might have known you were the mystery man. I might have known. . . ."

She looks at me an' frowns. But she still looks a picture. Whatever expression this dame has got on her face she still looks good enough to eat.

"O.K.," I tell her. "Well . . . I think the time has come when I can be on the up-an'-up with you, Amanda. Because there have been a lot of things poppin' around this neighbourhood to-night an' I think it's time we sorta got things straightened out."

"Yes," she says, sorta casual. "And what has been popping—if it isn't a very rude question?"

She pours out some whisky for Sammy an' me. We pick up our glasses an' take a drink. I see him look at me over the edge of his glass an' his eyes are twinklin'.

"Here's the way it goes," I say. "To-night we knocked off a guy who has been pretendin' to be workin' along with us. All the time this mug—a guy named Cleeve—has been playin' along with your boy friend Varley. See?"

She smiles at me. She shows her pretty little teeth. She says: "Maybe I do and maybe I don't." She lights herself a cigarette.

"All right," I tell her, "it does not really matter much what you see or what you don't see. Well . . . this guy Cleeve has shot some mug to-night. He tried to kid me that this shot mug was Varley. Maybe you know why he did that?"

She looks at me with dreamy eyes. She says: "You tell *me*, Mr. Caution. Because you interest me more every minute I listen to you."

I give her a big grin. "Lana or Amanda or whatever your name is, you are a saucy little so-an'-so," I tell her. "But it is not gonna get you any place. But if you want me to tell you why this guy Cleeve knocks off this mug—who is a sap called Enrique—I will tell you."

She says: "*Please* do." She throws me a wicked sideways look.

"This guy wishes me to think that Varley is not with us any more," I say, "because he knows goddam well that the real Varley is operatin'. That he is stoogin' around with those papers an' that the time has come when he is probably gonna hand them over to somebody. So I reckon you know all the answers now an' I reckon you know that there is only one thing *I* wanta know."

I light myself a cigarette. "The thing is," I tell her, "have you got those papers? Have they been handed to you or sent to you? An' do not try any funny business because if you tell me that you have not got them then I am gonna throw you in the cooler for about four hundred years an' how do you like that?"

She draws a long puff at her cigarette. She purses up her little mouth an' blows out a smoke ring. Then she says:

"Listen, Mr. Caution. Your friend and assistant Mr. Maynes here told me that there was a reward of one hundred thousand dollars for the documents. He told me that if I worked in with him and agreed to hand them over to the Federal Authorities if they came into my possession, then I would share the reward with him. He said I'd get fifty thousand dollars an' no questions asked."

She stubs out her cigarette. Then she gets up an' stands on the other side of the table, lookin' down at me smilin'.

"And now, Mr. Caution," she says. "Here's the truth. I've got those papers and now I'd like to hear from *you*!"

I get up. I say: "Nice work, girlie. I'm for you."

I turn around to Sammy. He is sittin' there as large as life with his glass in his hand, smilin' at us.

"Look," I tell her. "I think a little new introduction is now necessary. Miss Flash . . . *allow me to introduce to you Mr. Varley—the boy we been lookin' for all along—the silly mug who handed those papers over to you!*"

He does not say one word. He puts his glass down on the table. He looks at me with snakes' eyes. Then he says in a near whisper: "You bastard . . . so you were wise to me . . . you sonofabitch. . . ."

I say: "Yeah, pal . . . what do you think I am? Say . . . do you think I got cheesecake above my ears or what. Maybe you think my nut is fulla lead. How do you think a guy rates bein' a Field Agent in the F.B.I. if he was as nutty as you seem to think I was. I been wise to you for a long time. But I hadta get those documents an' this was the way to do it."

I give him a big grin. "You smart guys make me laugh," I tell him. "Just because I got a photo of Miss Flash here an' had a lot of dope written on the back of it about her bein' Amanda Carelli an' a lot more hooey you haveta fall for that. Because you think that if this babe is Amanda Carelli an' I am mug enough to pay over that reward you are gonna get half of it an' nobody is gonna know that you are Varley—the cause of all the trouble."

I light myself a fresh cigarette. "You are so goddam dumb that you do not know you are born," I say.

He looks at her. His eyes are glitterin'. Then he says: "So you're the Flash girl, are you?" He turns to me. "That makes her General Flash's daughter, hey?" he asks.

"Right," I tell him. "That's who she is an' a very smart baby too. When Cleeve an' me was havin' our interview with the General I got an idea. So I started talkin' about Varley havin' a sister. The General caught on that I was gettin' on to somethin'. He asked me to describe her. So I described his own daughter; spoke about her twisted little finger. An' he got it. He knew I wanted her put in over here as Varley's sister. He didn't know why an' neither did she. But she knows now an' he will goddam soon. They got brains, the Flash family."

He says quietly: "Yeah . . . so they got brains. Well . . . I hope they got brains enough for this!"

He jumps to his feet an' I can see the pistol in his hand. I hear the girl make a little hissin' noise between her teeth.

He says: "This is for you, Miss Flash . . . an' goddam you!"

I take a jump between him an' the girl as he squeezes the trigger. The flash nearly blinds me. Then I hit him a honey under the jaw with my elbow. He flops down on the floor an' the gun drops outa his hand.

I pick him up an' stick him back in his chair. He is right out. I pick up the gun an' put it in my pocket.

She says: "Are you all right? I thought for a moment you were hit. Are you sure you're all right?"

"Not too bad," I tell her. I hold out my hand. "You're Lalage Flash, aren't you?" I say. "An' I'm Lemmy Caution. I'm glad to meet you an' thanks a lot for what you've done. You've been terrific. I don't know what I'da done without you."

She shakes her head. "I haven't done a thing," she says. "I've just done what you indicated an' I must say you've been pretty good. The documents are upstairs—*and* they're the right ones.

I've identified them with the code that Father gave me. You see when I started on my way over here he gave me a note, told me that you always got away with it in the long run and that I was just to take my lead from you. Well . . . that's all I've done."

I give her a winsome smile. "Did he say anythin' else?" I ask her.

She smiles back at me. She looks at the writin' desk in the corner an' I can see a letter lyin' on the top of it.

"As a matter of fact he did," she says. "But I don't know that I'm inclined to tell you about that. Anyway, I think you ought to have a drink."

She pours out one an' I sink it. Then I say: "Look, lady. I am gonna take this thug in an' hand him over to the Dorking police. We have already got Cleeve there, so there's no more need to worry; after which I will come back here an' maybe you'll come for that little walk we never had. An' we can sorta talk things over."

She says: "I'd like to, Mr. Caution. It's a lovely night and there's lots I want to hear."

"O.K.," I tell her. "I'll be seein' you."

I pick up Varley, who is just beginnin' to waggle his head about a bit, put him over my shoulder an' carry him around to the car behind the *Square Bottle*. The air revives him a bit an' he starts comin' round. I stick him in the passenger seat an' bust him another one on the jaw just to keep him nice an' quiet.

Then I get in, start up an' roll off towards Dorking.

I reckon it's been a pleasant evenin'.

It is pretty late when I get back to the cottage. I have done a lot of telephonin' from the Police Station. I have talked to Herrick in London about takin' care of these thugs an' fixed to have the General telephoned in Paris that everythin' is O.K.

When I get to the cottage the front door is open. I go in but there is nobody in the livin'-room. I stand at the bottom of the stairs an' call out: "Hey . . . Lalage!"

She calls down: "I'll be there is a minute. You'll find some whisky on the table and cigarettes. And who told you that you could call me Lalage?"

I don't say anythin' to that one. I go inta the livin'-room an' pour a drink. I light myself a cigarette an' hang around. Then my eye falls on the General's letter on the writin' desk in the corner. I get sorta curious as to what the big boy has been sayin' about me.

I ease over to the desk nice an' quiet an' read what is on the page lyin' in front of me.

He says in the letter:

. . . and take your lead from Caution. He's our best man; damned clever and nothing ever stops him. He'll get these people if anyone can. But watch your own step—personally I mean—Caution's a great one for the girls and as you may know you are quite a good-looking young woman and just the sort of person he's likely to make a pass at. Just remember that, Lalage, and also that he is as cunning as a monkey and usually gets what he goes after. . . .

I hear her comin' down the stairs so I stop readin' an' ease away from the desk. When she gets in the room I am standin' by the table.

She is a sight for sore eyes. She has put on a little summer ermine coat an' she stands there with her eyes shinin' lookin' one hundred per cent. *plus.*

I say: "You are terrific. Me . . . I have not seen a dame like you in years, Lalage—or may I call you Miss Flash?"

She laughs. "Come along, Mr. Caution," she says, "and we'll have the walk. You may call me what you like."

"O.K.," I tell her. "I'll call you Lalage—which is a helluva pretty name. Let's get goin'. . . ."

We walk down the road towards the fields that run between Brockham an' the golf course. After a bit we come to a little lane with trees each side.

She says: "You're very quiet . . . what's the matter?"

"Nothin' much," I tell her. "But you gotta realise, lady, that I am a guy who is very poetic by nature an' that all I wanta do is to get as close to the beautiful things as I can."

She looks around her. She says: "But you are close to beauty. *All* this is beautiful."

"Yeah," I tell her, "but it is not the same thing."

Suddenly I lurch up against a tree. I give a gasp an' put my hand to my side. Then I let go a helluva groan.

She says: "My God . . . you're wounded. I knew it. I *thought* that bullet hit you . . . what can I do?"

I say: "Just come a little closer an' put your arm around my shoulder. Maybe I can get back to the cottage like that."

She says: "Oh yes . . . of course. . . ." She comes up to me an' she puts her arm around my shoulder an' I can see her eyes shinin' an' I get a breath of the perfume she is wearin'.

Well . . . what would you have done . . . hey?

I put my arms around her an' I give her one helluva kiss . . . and when I say kiss I mean kiss. Me . . . I have kissed dames in every part of the world but I am tellin' you that kissin' this Lalage is an experience that I have not met up with before.

She wriggles outa my arms an' stands lookin' at me. She says: "So you were lying. You're not wounded at all. Don't you think that was rather a mean subterfuge?"

"Look, baby," I tell her. "If I haveta use subterfuge to kiss you, then my middle name is Subterfuge. I would jump off the end of the pier for you. Another thing," I go on, "surely you did not think that I was mug enough to let that Varley loose with a gun. Why *I* gave him that gun."

She looks at me with wide eyes. "*You* gave it to him!" she says.

"Sure," I tell her. "An' it was loaded with blanks. I knew that mug would never look at the clip."

She gives a little smile. "You're very clever, Lemmy Caution," she says. "You know all the answers."

I put on a very sad look. "No," I tell her, "I am a very disappointed guy. I am a very unhappy guy an' I will tell you why. You were right in what you said just now. I got that kiss outa you by subterfuge an' therefore it don't really count. That's where I made my mistake. I'm always in a helluva hurry. Now I've fixed myself."

She looks at me. She says: "Exactly what do you mean?"

"Well," I tell her, "if, instead of pullin' that fast one on you about bein' hit by that bullet an' needin' support I hadda said to you 'Lalage ... I am nuts about you. You got everything. You are beautiful an' graceful an' wonderful, an' I like the way you walk an' speak an' every goddam thing about you, so, for the love of mike, give me a kiss!' ... well ..." I say, "you mighta done it. But now, of course, you'll never want to. You'd just hate it."

She looks at me again an' then she says sorta soft: "And how do *you* know, Mr. Caution?"

I don't say a word. I just gather her up in the moonlight. An' I'm tellin' you mugs that this baby is some bundle of woman. I reckon if old man Confucius hadda been there he woulda been doin' backfalls outa sheer jealousy.

She puts up her face to me an' I say: "Listen, Lalage ... when you are kissin' somebody there is only one thing you gotta remember. Just one thing. An' that is *give*!"

An' does that dame *give* or does she?

I'll say she does!

THE END

Lightning Source UK Ltd.
Milton Keynes UK
UKHW012001030322
399530UK00001B/152